CONTENTS

Chapter 1 – We Don't Save Lives, but THIS is an EMERGENCY   1

Chapter 2 – The Help Desk is Never HELPFUL!   12

Chapter 3 – Perfect Planning Pulverized   21

Chapter 4 – Audits Are Like Colonoscopies   32

Chapter 5 – Fresh, Organic, Non-GMO, Vegan, Gluten-Free, Fruit (and other audit snack food groups)   45

Chapter 6 – Finding Huge Mistakes is Every Auditor's Dream   61

Chapter 7 – Flexibility, What's That?   71

Chapter 8 – The Outlier Among Outliers (AKA Backup Staff)   83

Chapter 9 – Passive Aggressive Drinks   93

Chapter 10 – "Um, Guys...There's No Toilet Paper in Here!"   104

Chapter 11 – Really Stinky Overages   117

Chapter 12 – Moving Up   132

Chapter 13 – Never Eat Beef, Fish, or Dirt Again   147

Chapter 14 – Legal Matters   159

Chapter 15 – Sweet Revenge: The Auditors Strike Back   172

Chapter 16 – Another Steaming Mess   183

Chapter 17 – The Best is Yet to Come   196

Chapter 18 – Partner's Job is to Show Up and Blow Up 212

Chapter 19 – The Best Has Arrived 225

Chapter 20 – That's It? The Anticlimactic Push of a Button 239

Chapter 21 – Freedom! 252

All rights reserved © 2019 C.P. Aiden

Proofreading provided by the Hyper-Speller at https://www.wordrefiner.com

All characters and situations depicted in this book are purely fictitious. Any resemblance to real events or real persons, living or dead, is purely coincidental and unintended.

CHAPTER 1 – WE DON'T SAVE LIVES, BUT THIS IS AN EMERGENCY

> ***Staff 2 pinging Manager:*** We have an *EMERGENCY!*

Staff 2 sat with his eyes fixed on the instant messenger box for a full 30 seconds. No response. Manager's status said "offline", but he'd been "offline" for 17 hours and the ping went through, so maybe he was just ghosting as "offline". Staff 2 was just about to give up when the bottom of the messenger window changed to, "*Manager is typing a message...*"

YES!! Staff 2 thought aloud. *I'm going to get some help!* Then the message came through.

> ***Manager pinging Staff 2:*** *Hey, I'm just leaving home to head to the office. See you there in 25 minutes. Call my cell in two minutes if it is urgent.*

The two minutes felt like an eternity and Staff 2 was shaking with anxiety as he scrolled down his contact list to find Manager's number.

"Hey," said Manager. "Can you give me one second?"

Before Staff 2 could respond, he heard Manager saying goodbye to his wife.

"When do you think you will be home?" Manager's wife asked.

"It is just an APE today, so I should be home at a good time," Manager replied, hopefully.

"I don't know what that means anymore. One day a good time means 8:00 p.m. and other days a good time is 10:30 p.m. It would be great if you made it home before the sun goes down so you can watch the kids and I can go for a walk," Manager's wife let out, with a hint of frustration in her voice.

"I'm hoping 6:00 p.m., but I'll sandbag and say 7:00 p.m. just in case," Manager quipped. "On a happier note, I won't have to work tonight when I get home so I can watch the kids."

"OK," Manager turned back to the conversation with Staff 2. "I'm getting in the car. What's up?"

"Do you really think the APE will go that late today?" Staff 2 asked, intently.

"You aren't married, right?" Manager asked.

Staff 2 was a bit taken back by the question. After a short pause to collect his thoughts, he replied, that he was not, but that he was dating someone.

"I want to let you in on a little secret about expectations in relationships," Manager said, seriously. "I fully expect to be home by 5:00 p.m. tonight. There is no way Partner will let this thing go all day, but if I tell my wife 5:00 and something happens and I show up at 5:05, she's mad because I'm five minutes late. If I tell her 6:00, even if I show up later than I expect, say 5:30, I'm still a half hour early based on the time I gave. If you set the bar a bit lower and then convince others to believe the lower expectation, you can generally meet and exceed other people's expectations with ease. You can thank me for this little gem later."

"This makes so much more sense now," Staff 2 said, as the lesson sank in. "My girlfriend has been all up in my business about working too much, but it is because I keep getting home from work way later than I tell her."

"Works in relationships as well as in your career," Manager replied.

"Umm. Helloooo! I'm standing right here!" Staff 2 heard Manager's wife exclaim on the other end of the phone. Then he heard Manager's garage opening.

Oh, snap! thought Staff 2.

"Doesn't make it any less true," Manager told his wife, as the car started. "Love you! Bye! See you this evening!"

"At 5 P.M.!" Manager's wife shouted over the noise of the car backing out. "AND NOT A MINUTE LATER!"

"You seriously just said all that in front of her?" Staff 2 asked in amazement.

"Yeah, our meeting really won't go past 3:00 p.m. I'll be home by 4:00 or 4:30. I have a surprise for her tonight – I bought a swing set for the kids and the one good friend I have left from college is coming over to build it while she goes on her walk. I did all of that on purpose," Manager said. Then his tone became a little more serious, "But you didn't call to hear about how I try to keep my wife and kids happy. I'm assuming that nobody has died, but you did mention that this was an EMERGENCY!"

"Oh yeah...I got distracted," replied Staff 2, in a bit more panicked voice. "Huge EMERGENCY! I was sitting here at the office with everything ready – the agendas printed on nice paper, in color, nametags out, breakfast ordered for everyone, when there was a short double beep and a flash at the bottom of my screen. SM was pinging me."

SM was intense – he truly was a machine. SM was rated "Always Exceeds Expectations" (the highest rating possible and one that was next to impossible to achieve) since starting at the Firm.

In reality, SM was a regular, big firm workaholic whose entire existence was defined for him by the Firm – except for his dogs that he called his "children". He was 110% dedicated to the Firm, The Audit & Tax Firm (or TA&TF), and he could never understand when others were not so dedicated. SM worked at least 60 hours a week all year round, rarely took vacation, spent Christmas with his parents each year and complained that each year they "stole his computer so he couldn't work at all on Christmas day". All the pressure and stress he took on had turned him into a physical wreck. He was highly addicted to energy drinks – always had two or three tucked away in his laptop bag – and his left arm would twitch and his right hand would shake uncontrollably if he had gone more than six hours without one. And now, he was frantically pinging Staff 2.

> **_SM pinging Staff 2:_** _Did you see my comments on the agenda and the slide presentation?_

> **_SM pinging Staff 2:_** _I sent them over this morning. Mostly little minor stuff._

"Shoot!" Staff 2 exclaimed, grabbing the sides of his head. He hadn't seen them. Then he noticed he was not connected to the VPN and his email had not refreshed since 5:45 that morning when he left home.

Idiot! He thought as he anxiously typed in his login credentials, _I've been disconnected for an hour and a half now. He probably sent these comments at like 6:00 am!_ Staff 2 scrambled to get back on the VPN and refreshed his email and responded while the email was still loading.

> **_Staff 2 pinging SM:_** _I'm just looking at them now._

Staff 2 did not want SM thinking he'd completely missed the comments, even though he had.

There were 23 new emails in his inbox, mostly Firm newsletters and technical updates. "Where could these comments be?!" Staff 2 asked himself aloud, as he scrolled from the bottom of the new messages up. At last, he found them right at the top of his inbox. "Earlier this morning? You sent these LIKE 4 MINUTES AGO!" Staff 2 screamed at his computer.

> ***SM pinging Staff 2:*** *Let me know if you have any questions. I'll have internet access on the train for the next 20 minutes or so and will get to the office just before the meeting starts.*
>
> ***Staff 2 pinging SM:*** *Okay, I'll let you know if I have any questions.*
>
> ***SM pinging Staff 2:*** *Please address or respond to each comment and send the updated files back to me ASAP. I want to close them out before the meeting.*

Great, Staff 2 thought. *He finally decides to look at the agenda and presentation and now 45 minutes BEFORE THE MEETING he has comments? Well, there goes the $35 I paid the office store for printing these.* He quickly grabbed the agendas and rushed down the hall to the nearest shred bin to destroy the evidence.

Staff 2 looked at the time and realized he had 40 minutes until the meeting started. Then he actually opened the files.

"How on earth do you fit 32 COMMENTS on three and a half pages??!!" Staff 2 roared. "And another 25 comments in a 17-slide presentation?!"

At this point, he had pinged and called Manager to tell him about the EMERGENCY!

"This is pretty typical," said Manager, calmly, after hearing about Staff 2's morning. "Unfortunately, I'm unable to help you look through those while I'm driving. Is anyone else online?"

Staff 2 quickly checked to see if anyone else on the team was online. No such luck. He relayed that to Manager.

"Well, I guess you can call me back if you get stuck on any specific comments you see before I get there and we can talk through them as I drive in," said Manager.

C.P. Aiden

"Sounds good," replied Staff 2, as he sadly looked down at his phone screen.

With no one online and Manager driving, there was nothing he could do, but frantically try to clear all the comments before SM arrived.

Comment 1 – everything should be Arial 10, zoom at 80%, (this is true for all spreadsheets as well)

"Easy. Done. Don't see the point in changing the zoom since these are printed out anyways, but if he says so..." muttered Staff 2 under his breath. "If they are all this stupid, maybe I have a chance."

Staff 2 responded "updated" to the comment and moved down the page.

Comment 2 – This section should be at the top, with the section above two paragraphs down as the 3rd item to discuss. In fact, I think we need to change the whole order of everything. See the PDF attached to my email and re-order the sections accordingly

"So that is what that PDF attachment in his email is. He made a whole attachment to show me how he wants to rearrange this stuff and he couldn't have just rearranged it himself in the time it took to create this PDF? I suppose he thinks he's doing me a great favor by "coaching" me on this one. Great. Cut here. Insert there. Drag. Drop. Done."

Staff 2 responded "Done" to the comment and moved down the page.

Comment 3 – You put 'to' in this sentence "To many people have access to the bank account, you should have used 'too' as in a higher degree than is desirable, permissible, or possible; excessively. Please add the extra 'o' and watch out for these words that sound the same but are spelled differently.

Staff 2 was confused and frustrated. He lifted his hand up and shook it at the computer with his fingers spread out tightly in anger, "He couldn't just change this himself?! How hard is it to add the extra 'o'? It took 45 seconds to write the comment; it would have taken half a second to add the 'o'. I'm pretty sure I know the difference between too and to – like you don't have '**TO**' type out an actual definition of '**TOO**' for me to get it! Now I've had to take 15 seconds to read the comment, a half a second to fix it and I'll be raging for the next two to five minutes because of it! AND, it is called a homophone when words sound the same but are spelled differently! You want to distinguish between 'to' and 'too' so much, but you have to type out that whole definition of a homophone because you don't freaking know what a homophone is!"

Staff 2 then responded to SM's comment within the document. "Great catch. Thank you for the comment. I will watch out for these homophones going forward."

Then Staff 2 went back and deleted "homophones". Calling SM out as if he didn't know what a homophone was would be too sassy and would likely give a bad first impression. "I will watch out for these going forward." Next.

Comment 4 – If you haven't spell checked already, please do that – this needs to be perfect – see comment 3

"Comment 3 wasn't a SPELLING error! 'To' was spelled right and spell check never would have caught it even if I HAD run spell check," Staff 2 pounded out on his keyboard in response.

Then, deleting the whole response and saying to himself "stay calm, just stay calm," he typed "Thank you. I ran spell check and it identified two actual spelling errors in the document. Great catch." Then he went back and deleted "actual". Moving on!

Comment 5 – Shouldn't we list out the Tax and IT audit teams down here?

Staff 2 suddenly flared up again, yelling aloud, "THEY WERE HERE…UNTIL YOU DID YOUR LITTLE CUT AND PASTE JOB MOVING EVERYTHING OUT OF ORDER!!! They are now in the section above – exactly where you put them in your PDF!"

Staff 2 quickly realized he had just screamed out at his computer and the door to the conference room was wide open. He ran out to look up and down the hall to make sure no one had heard him, then rushed back to his computer and quickly typed out, "These were moved to the section above based on the PDF reordering you provided. I am happy to move them back down here if you would like."

The list went on and on and on. Staff 2 was losing his mind. Just over a half hour to go and he had 29 comments left in the agenda and another 25 in the power point presentation.

Just then, Senior 1 and Staff 1 arrived.

Senior 1 was in charge of running part of the day-to-day audit. She was Staff 2's direct supervisor. At first glance, Senior 1 was reserved and quiet, but tough. She had grown up on the East Coast in a rough neighborhood and would not take nonsense from anyone. Senior 1 was smart and rarely got upset, but when she did, it did not take very many words to let the team know it. She was married and had two young children. Her husband worked at a grocery store pharmacy so worked the hours he was scheduled, nothing more. He also received this crazy thing called overtime pay whenever he worked more than 40 hours a week. He never understood why Senior 1 had to work so much for so little, but Senior 1 was a professional and wanted to succeed in her career. So far, she had been willing to make the sacrifices to do what it took to get the job done. Senior 1 wanted to balance being a professional and a mom and had come to TA&TF because during the recruiting process they had been most vocal about offering 'flexibility' at work.

Staff 1 was a brand-new staff. She was a little older than a typical first-year staff and already had two kids. Her husband had just started a nutrition consulting company, which meant he had a very chill job that bled a lot of money. As a result, the family was going to be pretty reliant on Staff 1's salary. Staff 1 liked the hippie things Hippie Town offered. Since she'd only been at TA&TF for two weeks, she still had the first-year excitement and enthusiasm for the job.

"Good morning!" Senior 1 said, cheerfully, as she and Staff 1 walked in, found their assigned seats, set down their bags and started pulling their laptops out.

"No, it is not!" retorted Staff 2, not even looking up from his screen. "SM just blew up the agenda and the slide deck. There's like 50 comments we still have to clear in the next half hour."

"What can we do to help?" Staff 1 asked, enthusiastically.

Senior 1 and Staff 1 quickly set up their laptops as Staff 2 described the situation. They decided that Staff 1 would work from the bottom of the agenda and meet Staff 2 in the middle while Senior 1 went through the comments on the slide deck.

"Oh my," said Staff 1, as her jaw dropped a bit when she opened the file. "Who doesn't know what a homophone is?"

"Apparently, he doesn't," replied Staff 2, in a very annoyed voice and then catching himself added, "But don't point that out to him when he gets here – best not to make the audit leaders (that's Managers, Senior Managers, and Partners) look or feel stupid. I thought you were working from the bottom?"

They worked together and made it through several more comments. It was now 7:38 a.m., just 22 minutes to go. Another double beep and SM's face popped back up on Staff 2's screen.

"Great! What is it now?" moaned Staff 2, throwing his hands up. The others looked up with concern, "SM needs someone to go and get him breakfast."

"Didn't Administrative Assistant order breakfast for everyone?" asked Senior 1, a little snidely.

"She did," replied Staff 2. "But SM apparently hates the place we ordered from. The food needs to come from his favorite, little, specialty place down the street. Luckily, it is only about a half-mile away."

"I would be happy to go grab that if you'd like me to!" Staff 1 piped up, as she grabbed a pen and paper to write down the order and addresses.

Just then, Intern walked into the room.

"I need you to run to pick up SM's breakfast," Staff 2 said, anxiously.

"Great!" said Intern, cheerfully. "Where am I going and what am I getting?"

Staff 2 scribbled out the orders and handed them to Intern. "You need to be back at 8:00 so you are here before the meeting starts and it is still hot. Any earlier than 7:58 or later than 8:02 is a total fail."

Intern looked around the room a little shell-shocked, almost as if to ask whether or not Staff 2 was serious or if it was just a prank.

"He's serious," Senior 1 said, sternly, while turning to face Intern. "You'd better get going."

The panicked Intern was gone in an instant. The others chuckled a bit. They had all remembered being interns.

"I forgot what Senior 1 power looks like to an intern," Staff 2 told Senior 1, as they watched Intern rush down the hall towards the elevators.

Twenty minutes to go time and it was back to the comments. The occasional "Holy Cow" or "Wow, what kind of stupid comment is this?" was muttered, but for the most part, the room was silent.

With 10 minutes to go, Senior 1 suddenly smacked her palm on the table and burst out, "OH MY....WOW!"

This is trouble, thought Staff 2, as he raised his eyebrows. He turned to Senior 1 and asked, "What is it?"

"The last comment on the slide deck," answered Senior 1, with her eyes widening as she read the comment aloud. "Didn't you see the announcement this morning? The Firm has changed its name to—"

"About time," interrupted Staff 2. "We always get made fun of for being The Audit & Tax Firm. Being called an acronym is horrible. Everyone is always asking 'which one of you is TA and which one is TF?'. Anything would be better than TA&TF."

"It gets worse," Senior 1 continued. "The Firm's new name is simply The Accounting Firm or TAF. All Firm marketing materials, signage, presentations, letterhead, apparel, etc. should be changed to the new logo and tagline immediately. Please see the email sent out by the Firm at 7:00 this morning for the new presentation templates and letterhead and adjust the agenda and slide deck accordingly."

CHAPTER 2 – THE HELP DESK IS NEVER HELPFUL!

"New Logo + New Letterhead + New Tagline + New Vision for the Future = The Accounting Firm," Staff 2 laughed, as he shook his head. "Are they serious?"

"Oh yes, they are," Manager said, chuckling, as he walked into the room. "Someone at the National Office needed to justify their existence."

"Ha," added Senior 1. "I'm sure this will make a huge difference out in the market. We don't just do Audit and Tax anymore. We do ACCOUNTING!"

They all laughed. Then Staff 2 pointed out that SM would be there any minute and ALL the comments had to be addressed, especially this last one. Staff 2 insisted that they would look pretty silly to do a presentation on the Firm's old materials, even if they had only realized there were new materials 10 minutes before the meeting. Manager agreed that Partner and SM would probably expect it because it would be nearly impossible to do.

Staff 2 opened the email with the announcement. There was a link to an internal shared site that was supposed to have everything on it.

The Good Audit

"Why isn't this link opening? Where is Senior 3 when you need him?" shrieked Staff 2, as he kept hitting the refresh button.

"The page doesn't seem to be loading," said Staff 1, frantically. "I'll keep refreshing!"

"All I'm getting is the blue circle going around and around," Senior 1 said, desperately.

"Okay," said Staff 2, standing up with excitement. "There is another link in the email farther down that says if you can't get to the website due to heavy demand, you can email the helpdesk to receive a packet of the materials directly."

"I'm on it," said Staff 1, as she quickly typed out an email on her laptop. "I just sent out an email...Oh wait, this is not good, the auto-response said that due to high email traffic, please expect a delay in response. Your direct email packet should arrive in the next two weeks."

"Why is the help desk never HELPFUL?!" moaned Staff 2. "And why do IT people, who are supposed to know so much about IT, never seem to see this type of thing coming? Of course, EVERYONE is going to want to switch over to the new logo and tagline and letterhead and all that right away. Plus, in two weeks, the website will work fine because no one will be on it anymore! Why couldn't they just include a small file with all the new stuff and attach it to the original announcement email instead of sending out an email with a link to a site that crashes when more than 105 people go there at the same time??!!"

"Wait," said Senior 1, clinching her fists. "There is one more option! 'Your receptionist will be sent letterhead that will arrive this morning to each office.' We could scan the letterhead, snip it, and paste into the presentation!"

"Brilliant!" exclaimed Staff 1.

Staff 2 was already out of the room running down the hall towards the reception desk. He came back panting 30 seconds

13

later. "No good," he said. "She was dealing with the people getting our breakfast set up when the delivery guy came. Apparently, she had to sign for the package. The delivery guy did the 10-second countdown and left with the package and it won't be back until the 2 p.m. delivery. We're hosed. Ping anyone you see online and ask if they have the packet downloaded yet!"

Manager didn't seem to care about all the fuss. He was jovial and laid back. No one was quite sure why he was in public accounting. He was as much a family man as one could be while working at any big firm. He wasn't serious or anal like most other audit managers and almost nothing could make him really panic. He often got a bad rap for being so laid back and partners often prematurely pegged him as lacking the professionalism needed to be a serious accountant. As a result, and to the significant disappointment of those partners, Manager would always fall short of his potential to be an "auditing superstar". Notwithstanding this stigma, most people on his teams and at clients loved working with him. Since he wasn't so constantly caught up in the minutia of pointless and meaningless details, he was seen by others as way more practical and pragmatic than any other auditor they'd ever met.

While everyone else was frantically trying to find a way to get the new logo, Manager started satirically reading the announcement aloud.

"Dear Esteemed Colleagues, it starts out. Wow, this change is great! We are all 'esteemed colleagues' now. I've never been treated like an 'esteemed colleague' before. I hope I get to feel the full impact of this life-altering change. Do you feel any different?"

Everyone else was too frantic to pay much attention to Manager, but he was having a good time.

"We are pleased to announce exciting, new changes with the naming and branding of our Firm, including a new logo, tagline, and plan for the future. This exciting, new naming, look and feel in the way we present our Firm will enable us to continue building on the past while forging a brave, new future of positive client interaction and service," Manager continued. "For additional details about today's news, and to download the new Firm logo, letterhead, and marketing materials, click here."

"Except when you click there, all you get is the blue circle of death, spinning around and around mocking your effort to have a perfectly, updated presentation," Staff 2 cut off Manager's reading, as he pulled down his eyebrows in anger and frustration.

"Extensive time and research went into making such a drastic change to the way the Market will view our Firm and our brand going forward. We believe that our people are what truly makes our Firm and our brand so unique and special! Check out what some of our people who worked on this project have to say."

"They have actual testimonials from people working on the project?" Senior 3 asked, earnestly, as he walked into the room.

Senior 3 was one of the smartest people anyone on the team had ever met. Everyone liked him. He always found a way to give people the benefit of the doubt, no matter what. Maybe it was his very dry humor combined with his smarts or his very literal take on everything or perhaps it was something else, but somehow everyone always seemed to think that he knew a lot about IT. This drove him crazy because while he was very smart, he knew no more than any other team member about IT.

"Check it out," said Manager, turning his laptop screen towards Senior 3 and pointing at the testimonials. "Look at these people. Can they be for real? I always wonder if the Firm just makes them up and inserts random 'feel good' stuff into these emails."

"For real? They are in an email announcement from the Firm. They have to be real. The Firm would not just make stuff up to publish for an announcement like this," replied Senior 3. "This

15

National Office Guy went to school with me – look what he says: 'This experience has been so challenging. We've analyzed all the market data, the impact name changes have had on other accounting firms—' "

"Zero impact. End of story," interrupted Manager in disgust.

Senior 3 cleared his throat just slightly and continued, "and presented our conclusion to Firm leadership. Those leaders truly listened to us and today's announcement makes it all worth it – a huge capstone to all our effort."

"There is no way he said that," said Manager in disbelief.

"He could have said it," responded Senior 3, looking up from the screen. "He was always pretty excited about everything in school and he is in the National Office now. Look he is online. I will ping him and ask."

"If I were that guy, I would not show up as online right now, or I would at least appear away or something. With an article and quote like that, I'd be looking for somewhere to hide," Manager replied. Then, he muttered under his breath so that only Staff 2 could hear, "Anyone at the Firm who remotely knew you would be pinging you to find out if you'd seriously said it."

"He responded!" cried Senior 3, waving his hands in the air. "And he remembers me! Although, for some unknown reason, he is shocked I am in the Audit Specialty Services group. He thought I did the IT stem of the program. He said that he was required to read that statement in a short video clip about the project and then they quoted the video as if he had said it on his own."

"That is hilarious," said Senior 1, who had finally taken a moment to look up from her efforts to find the new logo.

"Them quoting him or the fact that he thought Senior 3 did the IT stem of their program in school?" asked Manager, sarcastically, while jabbing his elbow towards Senior 3.

"Zinger!" replied Senior 1, laughing out loud. Senior 3 completely missed the joke. He was frantically pinging with his old classmate at the National Office.

"Ask him if he has all the new stuff he could send us," said Staff 2, not amused at all with the conversation. "We absolutely need it for the presentation and agenda and the website is totally crashing."

"He is sending it to me now," Senior 3 answered, triumphantly. "I will forward to everyone."

"Look at that! Senior 3 managed to be our IT fix-it-guy after all, right Staff 2?" said Manager with an amused look on his face – he was mostly amused at the whole fuss over the logo, but partly amused at how clever his IT jab was.

Senior 3 picked up on the joke this time and was irritated, "You know I am not an IT guy, Manager. I've told you this several times already...today...like this morning."

"I know," Manager smiled. "I just enjoy getting a rise out of you way too much. Why don't you ask your friend how much they paid him to do all this research and how much it cost the Firm."

"I doubt he would tell us. I think that type of stuff is supposed to be SUPER confidential and I can't imagine National Office Guy telling me something like that," Senior 3 replied, and then after pausing to think for a moment added, "But why not? I will ask."

Senior 3 started pinging National Office Guy.

"Just think of the costs, all the Market research, new signs, new letterhead, new recruiting swag, new business cards. I mean, TA&TF—I mean TAF—employs 165,000 people worldwide. Now you have to get each of them a whole new pack of business cards with the new logo and Firm branding. At five dollars a pop, we are talking...", Manager paused to get his calculator pulled up on his screen and then punched his 10-key.

"That is $825,000 just on business cards! Then you think of all the letterhead, the signs on office buildings, the logo on the wall by the reception desk at every office, it just goes on and on," Manager said, as he stood up and went to the whiteboard to start adding things to the list that would have cost TAF tons of money to switch. "Business cards are the tip of the iceberg, really. The real question is all the fluffy stuff, like market research, your buddy was doing—must have cost a fortune!"

"Oh my," shouted Senior 3, excitedly. "He told me! Well, at least for his part of the project. His charge code for research on the Market impact of the name change has $7.6 MILLION in it! That is just for the research study internally. He says they also paid outside consultants an additional $9.3 million. That is INSANE!"

"$7.6 million!" said Senior 1, in shock. "They could have paid me $7.6 MILLION and I would have given them a very fancy answer!"

> ***Manager pinging Senior 1:*** *No impact. Please pay me $7.6 million...* 😊
>
> ***Senior 1 pinging Manager:*** *Exactly*
>
> **Manager pinging Senior 1:** *Never ceases to amaze me that there are people employed by this Firm who have so little to do that they make up reasons to pass stuff like this off as a good idea so they can justify their existence.*

"I bet the whole thing costs over $100 million, just to change from TA&TF to become TAF. The email even continues to say that the Firm will still be referred to as TA&TF or The Audit and Tax Firm, due to the name recognition in the market," said Manager to the whole team. "Well, just don't say anything to Partner about the cost. Most partners will see this as money the Firm spent that is taken out of their distributions."

"I heard it was actually closer to $150 million," SM said, as he walked in the room. He then added, "Manager is absolutely right about not saying anything to Partner about the cost. Anyway, where's my breakfast?"

> _**Staff 2 pinging Manager:** It is outside on the table just like everyone else's._

Manager laughed out loud at the ping from Staff 2 and the rest of the team just stared at him blankly.

It was 7:58. Thankfully, Intern was a good intern and she walked in the door within 10 seconds of SM asking about his personalized breakfast.

All the comments were closed and the updated presentations were in SM's inbox when he opened his computer. He thanked Intern for having his breakfast timed perfectly to still be hot.

"Where is Partner?" Manager looked at SM and asked.

"Partner is coming 20 minutes late. He had an unexpected conference call this morning," replied SM, nonchalantly.

Suddenly, the right-hand corner of Manager's screen lit up. Manager clicked the box to find that Staff 2 was RAGING.

> **Staff 2 pinging Manager:** _Partner had a conference call this morning and HE KNEW!!!!??? Why didn't he tell us? Do you know what 20 more minutes would have done for my blood pressure? Here I am nearly having a heart attack and he just blatantly doesn't mention that Partner is coming 20 minutes late?!!!_

> **Manager pinging Staff 2:** _How else was he going to have time to close out his comments before the meeting started?_

> _**Staff 2 pinging Manager:** Did you know?!_

> **Manager pinging Staff 2:** _Nope, but I'm not surprised. If SM wasn't going to be here until right on time, Partner was probably coming late._

Staff 2 pinging Manager: *Unreal, but I guess that makes sense. I suppose you learn these little secrets as you go, right?*

Manager pinging Staff 2: *Just like setting expectations for others, you have to lower all expectations of being surprised by partners and senior managers. Something you need to get used to – partners work on their very own schedule, basically ALWAYS. And you, as someone who is not yet a partner, just have to deal with it. Pretty much the only thing they are ever on time for is meetings with other partners or lunch meetings with clients.*

SM flew through closing out his comments and the new agendas were printed (on normal copy paper and in black and white this time) and the presentation was up and ready on the big screen by 8:15. The team sat and silently waited for Partner's arrival and the start of the meeting.

CHAPTER 3 – PERFECT PLANNING PULVERIZED

Partner was just wrapping up his conference call when he walked in.

"Thank you, everyone. We are very excited about these new changes! We look forward to implementing this change in our office," Partner said, enthusiastically. "Bye."

"Was that a call about the Firm's name change?" Manager asked, excitedly.

"Yes," replied Partner, energetically. "The name change is the big news everyone is talking about. Except no one will give any details on how much it cost to make the change. It can't be small, but no one part of the regional leadership team on that call would say anything about how much it cost. At least six of us tried asking in different ways to pry the information out of them. Makes me wonder if they even know, or if it is just so massive that they won't say anything."

Senior 3 saw this moment as the perfect opportunity to be impressive and he raised his hand like an excited but timid child in school hoping to get the teacher's attention by saying something meaningful, "I have a friend from school who is now in the National Office. He was on the market research team that analyzed the impact of the name change on the way the Firm is perceived in the outside market."

> **Manager pinging Senior 3:** *Dude, you cannot tell him that we found out how much it cost.*

> **Manager pinging Senior 3:** *STOP TALKING!*

> **Senior 1 pinging Senior 3:** *Are you really going to tell him what your friend told you it cost? I don't think that is such a good idea.*

> **Staff 1 pinging Senior 3:** *Manager and Senior 1 both look very worried and looks like SM is trying to get your attention.*

> **Manager pinging Staff 2:** *If he doesn't shut up, I will regret the expectation I set with my wife this morning.*

> **Staff 2 pinging Manager:** *Seriously, we will be here all day talking about this the second Partner gets a number in his head.*

Senior 3 was looking up at Partner so did not see any of the pings flashing on his screen. Partner rarely looked interested in anything a senior was saying, so Senior 3 was eating up the attention.

"My friend told me that the code he was using had—"

At this, SM, who was standing behind Partner finally got Senior 3's attention. He was waving his arms frantically and then motioned his hand across his throat to silently scream "STOP!"

After a pause to regroup himself, Senior 3 continued, "—a huge balance."

"See!!" Partner exclaimed, as he threw his arms out. "Nobody will tell anyone anything! It just makes me think it must have cost a ton! It will probably mean a 5-10% drop in my partner distributions this year."

The Good Audit

> **Manager pinging Senior 3:** *There is no way the partners take the hit themselves. Get ready for a change to the expense policy, lower performance bonuses and really bad raises this year.*

> **Senior 3 pinging Manager:** *We'll see. I think they will be fair to us as employees.*

> **Manager pinging Senior 3:** *You just keep telling yourself that. The last time the Firm wasted millions of dollars on pointless endeavors, they changed the breakfast reimbursement amount from $25 to $15 and stopped reimbursing for CPA license renewals.*

Senior 3 had now seen the pings from everyone and he responded to Manager.

> **Senior 3 pinging Manager:** *I don't see what the big deal is with telling Partner about the $7.6 million.*

> **Manager pinging Senior 3:** *Do you want to have a planning event or talk about the Firm's name change all morning and get nothing done? I would like to go home tonight. In fact, I need to be home tonight before 5 o'clock because I have a surprise for my family – yes, those other people in my life that this job takes me away from too often. If Partner doesn't sign off on planning today, it won't get signed off on until March 28, and I promise that you do NOT want to be clearing planning comments during the last two days of the audit.*

> **Senior 3 pinging Manager:** *That is fair.*

In the meantime, Staff 2 had handed out the updated agendas.

"How did you get the new logo on here this morning?" asked Partner, in shock, when he saw the logo added to the agenda. "I heard that the website to download everything crashed about two minutes after the announcement went out. Impressive."

Staff 2 beamed with pride. At least he was getting credit for something.

"Senior 3 had a few IT tricks up his sleeve," Manager laughed. "He—"

"I have no IT tricks, Manager!" Senior 3 interrupted. "Remember, I am not an IT guy! I have told you this several times this morning already. My friend at the National Office sent them to me."

"I suppose you deserve a gold star then," Partner said to Senior 3, as he smiled. Partner then pushed his hand forward with his thumb up a little and pressed a pretend gold star through the air towards Senior 3.

> **Manager pinging Senior 3:** *I hope a smile and mid-air pretend gold star makes you feel happy because it is all the thanks you will ever get from Partner for accomplishing a nearly impossible task.*

> **Senior 3 pinging Manager:** *I think he will reward us fairly for our efforts.*

Staff 2, who was now looking very deflated, was anxious to move on. He quickly cleared his throat and said, "Ok, I guess we should get started. Everyone has the agenda in front of them, so we'll just go down that. I'm Staff 2 —"

Staff 2 was interrupted by a voice from the phone that was sitting in the middle of the table, "I don't have an agenda. Did you send that out with the meeting invite? If not, will someone please send me a copy?" The voice was AQR, who was the Audit Quality Review Partner on the engagement.

> **Manager pinging Senior 3:** *How long has AQR been on the phone? Long enough to hear about your $7.6 million?*

> **Senior 3 pinging Manager:** *I don't know. I hope*

not.

Staff 2 had forgotten that AQR was on the phone. His face went pale and he was speechless for a couple seconds.

"I'm sending it to you right now." Staff 1 piped up. "Let me know if it doesn't get to you in the next 30 seconds."

> **Manager pinging Senior 1:** *And that is how you know we have a good staff 1. She jumps in to save the staff 2 just like that.*

"Got it. Thank you," said AQR.

"Well," said Staff 2, "to start off, I thought it would be a good idea, especially given this is a first-year audit, for everyone to introduce them—"

AQR interrupted Staff 2 midsentence, "Remind me who this client is and what they do."

"Widget Maker – a large manufacturing company that makes widgets." Staff 2 began, "They are a—"

"Wait!" interrupted Partner. "All they do is make widgets? I thought they also made gadgets."

"Nope, just widgets," Manager replied, patiently. "They told us in the bid process that they are looking into making gadgets, but they need more cash flow from widgets before they can make gadgets."

> **Manager pinging Senior 3:** *$2 Billion in sales of widgets and about $500 thousand in operating cash flow. What a fabulous business! Looks like they will never be making gadgets.*
>
> **Senior 3 pinging Manager:** *Ha! Although, I suppose if you have $3.5 BILLION of assets on your balance sheet, you are doing something right.*
>
> **Manager pinging Senior 3:** *Given that my first grader could manage that much money and produce*

better results, I think you will be surprised at just how much will go wrong.

"Ok," said Staff 2. "No gadgets, just widgets. Widget Maker is a $3.5 Billion company that manufactures widgets all over the world. These widgets are primarily sold to makers of gadgets."

Staff 2 pulled up the presentation deck and displayed the slide with a few pictures of the company's warehouses.

"Ok, I remember now," said AQR. "I took these guys golfing when I came up to give our presentation for the bid. Speaking of golfing, I am just pulling up to my country club. I am meeting one of my clients here in 15 minutes. Aside from the $7.6 million of internal research costs and the $9.3 million to external consultants to change the Firm's name to TAF that you all found out about and were discussing earlier, what else do we need to cover before I drop off?"

"Wait. WHAT?!" exclaimed Partner, as he looked around the room in total disbelief. "You mean to tell me you guys had two real numbers and you didn't say anything!?"

The room was silent. No one dared to say anything. They could all feel Partner's frustration building. Senior 3 lifted his head momentarily and mumbled something completely inaudible and then went silent again. The silence went on for at least 10 seconds. No one dared to make eye contact with Partner. Finally, to the total shock of the entire team, AQR piped up over the phone.

"Did I lose you? Or, did the room go silent?" he asked. "If I lost you, I'm very disappointed that I'm not hearing what is going on in the room right now."

Manager pinging Senior 3: *We are in trouble now!*

Senior 3 pinging Manager: *I think I'm going to be sick, literally...* 🤢

"No, the room has been silent," Partner replied, but before he could get anything else out, AQR spoke up again.

"From what I heard, the team was very concerned the number would be upsetting to us partners, and the team was right," AQR said, with a chuckle. "I would not be upset at the team for keeping that information to themselves, although Senior 3 came dangerously close to disclosure."

> **SM pinging Manager:** *I hope your resume is up to date*

> **Manager pinging SM:** *My sentiments exactly*

"Oh, I completely agree," responded Partner. Manager's head was swirling – *how could he completely agree with what AQR had just said. He looked furious.* Manager thought they were all going to be fired on the spot for knowingly withholding information from a partner and then being called out on it by another partner.

"I don't blame the team at all for not saying anything. If I were in their shoes, I would have done the exact same thing," said Partner, coolly, as Senior 3's and Manager's jaws raced each other to the floor.

"I don't doubt the information is good and it makes me angry that the Firm just blows money like crazy on something as perfunctory as this name change. All of that comes out of the partners' distributions this year, and probably some for each of the three years to come," Partner added, angrily, and then started shaking his head. "I'm going to need to find a way to get more fees."

"The team covered all these points in their discussion earlier," replied AQR in his matter of fact tone. "And sadly, I think Manager is right on the money that Firm leadership will now look for any way possible to cut costs in other areas to make up for this astronomical sum. If internal research alone was $7.6 million and external consultants for that research were $9.3 million, the whole thing easily goes over $100 million and maybe approaches $200 million."

While all of this was going on, Staff 2 stood paralyzed in front of the room and he was clearly getting flustered. He hadn't even hit the first agenda point (team introductions) and now he had to figure out everything AQR needed to discuss in the next 12 minutes and pull those things up first. He was overjoyed when Manager piped up.

"We just need to go over estimates, fraud and other major risks, scoping, planning materiality and timing," he said, as he raised one arm towards Staff 2 and then gestured to the screen. "Go ahead."

"I looked at the scoping documents while I was waiting for the meeting to start," said AQR. "Will you please add some good documentation over our basis for setting materiality?"

> **Manager pinging Senior 1:** *"Good documentation" means we need to add about three pages of fluff to that file. Will you please put that on your list to do?*

> **Senior 1 pinging Manager:** *Sure, I am so happy I have over $100k in student debt for a Master's degree in accounting! All that for a housekeeping role at a large, prestigious firm. I feel like I am fluffing things up all day every day.*

> **Manager pinging Senior 1:** *It only gets better, after years of fluffing, you can look forward to "taking out the trash" and dealing with theoretical "messes" that guests (aka clients) leave everywhere for you.*

"We will add that in the scoping document and send you the updated wording," said Manager.

"OK," Staff 2 tried to push the discussion forward. "Let's talk about fraud and significant risks."

"This is supposed to be a brainstorming discussion from ALL members of the team," said Partner.

> **Partner pinging Manager:** *What's the staff 1's name?*

> **Manager pinging Partner:** *We call her Staff 1*

"Staff 1," Partner said, pointing at Staff 1.

Staff 1's face lit up. Inside, she was quietly thinking, *oh wow, Partner knows my name. I feel so valued and appreciated! Control the emotions, don't do anything stupid, need to impress here....*

"Will you please take notes on this discussion?" Partner asked.

"Certainly! I would love to!" Staff 1 replied, as she pulled up a blank document on her laptop and started typing.

"I'm about out of time," AQR remarked, hastily.

"I think we've covered everything you need to be a part of," Partner replied. "The team can catch you up later on any other important items that may come up."

"Sounds great! I've got to go," said AQR, as the team heard a car door shut.

"We didn't get through significant risks, estimates or timing!" exclaimed the flabbergasted Staff 2. He was clearly panicking now – his hands reached out grappling thin air between himself and the phone. The whole meeting seemed like it was falling apart.

"Have a great rest of your day!" said AQR, hurriedly. Then, with a double beep from the phone, AQR was gone.

> **Manager pinging Senior 3:** *$20 says we don't hear a thing from AQR until the last day of the audit when he sends us his comments on the financial statements.*

> **Senior 3 pinging Manager:** *I think he will be heav-*

ily involved given this is a first-year audit.

Manager pinging Senior 3: *Him calling into the Audit Planning Event makes him more heavily involved than half the review partners I've ever worked with, but I guarantee you his involvement in this audit is basically over.*

Staff 2 looked at Manager and SM, almost begging for them to help him figure out what to do next. Manager just grinned back at him. To Staff 2's total surprise, SM took pity on him.

"Why don't we go back up towards the top and move through the rest of the agenda?" he suggested. "Although I think we can skip Introductions, Understanding the Business... oh, and Flexibility."

Staff 2 went back to cutting and pasting the slides of the presentation. This was the fourth time he had done it since waking up so he was getting pretty fast.

Senior 3 pinging Manager: *Did he just say we are skipping flexibility?*

Manager pinging Senior 3: *Yes. I can't tell you what that implies for how this audit is going to go, but I can take a guess.* 🙂 *The life of working for a machine. My wife hates using 'flexibility' and the Firm in the same sentence.*

Senior 3 pinging Manager: *I think we will get the flexibility we need in the end.*

Staff 2 was now ready and standing back in front of the room. The team went through the agenda quickly glossing over the rest of the areas as "check the box" items.

After about two hours, Partner told the team he thought they'd been through all the "critical areas", stood up, packed his laptop in his bag and walked out of the room. SM was not far behind.

Everyone told Staff 2 what a great job he did leading the meeting. Manager stayed in the room working as Staff 1 and Staff 2 cleaned everything up.

"Nice work," said Manager. "APE's never do what you want, especially the big APE's at The Accounting Firm."

"Ha," replied Staff 2. "Good to know. We didn't even cover half the things on the agenda. I feel like the whole meeting really got away from me."

"I wouldn't say that," said Manager. "Especially given that you are a staff 2 and a senior usually runs the meeting, I think you really did well."

"Really? Thanks!" said Staff 2, beaming.

"I mean, it is only 2:00 p.m. I have another hour or so of work to do before I leave, but I should make it home earlier than I've been home in over 6 months," replied Manager with a grin. "And I will have easily beat expectations for my wife…for one day at least."

"I hope the kids like the swing set," said Staff 2, as he picked up his bag and turned to the door. As he reached the door, he turned back and added, "And that you can get it all built tonight, since life at the Firm is about to get crazier with this new client. See you next week at the Widget Maker office."

CHAPTER 4 –
AUDITS ARE LIKE
COLONOSCOPIES

The following week, the TAF audit team was gathered in the up-scale board room at the Widget Maker office anxiously awaiting the finance team.

"They are almost 20 minutes late!" Manager exclaimed, as he, Partner, and SM peered out the conference room window that looked over an exquisite golf course sprawled out below.

As they continued waiting for the Widget Maker finance team to arrive, Partner told SM they would all have to go play the course sometime. Partner played there at least once a week whenever his schedule permitted – he claimed it was to schmooze with clients, but SM and Manager could both tell that golf was the one and only hobby Partner had left. As they looked out, they saw two golf carts approaching the hole nearest them. The trio watched as two people hopped out of the first cart.

"That looks like CFO," Partner blurted out, as he pointed towards the first cart. "And I'm almost positive that is Finance Manager!"

"Isn't Finance Manager the one that made Manager at our firm and left right before Busy Season and one day after his promotion a few years back?" Manager asked Partner, mostly for the benefit of SM.

"It wasn't exactly right before Busy Season," Partner replied. "More like he was promoted to Manager, collected his promotion bonus and had his new pay rate effective 15 days later, and then he gave his notice the following day."

"Wow," said SM. "That is like dousing the bridge with gasoline and then throwing a match on it."

"You generally have to do something pretty awful to burn the bridge with the Firm. We kept the relationship alive and well," Partner sighed, as he shook his head slightly. "The Firm really wanted this client, so we pushed to keep the relationship. He became our foot in the door that gave us the opportunity to bid on this new work. It just goes to show that even having someone quit at a really bad time won't keep us away from a relationship if there is huge fee potential involved."

"Who are the other two golfing with them?" asked SM, as the two in the rear cart emerged with their clubs.

"One is Assistant Controller," said Partner. "I'm pretty sure the other one is Inventory Manager."

"Aren't they all supposed to be in this meeting – the meeting we were all on time for that was supposed to start 20 minutes ago?" asked Manager, dumbfoundedly.

"Yes, they are," said Partner, irritably. "I hear this is somewhat typical of CFO. She will likely walk in and apologize and say that another meeting went long. CFO is very sharp – much smarter than she comes across – she went to some Ivy League School for an MBA, spent about three years in management consulting before moving out here. She did about 10 years in private equity and then took the job as CFO here. I've heard she doesn't care much about what other people think. I've also heard she does things the way she wants unless someone can really convince her of a stronger position or better alternative."

Partner took a half step back away from the window and then texted CFO.

> **Partner to CFO:** *Our whole team is here and ready whenever you are! Looking forward to meeting your team!*

Partner showed the text to SM and Manager as they backed away from the window a couple steps to watch CFO without being seen from below. They saw CFO calling the rest of the group into a huddle and showing them her phone. They all busted up laughing. CFO started typing a response. She appeared to be interrupted by Finance Manager and Inventory Manager several times. Suddenly, Assistant Controller was laughing so hard he tripped on his bag of golf clubs and fell over right as Partner's phone buzzed with a new text.

> **CFO to Partner:** *We are in a very strategic meeting that is going long but very well. We will be there as soon as we can.*

"I met Assistant Controller at a networking reception about a month ago," Manager said. "I guess he has been here for about ten years. He did two years at some tiny firm and then moved out here. His wife works for the company as well – HR or Legal, nobody really knows. The dude is quirky though, often says stuff that doesn't make sense or that seems out of place."

"What do we know about the Inventory Manager?" asked Partner.

"Pretty funny guy, but a bit of a conceited hotshot – like super arrogant and acts like he knows everything," Manager replied. "He's one of those people who acts very professional in front of those he views as 'above him' but will treat anyone else like they don't know a thing."

The foursome finished playing the hole – Inventory Manager three-putted the green while Assistant Controller continued to trip over his own golf clubs – and the two golf carts headed towards the building. 10 minutes later, six members of the accounting department walked in. Along with the four golfers, came Financial Reporting Manager (or FRM) and Senior Accountant.

"I'm sorry to be a few minutes late," said CFO, nonchalantly, as the team walked in. "We had another meeting that ran over."

"No problem," replied Partner. "We are just so excited to be here and kick off this year's audit with you. We can't imagine what we'd all rather be doing right now!"

> **Staff 2 pinging Manager:** *Speak for yourself, Partner. I can imagine lots of things I'd rather be doing.*

> **Manager pinging Staff 2:** *I bet these guys would rather be finishing their round of golf! And, I don't know what world she's living in if coming 25 minutes late to a meeting with your auditors is only "a few minutes late".*

"It is a beautiful view from this conference room!" Manager exclaimed. "Makes me wish I were out there on the golf course—"

"Let's get started," CFO interrupted Manager, as she took the seat at the head of the table. "I believe you've met Finance Manager, Inventory Manager, and Assistant Controller. Why don't we have the others in our group introduce themselves? FRM, why don't you start."

FRM stood up and gave an awkward wave arching left to right.

"Hi, I'm FRM," he said, and then sat down.

"Tell everyone a little bit about yourself," insisted CFO.

"Um. Ok," said FRM, standing back up again and repeating the exact same awkward wave. "Well...I'm not sure what to say. I'm FRM. I've been at the company for what? ...four weeks now? Yeah, something like that. I came from An Audit Firm where I was an audit senior."

"So, you came from *AN* Audit Firm not THE Audit & Tax Firm?" Partner asked with a smile.

"Yep!" FRM said, unfazed by the question. "My wife and I are expecting our first baby in April, so the audit needs to be done by then."

"Congratulations!" Partner exclaimed, as he looked directly at Manager, "Having a baby AFTER you've left public accounting is the perfect thing to do. Parental leave is such a drag on billable hours."

Manager, who had just returned to work from parental leave for his third child, rolled his eyes. The whole room gave an uncomfortable half laugh. FRM quickly took his seat.

"I guess that means I'm up," said Senior Accountant – she did not stand up and her wave was sort of an off the shoulder salute. "I'm Senior Accountant. I am not going to stand up because if you can't tell, I'm fairly pregnant – due in December!"

"Congratulations," said SM. "Is this your first?"

"No," replied Senior Accountant. "This is number four – four under five."

> **Staff 2 pinging Manager:** *4TH?!, Did she really just say 4th? How do you work a job and have four KIDS?! Maybe her husband is like a stay at home dad?*
>
> **Manager pinging Staff 2:** *How can you afford a husband and four kids on Senior Accountant money? I bet she's only making like $65,000 a year.*

"Wow," replied SM. "You are looking good for having four kids! And four under five!! How do you stay sane??! And looking so fit?"

Manager pinging Staff 2: Awkward!

Staff 2 pinging Manager: No kidding, LOL

"The doctor has me resting quite a bit," answered Senior Accountant, as she blushed slightly. "I'm only working about six hours a day now. I worked all the way up until delivery for the last two. My husband only works about 20 hours a week, so he has the flexibility to stay with the kids, but I keep working to pay the bills."

"That's impressive," said Partner, not really knowing what to say.

> **Manager to Staff 2:** *She has four kids and that is "Impressive", while me having three kids is annoying since I had them all at the Firm and missed two weeks of work for each one?*

> **Staff 2 pinging Manager:** *Yep. That's exactly what I heard.*

"Yeah," CFO said with a smile. "She was pushing the send button on an email to the auditors last year and pushing the baby out at the same time. No pain medicine at all. No kidding."

> **Staff 1 pinging Senior 1:** *I would have died if I had done that! That is just CRAZY!*

> **Senior 1 pinging Staff 1:** *I know! With my second daughter, I was so drugged up and out of it, I would have written a fabulous email to the auditors. LOL.*

"We don't want that to happen again," said Finance Manager. "So please get all your requests to Senior Accountant ASAP. She'll get everything she can for you right away and then be back from parental leave in March to help wrap up the audit."

"While we are talking about requests, I'd like to make one of my own," Inventory Manager said, aggressively. "I'm super busy. I will answer your questions one time, but I can't answer them more than that. I really do not have time to teach auditors everything."

"Inventory Manager is the busiest person in our group," said Finance Manager, in an effort to tone down Inventory Manager's aggressiveness. "He will get you what you need as long as he isn't in the middle of close each month, which is the first two weeks. During those weeks, please only bug him in emergencies. Ask FRM your questions those weeks."

> **Manager pinging SM:** *Great, first day and we don't have access to inventory accounting half the time and Senior Accountant is going to be out half the audit answering emails while on bedrest. SMH.*

> **SM pinging Manager:** *With how demanding Inventory Manager seems to be on our question asking, it may not be a bad thing we get a break from him every few weeks.*

"Great!" said CFO, looking around the room. "That covers the people on our side. Let's hear about your team. Partner, would you mind introducing everyone?"

"Hi everyone," Partner said, standing up. "I'm Partner. I've been with THE Audit & Tax Firm, I guess I should say THE Accounting Firm now, for just over 20 years and have been a partner for the last seven years."

"Next to me," said Partner, pointing at SM, "is SM, our Senior Manager. If he ever looks out of it, just give him an energy drink or ask him about his dogs. We are very excited to have him on the team this year to help me oversee the audit and with my overall review."

"Next to SM is Manager, our audit Manager," continued Partner, gesturing towards Manager. "He's a bit strange for an accountant. He actually gets along with people and likes being around them. As a result, any issues you have with the team or with how the audit is going should go through Manager. He just moved back to town about a year ago."

"Why on earth did you move back here?" asked Inventory Manager – it came out very blunt with only the slightest hint of sarcasm. Thankfully, Manager's parents were family friends with Inventory Manager's parents and Manager had known Inventory Manager for several years. He took the question in stride.

"After we had our second son, my wife started looking for an opportunity to move back here to be closer to her family," Manager replied, enthusiastically. "Given how much I work, she really appreciates the family support she gets here."

"We are glad it worked out," said Partner – he was visibly uncomfortable with Manager talking about his family in front of the client and tried to move on quickly. "Next to Manager is Senior 3, our lead audit senior. Several people confuse him for an IT guy, but he doesn't like that, so please try not to. This will be his fifth Busy Season with us... Oh, yeah, one last thing – if you see him looking at his phone, just say 'swipe right'."

The delivery wasn't there on either joke, but the whole room gave him a courtesy laugh and Partner looked very pleased with himself. Senior 3 looked less happy, but forced a smile and said, "very nice to meet all of you."

> **Manager pinging Senior 3:** *LOL. Which one was better, Partner taking me up on the "don't confuse him for an IT guy" piece of the introduction or the one about swiping right that he came up with on his own?*

> **Senior 3 pinging Manager:** *ha-ha – so funny, Swipe right had to have come from Staff 2. Partner has no idea what Dating App even is.*

> **Staff 2 pinging Senior 3:** *Did you meet the receptionist this morning? If I weren't already dating someone, I'd swipe right on her.*

> **Senior 3 pinging Staff 2:** *Very funny...NOT!...She was kind of cute though.*

Partner then pointed across the table to Senior 1. "This is Senior 1," he said. "She has been with us for almost three years now. She may seem quiet at first, but she really knows her stuff."

"Next to Senior 1 is Staff 2," Partner continued. "Staff 2 manages some of his own rental properties. He gets random calls from tenants at very strange hours. The good news there is he is used to answering the phone and dealing with unreasonable requests or demands at all hours, day or night. Feel free to call him with questions whenever you'd like."

> **Staff 2 pinging Senior 1:** *Wow, Partner actually knows something about me. I'm feeling a little Firm pride now.*

> **Senior 1 pinging Staff 2:** *Oh, he got that from Manager. Before the meeting started, he asked Manager about how he should introduce everyone. Also, he just gave the client permission to call you 24/7.*

> **Staff 2 pinging Senior 1:** *Ok, feeling deflated again.*

"On this side of me is…"

> **Manager pinging Partner:** *Staff 1 – started last month, just finished CPA exam. At the end of the table is Intern – tennis scholarship.*

"Staff 1," said Partner, pointing towards Staff 1. "She started with us just last month after finishing up her degree. She just passed her final CPA exam last week."

Staff 1 beamed with pride, but Partner had already moved on to Intern before anyone could tell her congratulations on passing her exams.

"Finally, at the end of the table is Intern," said Partner. "Intern is currently on a tennis scholarship at school and has one more year to wrap up the program there."

"Awesome," said CFO, cheerfully. "It is great to meet all of you and we look forward to working with each of you. Before we get down to business, I just want to say that my door is always open to any of you."

"Wonderful," said Partner. "We really appreciate it and we are committed to having an open and honest dialogue throughout the audit as we work together. We want to build a great relationship and be collaborative in working through issues as much as possible. We want your team to feel free to reach out to us whenever an issue or technical question arises."

"I think this will be a great year," replied CFO. "We know that there are several accounting firms that could provide us with basically the same audit at basically the same price. I want you to know that we chose your Firm in large part because of how impressed we were with how open and direct your team was through the bid process."

"Thank you," said Partner, happily. "We do appreciate hearing that we were selected due to our—"

"And with that," CFO cut Partner off and looked towards Staff 2, "do you have an agenda for the meeting?"

Staff 2 passed the agenda out to everyone. Staff 2 had printed the agendas on 40 lb. paper and SM even let him run the cost through as a reimbursable expense!

"I like the new logo," said Finance Manager. "It seems fresh and energetic."

"I completely agree," replied Partner. "This logo seems to scream 'creative accounting firm'. I really like it!"

> **SM pinging Manager:** *He did not just say that. "Creative accounting firm"? Oh SNAP!*

> **Manager pinging SM:** *ROFL!!! Biting my tongue super hard*

The only other person in the room who seemed to get what

Partner had just said was Inventory Manager. His hand was covering his face, his palm was pressed hard against his lips, and his head was shaking. When Manager caught his eye, he almost lost it.

"Looks like the first item on the list is the Client Support List," said Finance Manager. "Did you guys send that over already?"

"We did last week," Senior 3 answered, pleasantly. "You replied saying you would get right on it."

"I did?" Finance Manager said, scratching his head before a light seemed to come on inside his mind. "Oh wait…I did see that. I distributed it to the group and I think we put a few things up on the shared drive, right guys?"

"I added the July 31, trial balance yesterday," said FRM. "I—"

"I don't think that was ready yet," Assistant Controller interjected. "I still had a couple adjustments to push through so numbers will still be changing."

> **Manager pinging SM:** *Great, here we are in the middle of September and they are still adjusting July. This is going to be awesome! (sarcasm)*

> **SM pinging Manager:** *Hopefully, it is some one-off items and not that big of a deal*

"What still needs to be adjusted?" SM asked Assistant Controller, respectfully. "Generally, for interim testing, it is ok if a few one-off items are still moving around."

"Well, I've been pretty swamped trying to rework our consolidation file, so I still need to book depreciation, amortization, reconcile AP and post all the equity transactions – that's new investments, shares issued, and dividends paid – for the month of July," replied Assistant Controller, in a matter of fact tone.

"Oh," Senior Accountant jumped in. "I've got to reconcile the bank accounts still. As I said earlier, this pregnancy has put me a bit behind."

> **SM pinging Manager:** *That is not what I expected.*
>
> **Manager pinging SM:** *We are pretty much screwed.*
>

"We will continue to upload stuff as it gets done over the next couple weeks," said Finance Manager. "Let's move on to talk about timing."

"Sure," said Senior 3. "We are going to work through the rest of our planning over the next week and then we expect to come out here for a few weeks. We'll also be here at the beginning of November for Interim testing. At year-end, we plan to be back the first week of February and be here until we issue on March 31."

"You mean to tell me that you sent us the Client Support List before you guys finished planning?" Finance Manager asked Senior 3, with a look of surprise.

"As CFO pointed out, an audit is an audit," SM said, indifferently. "Our planning won't impact 90% of the requests anyway."

"Ok, good to know that planning is such an important aspect of the audit…Oh, I thought of one other thing. Please remember that Inventory Manager will be in close in a week and a half, so please take care of his walkthroughs first," said Finance Manager. "Did you send requests for the walkthroughs yet?"

"Yes," replied Staff 2. "That was all on a separate tab."

"I guess we totally missed that," said Finance Manager, chuckling to himself. "We will have to work through finishing July close, getting your audit support requests, and then get started on these walkthrough requests."

> **Staff 2 pinging Manager:** *So far, they have uploaded a total of 7 files to the shared drive and 4 of those are completely useless based on what Assistant Controller was saying.*

Manager pinging Staff 2: *Yep. Great start!*

"Ok," said CFO. "It sounds like we've started to provide some things. Hopefully, we will have more by the time you get through your planning and you can stay busy when you come out here. Is there anything left to discuss?"

The room was silent. The audit team was too shocked at the complete lack of preparation or support from the finance team to have any response.

"Alright," said CFO. "If that is it, then let's wrap up. We are very excited about working with your team and once again, please let me know if there is anything I can do to help move things along. We will do our best to make the audit go as smoothly as possible. We are very committed to giving you our full support."

"I'm excited too," said Inventory Manager, very sarcastically. "I mean, an audit, especially a first-year audit, is really like going in for a colonoscopy. Nobody really enjoys it, but If you HAVE to have it done, you may as well like the proctologist."

> **Staff 2 pinging Manager:** *He really compared an audit to getting a colonoscopy?*

> **Manager pinging Staff 2:** *Indeed! Pretty awesome dude that Inventory Manager! SMH.*

"Thank you all for coming today," added Finance Manager. "I think this will be our best audit yet! I'm looking forward to working with all of you."

CHAPTER 5 – FRESH, ORGANIC, NON-GMO, VEGAN, GLUTEN-FREE, FRUIT (AND OTHER AUDIT SNACK FOOD GROUPS)

The entire team showed up at Widget Maker a week later. After waiting for nearly 20 minutes in the lobby, CFO, Finance Manager, Inventory Manager, and Assistant Controller came through.

"Did another meeting go over?" Manager asked, as he looked at Inventory Manager's hands clutching, and trying to hide, a golf glove.

"A very strategic meeting," CFO replied, quickly. "Finance Manager and Assistant Controller, why don't you show the team the conference room they'll be working in!"

"How has the name change been working? Do people call you TAF now? Or are you using the full name, The Accounting Firm?" Finance Manager inquired, eagerly.

"TAF is a perfectly acceptable acronym for the firm name," Partner replied as he smiled widely.

"Great!" Finance Manager said, energetically. "Let's show you to the room."

The "conference room" for the audit team – if you could even call it a conference room – was more like an oversized storage closet that was down in the basement of the building. It was right next to the boiler room, had no windows and very little ventilation.

"The service elevator is broken," said Assistant Controller, as he pointed towards a cage-like thing that must have been the service elevator. "For now, you will have to use the stairs."

Inside the room was a disheveled mix of old desks and office chairs, most of which were in some way dysfunctional or broken. Manager sat on one of the chairs that looked ok and two things happened. First, the chair sunk to the floor. Second, the back of the chair fell right off. He quickly got up and moved the broken pieces to the far end of the room where there were some other clearly broken items.

The only things on the wall were two mounted moose heads. Staff 1 was disgusted and repulsed and slowly moved away from the heads and sat as far away as she could get facing the opposite direction.

"Oh, those are the CEO's" Finance Manager said, pointing at the moose heads. "He's a hunter, but his wife doesn't like having them in the house and CFO told him it was distasteful to have them in the big conference room where we had our kick-off meeting a week ago, so they ended up down here. Occasionally, he'll come down to show them to an investor, especially if it is one of the investors he goes hunting with."

The room was lit by two fluorescent light fixtures that dangled from the ceiling. One of the cords that held the lights was fraying badly and looked like it could break at any moment.

The light connected to that cord flickered slightly every few seconds. Various water pipes ran across the ceiling as well. Suddenly, there was the sound of draining water that lasted four or five seconds, followed by dripping noises for another 10 seconds or so.

"Well, now, I am feeling flushed!" Finance Manager said, giggling, as he looked up at the pipe.

"Oh, I forgot to show you," Assistant Controller said, moving towards the far wall of the room. "There is internet in here. The wireless doesn't get down here so we had to run some hard wires. Let's see…oh, there it is. It comes right down this wall to this router. There you go. Also, we have a mini-fridge for you."

The mini-fridge shook just a little and started humming loudly for thirty seconds, then went quiet again, then repeated the cycle every five minutes.

"The best thing is that you don't have to walk upstairs to go to the bathroom. There's one right here! We'll probably have to get some soap though," said Finance Manager, pointing at a cracked door.

Inside was a toilet and sink that looked to be at least forty years old. The tile was cracked everywhere and as Finance Manager turned on the water, it spurted reddish-brown water off and on for a good ten seconds before it became a solid, clear stream. He tried the switch for the ventilation fan and nothing happened. He then cracked the door again, which is when the team noticed the door frame was much taller than it needed to be and the door hung with a full, five-inch gap between the bottom of the door and the floor.

"Finally," announced Assistant Controller, pointing at the desk by the router. "We put this phone down here so we don't have to walk down here to talk to you. I'll get you a contact list with everyone's email's and extensions so that, in theory, you would never have to leave 'the cave' except to go home at night (if you ever get to do that)."

"Well, we will let you get settled," said Finance Manager to SM. "Hope it works out for you guys down here."

Then turning to the whole team, he added sarcastically, "Better than any audit room I ever had."

Finance Manager and Assistant Controller left the room. The audit team could hear them laughing all the way up the stairwell.

Partner looked around the room and then put his computer back in his bag, "I'm going to go work from the office," he said. "Let me know if you need anything. Hope that you can find enough chairs and desks in this mess to have decent workstations....oh, and one last thing...let's make our first team rule that no one uses that bathroom...EVER...for ANYTHING!"

After Partner left, the rest of the team, except Staff 1 who had already found her chair and desk, moved around the room testing out the desks and chairs and looking through the rest of the random stuff in the room. The most interesting things discovered in the cave, aside from the moose heads, was the sports paraphernalia. There were signed jerseys, a signed photo of Mickey Mantle, a signed Michael Jordan rookie card in a frame and a few random golf clubs.

"I guess his wife doesn't like sports either," said Manager, gazing down at the Mickey Mantle photo that they'd found in a drawer of one of the desks. "Some of this stuff is probably worth a lot."

"You would think that a company as big as Widget Maker would have a decent conference room to have the auditors use," said Staff 2, a little annoyed, as another chair started sinking on him as he tried sitting on it.

"They pay us a blended fee that is a lot of money. If they want some of those hours to be us walking back and forth from this hole to their offices upstairs, that is their choice," said Manager, trying to make the best of things. "Every client I've ever worked on has put the auditors as far away from their finance department as possible."

"Let's get all set up and settled in and then go through what we need everyone to do today to get things rolling," said SM, as he settled on a desk and an old fabric chair that looked like it had been in the basement since the seventies. It didn't sink because it didn't adjust up and down at all. SM then found a desk that was the right height for the chair and dropped his laptop bag on it. The desk broke right in half with the weight of the bag. The halves were hauled off by Senior 3 and Staff 2 and SM found a sturdier looking desk and sat down.

The team spent the next 20 minutes or so finding chairs that were functional, booting up, trying to get the internet to work (which eventually did, but was VERY slow), and opening up the Widget Maker audit file and shared drive. Once this was all done, SM called the room to order and started making assignments.

"Manager, I need you to start on the budget. Evaluate what the setbacks in requests are going to cost us as far as margin, see if we need to submit a write-off, and increase the budget for all of Assistant Controller's assigned areas," started SM.

"Just his areas?" asked Manager, a little surprised. "It seems we probably need to raise budgets for his, Inventory Manager's, Senior Accountant's and FRM's areas based on how the kick-off meeting went."

"That's fair," replied SM. "we'd better get it all out in the open now."

> **Senior 3 pinging Manager:** *Wait, why are we raising the budgets? On our first day here? Things might not be as bad in reality as they sounded in the meeting.*

> **Manager pinging Senior 3:** *You are right!*

Senior 3 pinging Manager: *I am?*

Manager pinging Senior 3: *They will probably be much worse. I had a manager once who would always tell me that you can't fix stupid. One thing to learn this year as you prepare to make the jump to the manager level – the earlier you identify negative variances in the budget, the less trouble you get in later...oh, and ALWAYS save positive variances for the end.*

Senior 3 pinging Manager: *Aren't we supposed to adjust either way, according to Firm policy?*

Manager pinging Senior 3: *Have you ever met anyone who really got upset about being pleasantly surprised?*

Senior 3 pinging Manager: *I guess not.*

Manager pinging Senior 3: *The longer you wait on bad news, the worse it generally gets. When Congrieve said "hell hath no fury like a woman scorned" he had never dealt with an audit partner whose team waited until the end of an audit to report that they were way over budget on hours and they lost all the margin on the job. That little nugget is the best piece of career coaching you've ever received from me.*

Senior 3 pinging Manager: *So, we came into this audit forecasting 50% margin on this engagement and now after day 1 in the field we will tell them that needs to drop to 40%?*

Manager pinging Senior 3: *More like 30%*

Senior 3 pinging Manager: *What is that going to mean for our hours out here then? If our profit margin is going down...*

> **Manager pinging Senior 3:** *Take a wild guess, but you need to prepare the team for the worst*

The whole time Manager and Senior 3 were pinging, SM had been giving Senior 3 instructions.

"Do you understand what you are doing Senior 3?" asked SM.

"Sorry," replied Senior 3, looking up from his onscreen conversation with Manager. "I was distracted. Could you say that again, please?"

"Okay," said SM. "Next time, stop setting up your date for tonight and start paying attention. I need you to go back through the request list and come up with the top priority items so we can give Finance Manager an "Urgent List". Also, go through the list and see what requests can shift from Senior Accountant to the others given how we will likely get no help at all from her."

"I'm on it," Senior 3 answered, energetically.

"Senior 1," continued SM, turning to look to the other end of the room where Senior 1 had set up camp. "I need you to start setting up meetings with process owners for walkthroughs. Ask if they have process narratives. Explain that we will want to walk through one transaction in each process from start to finish and that they will need to have support for us to illustrate each step of the way. Schedule an initial meeting for one hour and then schedule a follow-up meeting for additional questions."

"I can do that," replied Senior 1.

"Staff 2, figure out something for Intern to do and then coach her on how to do it," SM ordered. "And Staff 1, you will be creating account summary sheets for each group of accounts. I am very particular about how these should be set up for the optimal ease of review later on, so I will coach you on this and you will be a superstar on these from now on."

"I'm so excited!" exclaimed Staff 1. "Thank you for taking the time to coach me and help my performance!"

"Don't get too excited," replied SM. "It is just account summary sheets, but since I am going to make you a pro at them, I guess you can be a little excited."

> **Manager pinging Staff 2:** *How long before the excitement wears off? It has been too long for me to remember.*

> **Staff 2 pinging Manager:** *Some can carry it all the way through their first year, but given the fact that there is still a grand total of seven files in the shared folder, and we have SM and Partner to deal with on a first-year client, I'm giving Staff 1 three to five months max.*

> **Staff 2 pinging Senior 3:** *What should I have Intern do?*

> **Senior 3 pinging Staff 2:** *I don't know. Ask Manager.*

> **Staff 2 pinging Manager:** *What should I have Intern do?*

> **Manager pinging Staff 2:** *Start spending the client's money.*

> **Staff 2 pinging Manager:** *Huh?*

> **Manager pinging Staff 2:** *The engagement letter says they will reimburse up to $40 THOUSAND of expenses. I think this lousy room could use some audit snacks, the junker fridge needs to be stocked with drinks and we should plan to do team lunches every day!*

> **Staff 2 pinging Manager:** *Are you serious? Like free lunch, every day? For real? The highest I've ever had is twice a week except for at Oil & Gas Producer where they had a cafeteria, but they made us eat there every day which was horrible.*

Manager pinging Staff 2: *I'm serious as a heart attack. If they decided to stick us down in this lousy room, they can pay for our lunch EVERY SINGLE DAY.*

Staff 2 pinging Manager: *Awesome!*

Manager pinging Staff 2: *Have the intern gather requests for snacks and drinks. She can run out to a warehouse store right after lunch and pick it all up.*

Staff 2 pinging Manager: *You got it boss-man!*

Manager pinging Staff 2: *We will just have to figure out how to get it in here without the client seeing us. I promise you that if they know we have snacks loaded down here we will get three visits a day from half the department – not to help us with the audit at all – just to eat the snacks.*

Staff 2 pinging Manager: *I think I found a solution a minute ago when I was out exploring. There is an emergency exit door that goes into a stairwell on the side of the building. It is marked as an emergency door, but the wires appeared to have been cut. We tested it – no alarm.*

Manager pinging Staff 2: *Nice! That sounds perfect. We also need a list of decent lunch places around here. Intern could put that together too.*

"Intern, I have some great ideas for things you can do," Staff 2 called Intern over to his desk. "You need to get snacks for the team. In all, there are at least seven, audit, snack food groups."

"Hold on, I need to find my pen so I can write this down," Intern said, as she reached into her bag.

Senior 3 pinging Staff 2: *You know a good Intern by how fast they start writing instructions down.*

C.P. Aiden

"K. Got it," said Intern, bringing out a new pen and fresh writing pad.

"The seven audit food groups are; Dried Fruit, Gummies (including fruit snacks), granola and protein bars, M&M's and other chocolate, jerky and gum," Staff 2 explained.

"Wait, that's only six," Intern pointed out politely.

"You can probably skip the seventh category," Manager interjected. "There is always someone on the team who wants fresh, organic, non-GMO, vegan, gluten-free, grass-fed, free-range, cage-free, fair-trade, no sugar added fruit."

"There are organic fruits that are non-GMO, vegan, grass-fed, cage-free and gluten-free?" asked Intern, a little confused.

"No, I just added it in there because the companies that label their fruit with really dumb, uninformative labels are stupid," replied Manager. Then, getting on his soapbox, he added, "I have nothing against the labels themselves. In fact, I like my free-range, grass-fed beef, but everyone knows all fruit is gluten-free. You don't have to slap a label on the fruit and take credit for something that is so blatantly obvious and commonly known. It feels like an effort to take advantage of stupid people to charge a higher price for an attribute that the item they are selling inherently has."

"I see" replied Intern, looking up from the notepad – she had been writing down everything Manager was saying.

"I mean I saw a bag of tortilla chips – corn tortilla chips – the other day and it has this big "GF" on it," continued Manager, getting very into it. "Everyone knows that corn doesn't have gluten. It wasn't bread or crackers or something that a "GF" label might provide useful information on! All these natural grocery stores try to put a premium price on the same stuff you can get in the organic section of a normal grocery store just by adding five additional 'true but stupid' labels onto the piece of fruit. The best part is that all the sticky stuff from all the labels stuck to the fruit probably make it worse for you than just eating regular fruit! 'Please enjoy your gluten-free, non-GMO, vegan, no sugar added, grown in the USA, apple.' After that first bite, that tastes like the sticky part of an envelope, you hear a voice inside your head that says 'the stickers used to label this product contain compounds known by the state of California to cause cancer, birth defects or reproductive harm!'. In the end, you can pay regular price for an apple grown on trees that had pesticide and get cancer or you can buy an apple covered in all this great labeling and get cancer – pick your poison, literally."

Manager was out of breath after his long monologue and the rest of the team was sitting in shock. They could not tell how serious his ranting was so they did not know if he was being completely serious or totally sarcastic. Either way, no one wanted to say anything. Finally, Intern started laughing.

"That is too funny," she said in between gasps and laughs. "You like your corn-fed, grass-fed, free-range, no animals were hurt in the production of this packaging (except the cow the meat inside the package came from), but you think all the labeling on the fruit is total hoopla."

"Like I said, I don't have a problem with labeling what something is if it really is beneficial information to the consumer," Manager began defending himself to the team. "For example, if something is really non-GMO when most products similar to that item are genetically engineered, then knowing that about what you are buying is a good thing and can be useful."

"I agree," added Senior 3. "Labels can be really good."

> **Manager pinging Staff 2:** *Let's remind him that he said labels are good next time he gets mad at us for calling him IT guy!*

> **Staff 2 pinging Manager:** *Ha! Perfect*

"This seems like a very sensitive topic for all of you," said Staff 2. "Can we move on with the snack list now?"

"Ah, yes! Sorry," said Manager. "We were on the seventh food group. The problem with the fresh fruit is that it never gets eaten, especially when the other six audit food groups discussed earlier are readily available. Then it gets forgotten and three months later you find a huge pile of mold over in the snack corner covering what once was fresh, organic, blah, blah, blah fruit. Down here in the cave...my guess is that process would only take a week or two."

"Actually," Staff 1 spoke up, hesitantly. "I would totally eat the fresh, organic, non-GMO fruit. Like for real. I am from Hippy Town after all."

"Ok," replied Manager, laughing mostly at the Hippy Town comment. "Not my money, so I don't care, but I will bet you $20 that over half of the extra-special fruit gets all moldy by the time we come back in November."

"You are on," said Staff 1, and then, while looking nervously at Manager, she added, "But the fruit has to come from a natural grocer and include all the tags you mentioned."

"The gum can be sugar-free too, right?" asked Intern. "Then we'd have two, maybe three, depending on the granola or protein bars, of seven groups with no sugar added. The rest sounds like diabetes in a bag."

"Fine," said Manager. "Just fine. And to my earlier point, the sugar-free label on gum actually means something. It is informative and adds value to those who would rather coat their teeth with unknown chemicals than with sugar."

"Great," SM chimed in. "But I think you forgot the medicinal group."

"I haven't heard of that," Senior 3 indicated. "What is it?"

"Energy drinks, pain pills, allergy pills and, of course, those little packs of powder that you add to water and they give you like a power punch of Vitamin C and a bunch of other great stuff to keep you from getting the flu!" SM answered eagerly.

"Only you would lump energy drinks in with medicine," Manager joked. "Also, only you would think that the medicine category would fit in as a snacks category."

The comment came across more as an insult than intended and everyone in the room went quiet. Within five minutes, Intern circulated an excel spreadsheet that had the eight categories discussed over the top and each team member's name going down the rows in the first column.

Dear Team,

I have been asked to get audit snacks after lunch today. Please add what you would like in each of the seven audit food groups and what your favorite over-the-counter medicines are and I will pick it all up! If you want doubles of something, just relist it.

Thanks,

Intern

Five minutes later, Intern had her grocery list.

"You listed XL bag of peanut M&M's four times," Intern said to Senior 3.

"I want four big bags," Senior 3 replied, seriously. "I get hungry and those are my favorite – sugar, chocolate, and protein all in one. Plus, it isn't my money, so I want lots."

"You got it," Intern said, while trying not to giggle.

Next up was making the list of potential lunch places.

"Will you now also put together a list of decent lunch places within three miles of here?" Staff 2 asked Intern.

"I would love to," replied Intern. "Anything in mind? Favorites? Preferences? Dislikes?"

"There's a lot of stuff down by the mall that is good," SM piped up, quickly, as he was very particular about the places he would eat. "You have to add Mexican Restaurant – an awesome Mexican place down there. In fact, let's go there today, so we don't have to do a big long process to decide about where to go to lunch."

"Great!" said Intern, eagerly. "I will get the rest of the list going."

Ten minutes later, Intern sent the list to Staff 2 and asked him to look over it to see what he thought. The list included:

Mexican Restaurant, Slimy Meat Sub Place, Fast Food Burger Place 1, Fast Food Burger Place 2, Quick Burrito Place, Fast Food Burger Place 3, Fast Food Chicken, Fast Food Asian – the list continued with several other fast food places.

Oh, dear! thought Staff 2. *I've failed as a coach. She's still thinking like she's in college and that she is spending her own money for lunch…duh.*

Staff 2 kindly explained to Intern that she had made a good first pass at the list, that he had not done so well explaining what he wanted and then clarified the expectation. Look online and pick out restaurants within three miles of here that have over 100 reviews and get four stars or better. We have up to twenty-five dollars per person each lunch.

"Oh, you mean we are going to go to *NICE and EXPENSIVE* places!" shouted Intern, as her eyes widened. "I'm going to gain so much weight!"

"They don't call it the first-year fifteen for nothing," Staff 1 said, patting her stomach. "I thank The Accounting Firm when kids at church ask if I'm having a baby."

"With that said, who's ready to get out of this miserable cave and go stuff ourselves with a huge lunch?" asked Manager.

Everyone was ready and thirty seconds later the team left the cave and walked up the stairs.

The Good Audit

"How do we get back to the reception desk?" asked Staff 1, cautiously.

"Not just that," replied Manager, looking up and down the hall at the top of the stairs. "How do we get out of here without passing the accounting department?"

"We could go through the break room and down that hall," suggested Staff 2, pointing down to the right.

They started that way, but in the middle of the break room, Manager said, "No good. We'd be walking right past CEO's office every day that way."

"Wasn't there a hall back there that went past the bathrooms that would put us on the other side of the floor?" asked SM, as he pointed back towards the stairwell.

"Puts us pretty close to Inventory Manager," replied Manager, anxiously. "But it probably is the best route out."

"We could always go back down to the basement, out the emergency exit – the one that doesn't sound an alarm and crawl up the stairwell," suggested Staff 2.

"I don't want to do that all the time," replied Manager. "Let's just go this way."

The team walked down the hall past the bathrooms. Just as they turned the corner, they ran into Inventory Manager.

"Hey, guys!" he said, cheerfully. "Where are you all going?...wait a minute...look at the time. You must all be going to lunch."

"Yes," said SM. "I figure the first day of the audit probably merits a team lunch. There was a lot to take in downstairs in that... that...audit room."

"I see," said Inventory Manager, and then he stood in the middle of the hallway in complete silence with a huge mischievous smile on his face.

"Dude," Manager said, furrowing his eyebrows. "Are you gonna let us get past?"

"Where are you going today?" Inventory Manager asked, bluntly.

"This great place called Mexican Restaurant down by the mall," Intern piped up, before anyone could stop her.

"Really?!" said Inventory Manager. "Right out of the gate you are going to a nice, and very tasty, sit-down lunch with the whole team? I don't know if I should tell someone, maybe someone like CFO, that this is what you are doing with company money."

"What do you want from Mexican Restaurant?" asked Manager, a little annoyed as he realized what Inventory Manager was up to and saw no choice but to go along with it.

"That's more like it!" said Inventory Manager, with a grin that made Manager want to knock his teeth out. "I'll take a carne asada burrito with extra guac."

"Great," said Manager, trying hard to keep his temper from boiling over. "We will be back in about an hour or so."

"Perfect," said Inventory Manager, moving aside to let the team pass. "This is going to work out great. You guys can take my order every day. After all, the company is paying for it, right?"

As the team funneled into the elevator and the door shut, SM commented to Manager, "one is better than eight as long as he keeps his mouth shut."

CHAPTER 6 – FINDING HUGE MISTAKES IS EVERY AUDITOR'S DREAM

The following week, the audit team finally started meeting with the Widget Maker finance team to document each process. Staff 2 was in Assistant Controller's office going over the fixed asset process and things were not going well.

"What do you mean, the system just books the entry?" Staff 2 asked, sharply.

"Our old auditors never asked us so many questions," Assistant Controller said, squirming in his chair a bit while small beads of sweat started forming all over his face and a large blood vessel was quickly growing and bulging out of the middle of his forehead.

"Can you just show me how the depreciation entry actually gets recorded?" asked Staff 2.

"That is simple, and since I still have to do it for July, I will do that right now so this isn't such a huge waste of time," replied Assistant Controller.

Assistant Controller logged into the accounting system, went to the depreciation module, selected July and hit "run".

"See, the system automatically does it. I hit the button and I'm done. Now, are you done with your questions?" asked Assistant Controller, impatiently.

"Can I get a screenshot of that to show what is done in the system?" Staff 2 asked.

"Fine," said Assistant Controller, going back to his snipping tool. "You now have TWENTY-TWO screenshots in your inbox. Our previous auditors never even asked us for a single one! Now, are you finished?"

"Almost," replied Staff 2 – Assistant Controller's hands flew into the air and he let out a flabbergasted and annoyed sigh. "The last thing I need is to see the depreciation expense account detail so I can see the entry that you say the system just booked made it through to the general ledger."

"Easy. As I said, the system does everything automatically once I push that button," replied Assistant Controller, as he started punching account details into the system. "I suppose you'll want a screenshot of that too? Then will you be done asking me questions?"

"About depreciation? Yes," said Staff 2. "I do have some additional questions about those unrecorded asset tags sitting here on your desk though."

The very annoyed Assistant Controller pushed "Run" on the account detail report. It came back blank. "That can't be right," Assistant Controller said, with a look of disbelief as he started clicking more report options.

"Try just looking at the depreciation expense on the trial balance," Staff 2 suggested, trying to be helpful. Assistant Controller started spinning into a panicked and defensive spiral. The trial balance was also showing zero for depreciation for the whole year.

"Where could this be going?" Assistant Controller shouted aloud, shaking his fist at his monitor. "I guess I've never checked to see if the entry actually makes it to the general ledger – the system is just supposed to work."

"Did I just hear that right? You've NEVER CHECKED THIS?!" Staff 2 asked, bluntly, while shaking his head in disbelief.

Assistant Controller was now frantically looking through the system. "Oh, dear…this isn't good…I think I've found the problem," he said, looking up at Staff 2 like a sad, lost puppy with its tail between its legs. "The module seems to be set up for tax books only, so we haven't been recording depreciation on our financial books."

"Wait! Can you say that again? You've never recorded depreciation on your financial books?" Staff 2 asked in amazement.

"That's what I said. Yep, accounting books have nothing recorded," Assistant Controller said. "How big can that really be for this year though?"

"Well," said Staff 2, opening up his calculator. "If you have $1.2 billion of fixed assets at an average life of twenty years that is five million a month and we are nine months into the year comes out to about $45 million!"

"Yeah, but it doesn't matter anyway," said Assistant Controller, trying to convince Staff 2 that he could just brush it aside. "EBITDA is the only thing investors care about. The D in EBITDA is depreciation, so it is an add back whether it is $45 million or zero, EBITDA doesn't change!"

Assistant Controller looked proud for coming up with what sounded to him like a very reasonable explanation for why the auditors should ignore the mistake altogether, no matter the size. He sat quietly gazing at Staff 2 as if he were playing a game of chess and had just declared checkmate.

"We are auditing your financial statements, NOT EBITDA," said

Staff 2, in a tone that clearly told Assistant Controller that Staff 2 thought he was the dumbest person alive. "You still have to record depreciation!"

"Let's go ask CFO," replied Assistant Controller, upping the ante to assert himself and show Staff 2 that he was not willing to go down without a fight.

The two walked down to CFO's office and explained what was happening. CFO was shocked that the system could have been set up wrong and that nobody caught that depreciation had never been recorded. Ultimately, she agreed with Staff 2's position and told Assistant Controller to work with IT to fix the problem and report back to her. She also asked Staff 2 to send SM up to discuss the implication to prior years and if they'd have to get the former auditors involved. Staff 2 wondered how on earth the prior auditors could have missed the fact that the company had recorded zero depreciation expense on $1.2 billion of fixed assets.

CFO thanked Staff 2 for his hard work and for bringing this important issue to her attention. "We should ask our old auditors to give us back the fees we paid them. Totally useless. I can't believe they missed this for so long!"

Staff 2 thought to himself, *you guys totally missed this too, but sure, blame the old auditors for your problems. I guess it is sort of their fault too.* He then returned to the audit cave triumphant.

"We have our first BIG STINC!" he exclaimed, as he walked into the cave. "Like blow-your-mind, MASSIVE STINC!"

"Why are you so happy about a STINC?" SM said. "A STINC just means we have to do more work."

"What is a STINC?" asked Intern.

"Sorry, all these acronyms we use," said SM. "A STINC refers to the Summary of Things Identified that are Not Correct. It means we found a mistake that is large enough that we ask the company to record an adjustment to their books to fix it. When we find large errors, we accumulate them on a spreadsheet we call the STINC. If a company STINC's enough (or has big enough entries on the STINC), we are required to report the issues to their Board of Directors."

"Understood," said Intern.

"SM is right though," said Manager, jumping into the conversation as he saw an opportunity to provide coaching to the intern in front of SM. "The thing at The Accounting Firm that stinks the most is finding a STINC because it equals a ton of extra work."

"Why does it make us have to do more work? Isn't it our job as auditors to find the mistakes?" Intern was curious. "It isn't like we are the ones that have to go into the system and fix it, right?"

"It means we have to decide and document just how badly they messed up," replied Manager. "Usually means at least a five-page memo someone has to write. We also have to change our risk assessment over the account and usually do more test work. This also means we likely can't rely on their internal controls. All of that added together equals a big sloppy mess. In general, a huge and obvious error like this one Staff 2 just brought back makes us as auditors less comfortable with the presumption that the client is competent in any way, shape or form."

"That doesn't sound nice," Intern replied, uneasily. "I'm pretty sure you just called Assistant Controller incompetent."

"I'm pretty sure he is if his job is to book depreciation expense and it has never been booked in all of history," Manager said. "Can't fix stupid."

"I completely agree," added SM.

"Our job is to make sure the financial statements are correct," Manager continued explaining to Intern. "But we are really incented to not find anything as it causes us more work. More work translates into more hours. We generally have a fixed fee, so the additional hours will make our margin lower. Partner's distributions are a factor of fees and margins, so if those are bad, we won't likely get very good performance ratings on the job. As a result, we are effectively punished for doing a "good job" that leads to a "bad result" for the firm."

"I would think the company should have to pay for the extra work though, right?" inquired Intern. "Like, they screw up, we find it, their mistake makes us have to do more, and they don't want to pay for that? Seems like that is where the real value of an audit is?"

> **<u>Senior 3 pinging Manager:</u>** *I knew I liked Intern. She seems to just get it – no sugar coating!*

> **<u>Manager pinging Senior 3:</u>** *I know, she is going to be scheduled on all my jobs when she comes back as a staff next year (assuming I'm still here).*

"That's just it," said Manager, hitting his hand on the desk. "They generally think our documentation exercise for their error is a massive waste of time that they don't want to pay for. We can generally only charge them extra for it if there are several STINC's—like more than five would be a lot. On the flip side, finding a really big one is sort of like a badge of honor – a gold star!"

Manager then smiled, turned to Senior 3, and added, "A real gold star."

"Why is that?" asked Intern, a little confused. "Sounds like you are talking out of both sides of your mouth. First, it is bad because it creates more work and then it is some badge of honor thing?"

"Finding one proves to the team and to the client what we've known all along," Manager said. "We are way smarter and more competent than them and that they totally STINC at accounting!"

The Good Audit

"We are getting sidetracked here. I don't think it is super common to have a big STINC during a walkthrough of a process," SM said to Staff 2. "I'm concerned at how big you make it sound. Are you being over-dramatic again? How big is it?"

"I am NEVER overdramatic!" shouted Staff 2. "This is a BIG, FREAKING DEAL!"

"Okay, just hit me with it already," said SM.

"No depreciation has been booked...like ever," said staff 2. "Approximately $45 million not recorded this year yet that should have been, not to mention the massive cumulative amount not recorded in prior years."

"What do you mean?" asked SM. "I thought the system is supposed to automatically calculate that?"

"That is what Assistant Controller said – tried to blame the system for the fact that he has never once checked to make sure the entry gets recorded," Staff 2 replied, in the most overdramatic voice possible, while making huge gestures with his hands and arms. "I just can't believe that you never record depreciation and nobody notices, not even Ms. Ivy League CFO."

SM's jaw dropped and he put his head in his hands, "That is a big-STINC then. We probably have to tell the previous auditors that the financials they audited in prior years were messed up. They will have to restate the last two years."

"That is going to make everyone's life STINC," said Manager, dryly. Nobody laughed.

Staff 2 then explained to SM how CFO wanted to discuss the matter with him as soon as he was available.

Just as SM was about to head upstairs, Senior 1 walked back into the room.

"First blood of the audit!" she exclaimed, while slapping her notepad down on her desk, "I just found a MASSIVE STINC!"

C.P. Aiden

"Sorry, Staff 2 beat you by about 10 minutes," SM said, sadly, as he sat back down. "What is yours?"

"Well, it has got to be bigger than Staff 2's STINC," said Senior 1, a little taken back.

"Try me," replied Staff 2, grinning. "A $45 million error in the current year is a huge pile of STINC."

"WOW...," Senior 1 replied in shock. "That is bigger than mine."

"Will you please just tell us what it is already?" SM asked, getting impatient – he knew that CFO was probably expecting him up in her office several minutes ago.

"The company is amortizing goodwill," announced Senior 1.

"Why is that a big deal?" Intern asked. "I thought some companies did that."

"Companies following international standards can, but that type of amortization is not allowed in the accounting guidance here," Manager answered. "How much is it?"

"They have over-amortized $20 million of goodwill up through the beginning of the year with about $6 million recorded so far this year," Senior 1 said.

"I knew mine was bigger!" said Staff 2, cheerfully. "I don't think anything is going to come near it the whole year."

"Never say never," said Manager, wryly.

Just then, Staff 1 walked back into the room. "Guys, I think I found a major problem in prepaid assets."

"Great," said SM, sarcastically, while slowly banging his head on the desk. "More good news."

"I was upstairs walking through the prepaid asset process with Senior Accountant," said Staff 1. "They are booking prepaid assets for stuff they haven't paid for yet."

"How does that even work?" asked Senior 3, scratching his head.

The Good Audit

"I thought the word prepaid implies that something has been paid for in advance."

"That's what I thought too," replied Staff 1. "But Senior Accountant says that what they are doing is ok because it was approved by their previous auditors. Now, she doesn't understand why I would make a big deal out of it. She doesn't want to change it since they've been doing it this way for the past four years."

"How much is it off?" asked Manager, a little impatiently, as he just wanted Staff 1 to get to the point.

"About $700k," replied Staff 1, as she raised her eyebrows. "Big deal, right?"

"Huge," Manager said, encouragingly, as the others exchanged playful glances. They didn't want to deflate Staff 1 for only finding $700k when the other STINCs were so big. Truthfully, first year staff rarely found mistakes, so this was a pretty big deal.

"That makes three STINC'ers," Staff 2 said. Then, turning to SM with a smile, he continued, "I guess you have three things to talk to CFO about now, right?"

"I suppose" replied SM.

> **Manager pinging Senior 3:** *I thought we'd already identified three STINC'ers: One, Finance Manager, two, Assistant Controller and three, the biggest STINC'er of them all, Inventory Manager.*

> **Senior 3 pinging Manager:** *Not very nice, but a little funny, and you forgot FRM.*

SM returned from his meeting with CFO about an hour later. He was huffy, angry, disgusted and frustrated all at once. He was trying to calm himself with taking in big deep breaths, holding them and then letting them out slowly.

"After going through each STINC with her three times, I think she finally understands what kinds of problems we are dealing

69

with," SM said slowly, as he continued his breathing routine every few words, "She took no accountability for any of it though, nor would she blame her team. STINC 1 was the previous auditor's fault for not catching it. STINC 2 was the previous auditors who told them they could do it that way. STINC 3 was just a fluke and she claimed she knew about it during her review and they just hadn't fixed it yet. She wants to adjust it, but says it shouldn't be on our STINC."

"Did you tell her that each of the three errors is going to take us a ton of extra time to fix and document around?" Manager asked.

SM did not respond. The room went silent except for his slow, deep breaths as he tried to calm himself down.

CHAPTER 7 – FLEXIBILITY, WHAT'S THAT?

"She has no sense of the ripple effects these errors create," SM finally exclaimed, angrily. "It irritates me to no end! She acted like it was just depreciation or just goodwill and that any adjustment wouldn't impact anything else. How do you not realize that these things just snowball?"

Nobody dared to respond. Once SM took another three full minutes to calm down, he looked at Senior 1 and asked, "Would you mind helping Staff 1 document the STINC adjustments we've found so far?"

"I can, but I need to leave at 6:20 to pick up my kids because my husband has the night shift at the pharmacy on Wednesdays," Senior 1 replied, hesitantly.

"It would have been nice to know earlier," SM said, irritably, "so I could have been working under the expectation that you were planning to leave early today."

"I cleared it with Manager last Wednesday when you weren't here," Senior 1 replied.

"Wait, what? This is the second week in a row for this?" asked SM, his frustration building.

"Yes. It is," replied Senior 1, and then she kept her mouth shut, hoping she wouldn't have to explain her situation to SM.

"So, this will be an ongoing issue? Not just a one-time thing?" asked SM, furiously. "Will you please explain to me what is so important that it would make you miss work once a week? Is someone on their deathbed? Did you get approval to do some firm sponsored activity once a week? I'm dying to know!"

"My husband is a pharmacist," Senior 1 said, trying to hold herself together. She was now clearly upset. "One of the other pharmacists took another job so those left have to split the late shift that goes until 9:00 p.m. He got Wednesday and Saturday. On Wednesdays, the kids have to be picked up from daycare by 6:30."

"And you think that is a big enough deal to miss work for on a consistent basis? You don't have anyone else who can pick them up for you?" SM was now standing up. "You are going to have to leave early every Wednesday? How long is this going to go on?"

> **Staff 2 pinging Manager:** I wouldn't call leaving at 6:20 after showing up at 8 am leaving early… at least not at a normal job.

> **Manager pinging Staff 2:** *Unless you are SM, who works from 6 am until at least 10 p.m. EVERY SINGLE DAY because he has no life and thinks that others should be just as committed to the Firm as he is.*

"These are my children we are talking about! They need their Mom!" replied Senior 1, tearing up. "The kids are my responsibility."

"I guess you should have thought of that before you had them," said SM coldly. "Work is also a responsibility, and in my world, it always comes first."

"I don't live in your world," Senior 1 replied, now with tears streaming down her face in front of the whole team. "These are children, not just pets you can ignore and leave at home 24/7 as long as you refill their food and water bowls and let them out once a day to poop on the lawn!"

"When you are on one of my audit teams, you live in my world!" SM exclaimed, as his fist pounded on his desk. "Do you have a solution so I don't have to comment on it in your performance review?"

"The closest family I have is my mom, but she lives an hour away," said Senior 1. "I don't—"

"Couldn't you ask her to come down on Wednesdays, so you don't add more burden to the rest of the team by leaving early?" SM interrupted. "I mean, doesn't grandma want time with the grandkids?"

"She works a job too. The daycare is five minutes away from here," Senior 1 fought back. "The team has been staying until about 7:00 or 7:30 each night. I don't understand why I should ask my mom to drive over an hour each direction to allow me to stay an extra forty-five minutes!"

"You are part of a team," SM explained. "When the team leaves, you leave. If the team stays, you stay. If we start making exceptions, we have to start making exceptions for everyone!"

"The Accounting Firm has been promoting flexibility for years. I need to be able to go pick up my kids one night a week. I don't think it is too much to ask to leave forty-five minutes before the team leaves one night a week," said Senior 1, her tears now turning into anger.

> **Staff 2 pinging Manager:** *Why is he being such a jerk?*

> **Manager pinging Staff 2:** *b/c this type of stuff reminds him he has no family or life to go home to and he takes that out on those of us who do.*

> **Manager pinging Staff 2:** *I'm going to have to jump in to try to save her. Will probably get my butt chewed for it, but this has gone too far. Borderline workplace harassment even for TAF.*

"Look," Manager interjected. "I discussed this with Senior 1 last week. We agreed that she would do an hour of work from home on Wednesday nights in order to keep up with the team. She did the right thing here. As a manager, I can approve flexibility for the team, according to firm policy, can I not?"

"You should have asked me first," snipped SM, who had started his deep breath routine again trying to calm himself down. "The firm policy technically includes managers for approving stuff like this, but in reality, almost everything on the list of things a manager can approve should be brought up to the senior manager or even the partner. Senior 1's make-up work at home needs to be two and a half hours, not one, due to the flexibility factor."

"I was going on the low end of that at 1.5x since it isn't busy season and we are all working ten or eleven hours a day anyway, thanks to the 'flexibility' TAF required of us on account of this being a first-year audit," Manager stood his ground boldly.

> **Senior 1 pinging Manager:** *What is the flexibility factor?*
>
> **Manager pinging Senior 1:** *It is the number of hours you must work to 'pay back' each hour of flexibility taken*
>
> **Senior 1 pinging Manager:** *Is there some firm policy for that factor?*
>
> **Manager pinging Senior 1:** *No way. It is just one of the many unwritten rules of large firms.*
>
> **Senior 1 pinging Manager:** *I don't get that. I am paid salary for forty hours a week. I work fifty to*

fifty-five hours a week on normal weeks and way more than that during busy season. Didn't you just say the team is already being flexible?

Manager pinging Senior 1: *One problem with big firms is the group think mentality. Everything is relative to what the team is working. Since the whole team is also working fifty to fifty-five hours a week, then under these unwritten flexibility rules, you are 'taking' forty-five minutes to leave early Wednesday nights. Believe me, I think it is total garbage too, but it is what it is.*

Senior 1 pinging Manager: *The extra hour I work from home is like a 1.33x factor? You told SM 1.5x*

Manager pinging Senior 1: *Yeah, I rounded that to 1.5x for SM. Sounds like he is going for the high end of the flexibility range at 3x, standard range is 1.5-3x. Highest I've ever seen was 4.5x – busy season, week of issuing financial statements, the poor senior had a tooth break on him (like crumble in his mouth), the manager of that team made him work NINE hours (the whole night) to make up for the TWO hours he was at the dentist getting a temporary crown.*

"It really doesn't seem like too much of an inconvenience to ask your mom to come down, so you can keep working. At the rates we charge, our time is so valuable," said SM. "But if you feel like that is too much, you can work two and a half hours from home on Wednesday nights to make up for the flexibility taken."

"I don't see why one hour isn't enough," said Manager, really going to bat for Senior 1. "A 3x factor even during busy season is absurd and you know it!"

"Fine," SM said, coldly. "An hour and a half then. From here on out all flexibility requests go through me, understood?!"

Senior 1 pinging Manager: *Thank you!*

Manager pinging Senior 1: *You should not be thanking me for having to work an hour and a half from home every Wednesday just for leaving less than an hour before the rest of the team...especially after working ten and a half hours before going home.*

Senior 1 pinging Manager: *Better than the two and a half hours SM wanted!*

SM stood up and announced that he was going on a walk to clear his head and calm down – that the excitement of the past hour and a half really had him rattled. A minute after he was gone, Staff 2 asked Manager about the flexibility factor. Manager quickly asked Staff 1 and Intern to run to the gas station down the street and pick up some more energy drinks for the fridge.

"Wouldn't want those tender ears to hear what I'm about to tell you," Manager said after they had left.

"Oh dear," said Senior 3, putting his head in his hands. "Headphones are going in now."

"Basically," Manager began, "flexibility at big firms is never a two-way street – not a one for one give and take. Instead, I compare it to a freeway with six lanes coming one direction at eighty miles per hour with a tiny one lane frontage road going the opposite direction at thirty miles per hour."

"The firm's version of flexibility is the freeway and we get the frontage road?" Staff 2 confirmed.

"Exactly," said Manager, continuing from his soapbox. "All big firms take advantage of people as much as those people will let them. Why do you think everyone is on salary and no one gets paid overtime?"

"Interns get overtime," Staff 2 pointed out.

"There are two reasons for that. First, the Firm want interns to feel good about their internships, so they will accept an offer to come back full time (at an embarrassingly-low, base salary for anyone with a master's degree). Second, and more importantly, interns are temporary employees, so the firm is legally obligated to pay them overtime," Manager replied.

"It basically makes every hour we work over forty hours free for the firm," said Senior 1, in disgust.

"Bingo," replied Manager, half smiling. "Big firms generally over-schedule or oversell and then understaff on purpose. This is one reason we are 'required' to work fifty-eight-hour minimums in busy season. For at least three months (or in many cases, more like six months) of the year, they are getting at least 18 hours from each of us for 'free', and that 18 hours extra saves them from having to hire more people and pay them year-round. This translates to a 'buy four, get one free' deal for the Firm."

"Except it isn't just busy season," Staff 2 pointed out. "We've been working at least fifty-five hours a week here because 'it is a first-year engagement' according to Partner when he said the firm was asking us to be 'flexible' to accommodate the new client during a time of year that is generally slower."

"Precisely," said Manager, happy he was being understood. "They use this huge sense of urgency, priority and importance to convince you that you are letting the team down if you don't do 'your part' (aka get on the freeway and go eighty miles per hour like everyone else)."

"Then someone on the freeway looks over and sees Senior 1 heading the other direction on the frontage road for TWO SECONDS," said Staff 2, referring to Senior 1 leaving forty-five minutes before the rest of the team one day a week.

"And they cry bloody murder!" exclaimed Senior 1.

"They start honking their horns and yelling and screaming at Senior 1 in front of all the other drivers and then everybody demands that Senior 1 get back on the freeway and do a hundred and ten miles per hour until she 'catches up'!" Manager was really getting into this and the others could tell this was a passionate issue for him that he'd probably thought way too much about. "All the while, the firm is getting more and more hours for 'free'."

"It makes so much sense now. This is totally why SM gets a five-star rating each year." Staff 2 said, as if a light bulb had just lit up in his mind. "He barely ever leaves the freeway and when he's on it, he's in the left lane doing ninety-five miles per hour year-round. His whole life is basically flying down the big firm highway. He gets off to walk his dogs in the morning, hasn't taken a day of vacation this past year, works most holidays and takes his laptop with him while he's getting his car fixed or waiting at the doctor's office."

"As a result, the firm turns him into a poster child," added Senior 1. "Look at him! He is making a huge contribution to the success of the Firm! He has discovered the one and only real solution to work life balance by making work *equal* life. We need more of you to be more like him! His efforts carry his team to the finish line on every job! If you don't want to fail here, then you should aspire to be just like SM!"

"This is why I will never be five rated," said Manager, thoughtfully. "I care too much about my family and having a life to stay on the freeway all the time, even at seventy or eighty miles per hour. My sons need a father. My wife needs adult interaction after being with the kids all day and most of the evening – she is Supermom and deserves to be treated like it rather than being ignored just so I can go on auditing all night long – and for what? I don't want to miss my kids' childhoods or end up divorced like 60% of partners in the Firm. I mean, look 20 years down the road at the people who stayed on the big firm highway and see where that road took them: exotic vacations they can afford but can't enjoy, a family they don't know, clients calling them nonstop and constant fear of inspections from really stupid

The Good Audit

regulators – that life is not what I want for me or my family."

"At that point half your partner salary goes to pay alimony for the rest of your life." Senior 1 said, bitterly.

"Zero family is in the firm's best interest," continued Manager. "Legally, they have to say they support people with families, or at least that they don't discriminate against them, but who is really more profitable to the firm? SM who has no wife calling and texting to ask when he is coming home, no hobbies, no religious affiliation or commitments, no children to raise (dogs are not children – we can have that discussion later). Compare that to me, the guy with the amazing wife, the awesomely adorable and super-fun kids, the guy who takes all his vacation so he can actually spend time with that family, the guy who refuses to put the Firm's email access on his phone, etc. Who does the Firm really want?"

"No brainer if you are the Firm," said Staff 2, then, pointing his index finger at Manager while doing his best New Yorker accent added, "You're fired!?"

"Thank you, Donald," Manager laughed. "I come to work, I get the job done, I go home. I am profitable to the firm. However, I go to zero Firm-sponsored, social events. I don't get involved in any of the Firm extra-curricular groups. I am no longer allowed to do recruiting because the Firm doesn't like the straight-talk I give the candidates. I go to no team-appreciation events – even when spouses are invited (generally because the team-appreciation event is a result of the Firm requiring tons of 'flexibility' taking me away from my family and the last thing we want to do is take another four-hours to sit at a Firm propaganda dinner where the partners spend the whole time bragging about their 'fabulous lives' and disingenuously thank our spouses for letting them 'borrow us' in order to finish whatever fire drill the dinner is 'showing appreciation' for). If you really wanted to thank me, give me four hours with my family on some random weekday afternoon and the $200 you just spent on the overpriced dinner as a cash bonus, so I can pay to take my family to do something fun!"

"I can see how this would be a perfect place to work if you were single and had no life," Senior 1 thought aloud. "They basically provide you everything you need, twice a week firm-sponsored social events (if I left early two times a week to a firm-sponsored social event, SM would have no issue with me at all – in fact, he would encourage it and probably come with), three or four extreme events every year, free lunches many days, free overtime dinners almost every day, and work to keep you busy the entire weekend. All you really need is a bed to sleep in and as long as nobody else is permanently in that bed, the Firm wins."

"Yet, I am single, and I have plenty of things to do on the weekends without the firm giving me more work," said Senior 3, pulling the headphones out of his ears (he had been listening to the whole conversation but been pretending he wasn't until it was just too much for him to take). "I mean, I date and I have hobbies, so I also understand what you are saying to some extent."

"The point is that they sell 'flexibility' in recruiting as this amazing benefit," said Senior 1, trying to get back to the topic at hand. "Based on my experience, flexibility is just another tool the firm uses to squeeze more out of employees."

Just then Staff 1 and Intern came back with the energy drinks for the fridge. As they were loading the fridge up, SM also came back in from his walk. He looked worn out, but his face was somewhat calmer, but his right hand was twitching, and his left arm seemed to be having spasms.

"Oh great," he said to Staff 1, as he noticed the energy drinks. "I REALLY need one of those right now. I haven't had one yet today."

SM drank at least two energy drinks a day. Normally by that time in the evening, he'd been through his second.

"Well, I am a little calmer now," he said, and then stared at the moose heads on the wall. "I'm sorry to everyone for losing my cool a little earlier. It was unprofessional and unbecoming of a person at my level within the Firm."

> **Senior 1 pinging Staff 1:** *He can't even look at me! Instead, he chooses to apologize to the moose heads on the wall?!*

> **Staff 1 pinging Senior 1:** *Unbelievable, right?*

"As I've had time to clear my head and think about the situation we are in, I realize we are in trouble," said SM, as he sat down and opened his drink, "The adjustments mean that we cannot rely on internal controls. Also, our testing scopes come way down. Our sample sizes for audit testing are going to double if not triple."

"What does that mean for us?" Manager asked, very worried that any more bad news today might send Senior 1 into a total frenzy. He had also planned on going to dinner with his wife that night and did not want to have to cancel last minute.

"We will need to ask for a little bit more flexibility." SM said grimly.

"Flexibility, what's that?" Senior 1 mumbled under her breath, but she purposely said it just loud enough so that everyone could hear.

"We will need to start staying until 9 p.m. each night and work on Saturdays," SM replied.

Senior 1 had been packing up to go pick up her kids and she started walking out of the room.

"Where are you going?" SM asked Senior 1.

"We talked about this earlier," Senior 1 replied, tersely. "I've got to go pick up my kids."

"That was before all this happened," said SM. "Somebody else will have to go get them. Can't you call your mom? We are really in a bind and you're letting the team down by leaving."

"It is 6:25," said Senior 1, crossly. "My mom is over an hour away. If nobody picks up the kids by 6:35, they call Child Services. I cannot stay. Also, my husband works Saturdays, so I take care of my kids then too. I am happy to work from home on Saturdays if the team absolutely must be working, but I cannot come here on Saturdays."

"Why can't your mom come down on Saturdays?" asked SM

"BECAUSE SHE HAS THINGS TO DO TOO!" Senior 1 shouted, as she walked towards the stairs.

"Your choice," said SM. "But this is going in your performance review. You are letting the team down."

By now, Senior 1 was up the first half flight of stairs, "Get someone else then you…." The rest was muffled as Senior 1 had turned the corner to start the 2nd flight, but Manager was pretty sure he'd heard at least four or five four-letter words.

Everyone was quiet for a few minutes, then SM said, "maybe she's right. I should see if we can get another person to help out the team. We will really be screwed if she quits. I don't want to have to do this whole thing myself. I will ping Scheduling Lady to see if she can find us an extra staff."

"Scheduling Lady says there is a staff 1 with availability for the next three weeks," SM informed the team, as he continued to calm down a bit. "This is going to work out perfectly. He can come out here starting Monday."

"What's his name?" Manager asked, inquisitively.

"Backup Staff," replied SM.

CHAPTER 8 – THE OUTLIER AMONG OUTLIERS (AKA BACKUP STAFF)

There is always a little truth in stereotypes. Accountants are generally stereotyped as nice, but quiet people, good citizens, highly risk-averse, fiscally conservative, factually intelligent and somewhat quirky. They tend to get more than a little hung up in the details and will generally correct you (they think politely, but more often than not it is awkward) if you misspeak or say something that is not factually or technically correct.

An accounting major in business school might very well be considered an outlier on a normal curve of business students when compared to finance, marketing, operation management or even economics majors. Accountants generally earn much better grades than students pursuing these other majors. Some claim that is because they don't have nearly as much fun in college. Others think that accountants are simply better at picking out inconsistencies or false statements by nature, so they score higher on multiple choice exams. In any case, it is safe to say that in business school the accountants are sometimes looked at as being a few fries short of a Happy Meal.

Backup Staff was an outlier among outliers. If he were compared to that same Happy Meal, he'd have the toy, the cheese, and the box of apple juice – totally missing the burger, bun and ALL the fries. He usually acted the appropriate age for getting a Happy Meal too – like a four-year-old in an adult body. Backup Staff had no concept of socially, normal behaviors, particularly what was appropriate in group settings. He was bright, but ran on a very different processor. People often wondered how he took a set of facts and arrived at nearly opposite conclusions compared to the team – basic stuff was hard to figure out, but he'd pull the most random and fascinating observations out of things. He was definitely an accountant in that way – he found problems almost everywhere he looked – but the problems he so often latched onto were typically the very small and insignificant things while he completely ignored or missed the elephants right in front of him. Backup Staff was also a super nice guy – totally unassuming, well-mannered, and easy to talk to. He was married and had a couple young kids.

After SM announced that Backup Staff would be coming out to help for several weeks he asked if anyone knew him.

"I've met Backup Staff," said Manager, hesitantly. "He seemed like a nice kid. Not sure all his marbles are in the bag, but that never stopped you from auditing."

"Anybody else know Backup Staff?" asked SM, again, totally missing the insult from Manager.

"I think I went to a recruiting lunch with him," Staff 2 volunteered. "Can anyone find a picture of him?"

"Just look on the Social Network for Professionals," Manager suggested.

"You look on Social Network for Professionals," replied Senior 3, as defiantly as he could.

"I don't want him to know I was looking at his profile," said Manager point blank.

The Good Audit

"You can change your privacy settings so they can't see who it was that looked," Staff 2 pointed out. "Do you want me to show you how?"

"No," replied Manager, acting a little upset. "I know how to change the settings, but I don't want to because then I'd have to change them back. I want some people to be able to see I looked at their profiles."

> **Senior 3 pinging Manager:** *Like who?*

> **Manager pinging Senior 3:** *Like recruiters/head-hunters. Or CFO's at companies I might apply for a job opening at.*

> **Senior 3 pinging Manager:** *Does that really help you?*

> **Manager pinging Senior 3:** *Over two-thirds look at my profile within the next week and nearly half then connect with me, so I'd say so.*

> **Senior 3 pinging Manager:** *I will have to try that sometime.*

> **Manager pinging Senior 3:** *Yeah right, you are staying on the big firm highway forever.*

"I have his picture," Staff 1 volunteered, cheerfully. "They just sent a weekly, office-update email introducing my whole start class with bios and photos."

"I always just delete those," said SM, coldly, as if he didn't care about any of the new staff in the office.

"Me too," added Senior 3, sheepishly.

"Here he is. It is his whole family and here is his bio – we had to write these ourselves. They gave us some survey as an idea of what to write," said Staff 1, as she proceeded to read Backup Staff's bio aloud.

"Backup Staff comes to us, not out of school, but from the full-time workforce. He recently worked in a retail store as a loss prevention manager in a smaller city an hour away. He is proud to say that he put 52 people in jail over the course of two years in the position and theft at his store went down 90% over that time. Backup Staff went and personally visited all 52 criminals in jail and took each of them homemade brownies. A couple of the criminals came after he and his family when they got out a few days later, so now Backup Staff and family are part of the witness protection program (DON'T TELL ANYONE!)."

> **Staff 2 pinging Manager:** *Good thing nobody reads these things, so nobody will know that.*

"Backup Staff recently completed an online degree and can now sit for the CPA exam. Backup Staff and his amazing wife have been blessed with three children – two adorable daughters and one somewhat less-than-adorable son (he always looks like a mess because he's always into something. HAHAHA). Backup Staff's dream job would be working as a ride operator at an amusement park because when a ride gets stuck, they get to go behind the scenes and play with cool gadgets to fix the ride. However, said jobs do not pay nearly enough to support a family (not sure whether this one will either – ha!). Backup Staff's favorite color is neon grayish-aqua-marine. Ice cream is the best! Backup Staff is excited to join TAF and looks forward to meeting all of you! Hopefully, this wasn't too long and you made it through."

Everyone was speechless. Staff 1 was going around showing everyone the picture.

"That is hilarious," SM said, busting up. "I guess we will see how he is to work with on Monday."

Monday morning came and the team was quietly working away in the audit room. Keyboards, mouse clicks, the occasional flipping through papers and the random toilet flushes running through the pipes overhead were the only sounds in the room. Everyone had more work to do than could really be done, so there was no time for chit-chat. Backup Staff had a stack of papers a foot and a half high on the left of his laptop and a stack about an inch high on the right side. The papers were the supporting documents for the 90 expense selections the team requested and included purchase orders, vendor invoices, coding approval and copies of checks written to pay the invoices. The stack on the right-hand side was the items Backup Staff had looked through and had about 15 sticky flags coming out.

Staff 2 pinging Manager: *Are you seeing this?*

Manager pinging Staff 2: *No, I'm working. You should be too!*

Staff 2 pinging Manager: *I looked up a few minutes ago. His fingers are super flexible*

Manager pinging Staff 2: *So?*

Staff 2 pinging Manager: *Just watch. Every so often he takes his ring finger back and wraps it around his middle and index fingers – like all the way around the base of those fingers.*

Manager pinging Staff 2: *You are making this up.*

Staff 2 pinging Manager: *You can't make this kind of stuff up. Just watch him for a few minutes. Don't like stare, but pay a little attention and you'll see. His fingers stay that way for about 30 seconds to a minute and then he pulls it out and switches hands. The crazy thing is that he types one handed with the hand he isn't using. He has got to be the world's fastest, one-hand typist with either hand. He's about to switch to the hand on your side.*

Manager was shocked and horrified as exactly what Staff 2 told him played out right in front of his eyes. He pinged Senior 3 and told him to look for it as well.

> **Senior 3 pinging Manager:** *He is probably just nervous. This is his first day working on a new team.*
>
> **Manager pinging Senior 3:** *It is just crazy. I don't know how he does it!*
>
> **Senior 3 pinging Manager:** *What we should be worried about are those sticky flags coming out of his "done" pile.*

The pile on the right had grown an inch and there were now at least 25 sticky flags coming out the far side of the stack. Manager pinged and asked Senior 1 to see what was going on.

"Hey, Backup Staff," said Senior 1, inquisitively, as she looked at the stack on Backup Staff's right-hand side. "Looks like you are pushing through the stack. What are all the flags for?"

"Oh, those are just the things I have questions about," replied Backup Staff. "On my last job, they told me I was asking too many random questions all the time and that I should aggregate them and then bring up all my questions at once."

"Looks like you have several there," Senior 1 said, nervously, pointing at the flags. "Would you like to go through those with me? I think if there are recurring questions, maybe we can talk through them and save you the trouble of flagging things later in the stack."

"That would be great!" said Backup Staff, excitedly.

"Why don't you start from the beginning?" asked Senior 1, encouragingly.

"OK," Backup Staff began at the top of the stack to his right. "On this one, not everything on the PO made it to the invoice. In my mind, they ordered stuff and they are not being charged for it."

"We are just testing the expense line item we selected." explained Senior 1, patiently. "There can be multiple shipments and multiple invoices or even a single invoice can have things on it that are coded to different expenses and we just picked one of those expenses."

"Yeah, I saw that and flagged at least four of those," said Backup Staff, sounding a little confused. "But on this one, don't I need to see all the invoices to make sure the PO was right? That they didn't get shorted anything or given extra that they didn't pay for? How do I know this is right?"

"We are not testing the PO – we are testing the expense they recorded for what was paid for based on the invoice. The invoice should agree to the items that were actually shipped to them. The relevance of the PO is to verify they had actually ordered the goods or services they are paying for." Senior 1 continued to coach Backup Staff. "The receiving document shows how many from the PO they actually got, which should match what they are being charged for. If they were charging them for more items than we have receiving documents for, we would have to go ask for additional support showing more items were received from different shipments in order to support the invoice total going to the expense account. Does that make sense?"

"Well, that's just the thing," Backup Staff said, sounding a little panicked. "The invoice shows three of these items which agrees to what was on the receiving document, but the PO says they ordered five. Where are the other two? How do I know which three of the five these are?"

"As I said, we don't really care if the invoice quantity doesn't agree to the PO quantity as long as the PO shows that they had actually ordered the items received and that the invoice is only charging them for what they received," said Senior 1, growing a little impatient.

"I'm supposed to be auditing this!" exclaimed Backup Staff. "How can I be absolutely sure that these are the right ones?"

"Are they paying for something they received?" asked Senior 1, getting more annoyed.

"Yes", answered Backup Staff.

"And does the expense code seem to be correct based on the item they are paying for?" Senior 1 asked.

"I suppose so," Backup Staff answered, quietly, while straining his mind to try to figure out if this really made sense and if there was some other argument to be made for how this could be wrong.

"And was that item listed on the PO somewhere?" Senior 1 asked, growing even more frustrated.

"Five of them, not three of them!" said Backup Staff, desperately.

"But they are listed there on the PO, right?" Senior 1 nearly screamed at him.

"Yes, but—" Backup Staff's reply was cut off by Manager.

"You are done. The expense is valid. Move on," Manager said, conclusively.

"Ok. I'm not so sure about it, but if you," Backup Staff said, looking at Manager, "are ok with it, I think that will wipe out seven flags."

"Great! Next, please," said Senior 1, happy to move on.

"Manager didn't say it is ok," Backup Staff was confused.

Senior 1 rolled her eyes and looked over at Manager who wasn't paying attention anymore. Backup Staff also stared intently at Manager waiting for a response.

> **Senior 1 pinging Manager:** *Will you PLEASE tell him it is ok.*

"It is ok," Manager said, without looking up from his computer.

"Great, what is next?" Senior 1 asked Backup Staff

"They paid too much on this invoice," said Backup Staff, decisively, while pointing to the total on the invoice and comparing it to the copy of the check. "The invoice amount was $2,047.24, but on the check someone fat fingered it and they ended up paying $2,074.24 or $27 over. I can't find any evidence that this was fixed. Shouldn't I tell them? Shouldn't they fix this? Like ask for your $27 back – this is real money! I could get five $5 pizzas for my family and pay a tip with $27!"

"This is a company with $3.5 billion of assets," said Senior 1. "It would take more time to fix than it is worth. This is not a material difference, you can pass on it. Also, if they overpay an invoice, the vendor probably issues them a credit on the next invoice."

"It is wrong! I think I should at least let them know. I should tell them about it." Backup Staff insisted.

"Ok, you can tell them about it," said Senior 1, as she grabbed both sides of her head and pressed in. "But don't be surprised when they get mad at you for it."

"Why would they get mad?" Backup Staff asked, furrowing his eyebrows in confusion. "I just found them money."

"We've been talking about this for five minutes now," Senior 1 was visibly irritated now. "You fussed over this for 10 minutes yourself because it didn't match exactly. It will take you 10 minutes to go tell them about it. In total, my five minutes plus your five minutes talking just now plus your other 20 minutes it would take is 30 minutes of audit time. They will be mad because we bill at a blended rate of $150 an hour. They will ask why in the world we spent thirty minutes, costing them $75, to get them $27 back – especially if they get it back on the next invoice anyway."

"Oh," said Backup Staff. He was dumbfounded for a few seconds as this seemed to be slowly processing in his mind, "But it is an error, right?"

"Technically, yes," said Senior 1, letting out a sigh. "It is too small to amount to anything though. In our documentation, you do need to run an extrapolation and then explain that it is immaterial so we can pass on the difference."

"That will mean their financial statements are wrong!" Backup Staff said, insistently.

"All financial statements are wrong!" exclaimed Senior 1, now more frustrated than ever. "Our job is not to redo their jobs and fix every little thing. Our job is to make sure the financials aren't wrong by an amount big enough for investors to care about."

"If I were an investor, I'd want the $27," said Backup Staff scowling.

> **Staff 1 pinging Staff 2:** *The guy just had a senior and a manager tell him that something was not a big deal and should be ignored and he won't let it go.*

> **Staff 2 pinging Staff 1:** *Seriously*

"Well, you are not an investor, you are an auditor and $27 is not big enough to care about. We do not have enough time to care about it and it is not material, so MOVE ON!!" snipped Senior 1, very sharply.

It took another hour and a half to go through the rest of Backup Staff's flags. The whole thing was a frustrating ordeal for the entire room. Finally, it was time to take a break. The team needed to decide where to go for lunch.

CHAPTER 9 – PASSIVE AGGRESSIVE DRINKS

Just as Senior 1 was done going over Backup Staff's questions, Manager looked at the time – 12:15 – they were late for lunch.

"Where should we go to lunch?" Manager asked, as he patted his rumbling stomach.

The rest of the room seemed to have missed the question. Everyone continued working. They heard the question, but most of them were trying to get to a good stopping point so they could take a break and figure out lunch. The quiet went on for another five minutes. Even Manager had gone back to work, although his stomach was still growling and he was about to bring up lunch again.

"I've got it!" Backup Staff shouted out of nowhere.

Manager wondered if expense testing had finally clicked for Backup Staff and he'd figured out some answer to his own questions.

"Got what?" Manager asked.

"I know where we should go to lunch!" Backup Staff said.

Usually, the team wrote a list of restaurants on the whiteboard to choose from. Each person chose one place and added it to the whiteboard. If two or three people wanted the same thing, it was put on the whiteboard multiple times. Then, Intern listed everyone on the team in a spreadsheet and randomly generated numbers for each team member. The team then went in that order with each person eliminating a restaurant until there was only one restaurant left and that is where they went – the whole decision-making process took 10 to 15 minutes with the entire team involved. Nobody ever told the client that the audit team picking a lunch place was costing them $150-$200 a day in fees plus the cost of the lunch averaging $100-$150 a day.

"And where is that?" Manager asked. It was Backup Staff's first day on this job, so he had not been introduced to the standard selection process. Manager decided to humor him to see where he wanted to go.

"We should go to the Family Fun Center," said Backup Staff, his eyes filling with excitement. "They have the best pizza and burgers EVER!"

"Do you realize how far away that is?" asked Manager, mostly in shock, but with a hint of amusement. "That is at least fifteen-minutes each way. There are probably two-hundred restaurants between here and there. I'm sure some of them even have pizza!"

"Wait though…Just let me finish what I'm saying and see if you change your mind," Backup Staff insisted. "Not only is Family Fun Center a restaurant, there is also an ARCADE! The food is cheap, and you can buy tokens with lunch. If we hit the $25 per person limit, we'd each get like $20 OF TOKENS FOR THE ARCADE!"

Backup Staff looked at each person around the room and like an excited puppy, panted "Yeah? Yeah?" to each of them trying to get them on board with his plan.

Manager paused for a moment, mostly to keep from laughing hysterically about the way Backup Staff had just blurted out '$20 OF TOKENS FOR THE ARCADE!!!'. The whole room was struggling to keep it in, so no one was making eye contact.

"I think we all have more work to do than what we can really handle right now," said Manager, slowly and thoughtfully. "We do need to take a break for lunch, but I think driving way over there and playing games will take way too long. I think we should go through our normal decision process that our team does every day. You are free to put your choice on the list, but if it gets eliminated, that is it."

Backup Staff sat quietly for a minute after the entire lunch-venue-picking process was explained to him and then said, "Yeah, put that one on the list for me, would you Intern? And on the side of it, add 'ARCADE!!!' really big."

The rest of the list was made and SM was the first person to eliminate a restaurant. Without hesitation, he quickly crossed off Family Fun Center, with a special emphasis to completely black out the word "Family". Backup Staff was devastated, but there was nothing he could do now.

The team left for lunch to a place a couple blocks down the street. Except to order his food, Backup Staff did not say a single word the entire time.

The audit team returned from lunch and, after giving Inventory Manager the food he had ordered (the team was now getting him lunch every day, but so far, he had been smart enough to keep his mouth shut about the arrangement), they made their way back to the audit cave.

Backup Staff sulked for the entire afternoon. There were two very good consequences of his sulking though. First, he stopped messing with his ring finger. Second, he made it through almost three-quarters of the stack of expense testing support in about three hours – apparently being sad made him care less about things being off by a few dollars as he only had about twenty new sticky flags on the stack.

At five o'clock (when everyone at Widget Maker started heading home), the audit team started talking about dinner.

"Any thoughts on dinner tonight?" asked Senior 1, pulling out a marker to start writing people's choices on the board similar to the lunch venue selection process.

No response. The team was going full steam ahead. Senior 1 wondered if anyone had heard her. Then Senior 3's stomach growled. *Hmmm,* thought Senior 1, *Senior 3 heard me, at least subconsciously.* She asked again.

They were about to make a list when Backup Staff asked if there were any sushi places nearby.

> **Senior 3 pinging Manager:** *See! There is still hope for him. He's learned not to ask to go to places all the way across town.*

> **Manager pinging Senior 3:** *I noticed that.*

> **Senior 3 pinging Manager:** *MAYBE, we should break protocol on deciding where to eat and just defer to his suggestion for sushi.*

> **Manager pinging Senior 3:** *And look, right next to the sushi place down the road is a burger shop. I bet a milkshake would cheer him up.*

"I think Sushi sounds like a great idea," said Manager, enthusiastically.

"You do?" the shocked Backup Staff replied. "I mean…that's great!"

"I think we should skip the decision-making process tonight and just order sushi," said Manager, giving Senior 3 a sideways glance. "Backup Staff, it looks like you made it through quite a bit of that stack this afternoon. You could probably use a break to go pick it up for us. What do you say?"

"I would love to," said an exuberant Backup Staff. "Everyone, please send me your orders!"

"Let's just order a variety of rolls and share," Manager suggested. "Here Backup Staff, take my corporate card. I noticed there is a burger shop right next door to the sushi place. While you wait for the sushi order, would you run in there and get you and me milkshakes? I'll take a caramel one."

> **Senior 3 pinging Manager:** *That was really nice... making him get you a milkshake.*

> **Manager pinging Senior 3:** *Don't you see? I'm letting HIM get HIMSELF a milkshake. It would be weird to tell him to get one and not order one for me. Sheesh.*

"I want a milkshake," said Senior 1, quietly. "Is it ok if I get a milkshake too? I mean, technically we can charge it as part of dinner, right? Can I get a peanut butter one?"

"Oh, I want one too," added Staff 2. "Cookies and Crème."

Pretty soon, the entire team – even Senior 3 – had ordered milkshakes.

Backup Staff left the room, almost skipping, with a huge smile on his face to go pick up the sushi and milkshakes.

> **Senior 3 pinging Manager:** *Alright, I guess that was pretty nice. Sure cheered him up.*

Staff 2 was walking behind Senior 3's screen as he sent the message to Manager.

"Sure cheered me up too!" Staff 2 said, enthusiastically. "What a good idea, Manager!"

The whole room erupted in laughter.

"I just hope it doesn't violate the drink rule," said Senior 1, considerately.

"What is the drink rule?" asked Staff 1, curiously.

"When the team sends someone out to get dinner, there is an unwritten rule that you don't ask that person to bring back drinks," replied Senior 1, looking up from her screen. "Partners are the exception because most of the unwritten rules don't apply to partners – at least the unwritten rules I know about."

"But why is that?" asked Intern, curiously. "I've noticed that nobody orders drinks when I go pick stuff up. I've never understood why."

"First of all, the person picking up the food is already dealing with a food order for five to eight people. They are putting that somewhere in their own car. If you have to add drinks on top of that, it is just too much to deal with. Second, the drinks always come in those lousy drink carriers. Those things never stay flat on the seat, so they end up on the floor on the passenger side. No one should ask a staff or an intern to bring back a ton of drinks that will likely spill all over their car. Plus, most of our clients provide drinks for free or have a break room with vending machines where you can buy a soda or something if you really want one," Senior 1 explained.

"I get it," said Staff 1, looking around the room. "So…did we break the drink rule, having Backup Staff pick us up milkshakes?"

"I don't think so," Manager replied. "Milkshakes are smaller and thicker than normal drinks, should be easier – less spill risk. Besides, he's super excited about it. I think it is ok."

"I think it has been too long since you've had to pick up anyone's food," Senior 3 said to Manager. "And probably no one ever asked you to get drinks."

"You are wrong about both," said Manager, turning to scowl directly at Senior 3. "Do you remember Passive-Aggressive Senior? He left the Firm last fall."

"Yeah, what about him?" asked Senior 3.

"Last fall, right before he left the Firm, I got pulled onto a job with him," replied Manager.

"That is weird," said Senior 3, cocking his head back. "Wasn't he

The Good Audit

your same level back then?"

"Yeah. He had been on that client for several years, but the job wasn't getting done, and I had available time, so I got stuck on it to help him out," Manager shrugged his shoulders. "He was getting blamed for the delays and so he was under pressure. He really didn't like having someone his level come to one of his clients and show him up. He turned super passive-aggressive on me. I didn't really care. It wasn't really my client and I knew I was just there to help out, but pretty soon people figured out I knew way more than he did about how to run a job, so he started doing little, nasty things towards me."

"Right...Like what?" asked Senior 3 in disbelief. He had never worked with Passive-Aggressive Senior, but he doubted that anyone in the office would really be calculating and nasty towards another team member.

"Like trying to assert himself, boss me around and stuff – you know, see how far he could push me 'for the good of the job' he would always say," replied Manager. Then, seeing that Senior 1 wasn't biting, he added, "One evening, he says to me, 'Hey. The rest of us are all pretty swamped and looks like you are so fast you just finished what you've been working on. I think it would be most efficient if you went and picked up dinner tonight.' We all still had lots of things to do and, as you all know, it is generally the lowest person on the totem pole that goes to pick up dinner."

"He was your same level and he had the nerve to ask you to go pick up dinner with a bunch of staff there too?" Senior 3 asked, with a look of complete shock on his face – still wondering if any of this could be true or if Manager was just making it all up. "You told him no, right?"

"No, I went," said Manager.

"What?!" exclaimed Senior 3, as his mouth opened widely. "You just let him push you around like that?"

"I was so tired of being around him. A break sounded pretty nice. I totally understood what he was doing. He was passively-aggressively trying to pick a fight. I wasn't going to let that little turd get under my skin, so I just said 'Sure', took people's orders, and left. He was as shocked as the rest of the team," answered Manager, with a twinkle in his eye. Senior 3 still wasn't biting.

"I do not believe you," said Senior 3. "It is too convenient that the person the story is about has left the Firm. You are making all this up. Who can I verify this story with that is still at the Firm?"

"Short Staff 2. He was there," replied Manager, shaking his head. "You are such an auditor asking me to verify my own story. Audit away then."

Senior 3 looked up Short Staff 2 and started pinging him. Staff 2 and Senior 1, who had started paying attention to the story, crowded around his screen to see the response.

"Wow!" shouted Senior 1, as Short Staff 2 responded to Senior 3's ping. "You are not lying. He just verified the story. Unbelievable."

"Why are you so shocked?" asked Manager.

"Look!" Staff 2 blurted out, pointing at the screen. "He's asking if you told us about the drink part."

"Oh yeah," remembered Manager. "That is how we started this whole story-time discussion to begin with – the drinks! Just as I pull into the restaurant, my phone rings and it is Passive-Aggressive Senior. He asks me if I've left the restaurant already, and I'm thinking, 'no, you retard, I left the client five minutes ago. Of course, I haven't left the restaurant yet. I just got here!' Then I realized that he HAD to know that. He says to me, 'Hey man! Since you are still at the restaurant getting the food, would you mind getting me a ginger ale with just a little bit of ice, not a ton of ice? Oh, and Short Staff 2 wants something too.' I hear in the background Short Staff 2 saying he's good that he'll just go

The Good Audit

down to the FREE vending machine and get a root beer. Then the phone went silent for a few seconds."

"I've been pinging Short Staff 2 telling him everything you have been telling us to make sure you get this right," interrupted Senior 3. "He says that when the phone went silent, Passive-Aggressive Senior told him he had to order a drink."

"Exactly," said Manager. "Passive-Aggressive Senior gets back on the phone and says, 'Yeah, get Short Staff 2 a root beer while you're at it. Ice? No Ice'. I hear Short Staff 2 in the background – he's totally confused – he says 'ummm…sure, ice'. Then Passive-Aggressive Senior says 'really appreciate it, man! Thanks for being willing to take one for the team while it is all hands on deck back here with the rest of us finishing this audit'. I picked up the food, got the two drinks and headed back."

"Did you punch him in the face when you got back?" asked Staff 2, sarcastically. "I probably would have."

"No way," replied Manager. "I was never going to give him the pleasure of him thinking he was getting under my skin. I just dropped off the food and went back to work. No emotions. No nothing."

"Short Staff 2 said it was epic," said Senior 3, as he read from his onscreen conversation. "The whole time you were gone, Passive-Aggressive Senior was plotting it all out. He was purposely trying to get a reaction out of you in front of the team so he could hang something over your head and he says you came back in cool as a cucumber."

"Passive-Aggressive Senior was so mad when I didn't react that he didn't touch his ginger ale at all during dinner," said Manager laughing.

"Short Staff 2 says he went down to the free vending machine and got a can of ginger ale instead," said Senior 3, pointing at his screen.

"Oh yeah, I had forgotten about that," said Manager, "He stormed out of the room and three minutes later he has this can of ginger ale from the FREE vending machine. He pops it open and chugs the whole thing angrily in like 10 or 15 seconds. His ginger ale from the restaurant just sat there for like two hours."

"That is just crazy!" said Staff 2 in disbelief. "What happened to it? Did it just get tossed?"

"After two hours, I looked at his desk," replied Manager, starting to grin. "By then, he had like three empty cans of ginger ale sitting on his desk. I walked over so I'm kind of standing to the side of him at the back corner of his chair – sort of pinning him uncomfortably to the table – and say, 'Hey Passive-Aggressive Senior, looks like you've been so busy getting all your work done that you forgot about this ginger ale I picked up for you.' Then he looks up at me, kind of shrinking down into the opposite end of his chair and he was like, 'Oh…yeah, I guess so' all innocently shrugging his shoulders and putting his hands up to the sides of his shoulders. I looked at the empty cans on his desk in disgust and then I was like 'well, it looks like you've had plenty of ginger ale tonight. I guess I'll drink this one'. I reached over him, picked it up, and started gulping it down. I don't even like ginger ale, but I chugged as if it was the best thing I had ever tasted in my life. Passive-Aggressive Senior just sat there totally speechless."

Staff 2's jaw dropped to the floor and his eyes popped wide open, "Shut the front door! You did not!"

"He did though!" came a happy reply from Senior 3. "In front of the whole team, according to Short Staff 2."

"Nobody on that team really liked working with Passive-Aggressive Senior," said Manager. "He was always saying stuff like, 'I'm sorry guys, but this is just a really tough audit – all hands on deck tonight, nothing else we can do'. What I did shut him down so hard that I was an instant hero on that team!"

"I bet!" said Senior 1 in awe. "Until hearing this story, I'd never heard of anyone successfully putting Passive-Aggressive Senior in his place."

"One thing is for sure," said Manager, with a broad smile on his face. "I never went to pick up dinner again, and Passive-Aggressive Senior never asked anyone else to pick him up a drink with dinner after that!"

CHAPTER 10 – "UM, GUYS…THERE'S NO TOILET PAPER IN HERE!"

Backup Staff rushed back into the audit cave as giddy as a kid about to blow out candles on his birthday cake. He was carrying two large bags that were hanging from his wrists while both hands had drink carriers full of milkshakes. The team was surprised he had brought everything in one load. Staff 1 and Intern quickly jumped up to help him by taking the milkshakes out of his hands. Intern started handing them out to everyone while Staff 1 and Backup Staff started setting up the sushi on the far desk.

"I get to combine two of my favorite things into one big mix tonight!" Backup Staff said, excitedly, as he grabbed his stomach and swiveled his hips as if he was churning something inside. It was such a work-inappropriate motion that only someone as innocent as Backup Staff could get away with.

"I'm not 100% sure you are really supposed to mix the two," Senior 3 pointed out. "Are you sure you will be alright?"

"Milkshakes blend with everything," replied Backup Staff, happily. "At least in my world."

"To each their own. As a kid, I used to eat ketchup with almost everything – I even put it on cantaloupe, which was surprisingly awesome...I think, or used to think," Manager said, as the rest of the team gagged.

Accountants who work very long days only have the food to look forward to. On $25 per person, per meal, they could eat from almost anywhere. A mix of exhaustion and bitterness often causes them to take that 'use it or lose it money' and blow it on WAY more than anyone could possibly eat in a whole day. The team ate their fill and then ate some more and then there were still several rolls left sitting out as the team went back to focusing entirely on the audit.

The room had been quiet for over an hour. Backup Staff had finally reached the last check packet in his huge stack when he slammed his palm on the desk and yelled out, "I found another one! This one they overpaid $81 on. Fat fingered the 1 and the 9. I'm telling you, they need to know about these errors so they can go get their money back! I'm up to $108 I've found them now!"

"They won't care," muttered Manager under his breath, so that only Senior 3 and Senior 1 could hear him. Then, raising his voice a bit, he asked, "How much does all of it extrapolate to now? Are we still under the STINC limit?"

> **Staff 2 pinging Manager:** *Should we tell him that I found a $45 MILLION error the first week we were here?*

> **Manager pinging Staff 2:** *Nah, he'd probably call the authorities and turn Assistant Controller in for it.*

"Yeah," replied Backup Staff, a little deflated. "I think it is well below that. I just think the company should know about these. If this was an internal control, we would have two errors in our sample and we would fail the control."

"They don't have a control that says 'people don't fat finger things input into the system'. In fact, they don't have internal controls at all and we've already failed them on that point so it doesn't matter. Remember the discussion earlier," Manager asked, somewhat annoyed that Backup Staff was still hung up over this type of tiny error, "about not spending dollars auditing dimes? Just add it to the extrapolation in the workpaper documentation and then let's move on."

Backup Staff went back to being grumpy.

Manager remembered he left his milkshake in the freezer and went to grab it. Backup Staff continued sulking and staring aimlessly around the room. As Manager walked back in the room with his milkshake, Backup Staff suddenly snapped out of his chair and homed in on the milkshake, like a bloodhound. Then his head dropped, "I forgot, I finished mine earlier," he said, sadly. Then, raising his head and starting to smile, he added, "But there's still all the leftover sushi."

Backup Staff jumped out of his seat and went over to the desk the leftovers were sitting on.

"I'd be careful," Senior 1 warned Backup Staff, sharply. "That has been out for several hours now."

"We can't just toss it," Backup Staff said, ignoring the warning and filling up a plate. "This stuff was expensive and I hate to see good money going to waste."

"Not your money," Staff 2 pointed out. "Use it or lose it. If the Firm wants to allow $25 per person per night to be spent rather than just giving us an overtime per diem, you can always expect a lot of food gets thrown away. If they just gave us $15 a night for overtime meals regardless what we spent, we'd all get fast food, pocket $7 extra a night, (which is not inconsequential with what they are paying us) and it would save the Firm millions. I bet it could save the partners' distributions even with the cost of the name change. Save $10 a night with 25,000 employees getting overtime meals at least 200 nights a year on average is over $50 million!"

"On all my other jobs, I took all the leftovers home to my wife and kids," Backup Staff insisted.

"I wouldn't give my kids sushi that had been sitting out this long, that's for sure," Senior 1 said, grimacing.

"Oh, this is totally fine!" Backup Staff said, tossing some sushi in his mouth in defiance. "Still tastes great!"

Backup Staff ate an entire plate full and seemed to be much happier. He asked if anyone else wanted any or if he could take it home.

> **SM pinging Manager:** *I wonder how he'd react if I told him he had to throw it away.*

> **Manager pinging SM:** *Let him enjoy it. Nobody else is going to eat it anyway.*

The team all agreed that it was not advisable. In the end, they all said he could take it. Senior 1, who seemed to be most concerned, followed up with another warning about how long the food had been out and how it could present a health risk as Backup Staff collected everything that was left into a single box.

"Maybe you should put it in the fridge" she suggested, as Backup Staff set the box next to his computer.

"Great idea," replied Backup Staff, jumping back up to put the box into the fridge. "Just don't let me forget it. I will put it on this shelf here."

Backup Staff reached down to open the door to the mini-fridge. As he placed the leftover sushi on the door, closed the fridge and stood back up he looked extremely uncomfortable. He scrunched his face all up and both hands went to his stomach. Then, he let out something between a yelp and a cry that Manager thought sounded like 'He's gonna blow!!' and rushed into the bathroom. Before anyone could remind him about the rule to not use that bathroom, the door was shut, locked, and the team heard the toilet seat drop.

> **Staff 2 pinging Senior 1:** *Oh SNAP! Did he really just go in there?*

> **Senior 1 pinging Staff 2:** *I told him not to eat the sushi that was sitting out. He didn't listen.*

> **Staff 2 pinging Senior 1:** *Now we all get to listen!* 💩🤢 *That five-inch gap at the bottom of the door is going to be wonderful.*

Over the next several minutes, the team heard everything. As soon as the toilet seat dropped, they heard Backup Staff land on the toilet. Then came a groan and the rapid-fire explosions started. Plop. Plop. Plop. Plop.

> **Staff 2 pinging Staff 1:** *BOMBS AWAY!!! MAN DOWN!!!*

Staff 1 couldn't contain herself and started laughing out loud which led to the whole team laughing as silently as they could – the kind of laugh that makes the whole body shake due to the effort of preventing the laugh from audibly leaving one's mouth.

This was followed by a couple seconds of silence.

"CEASE FIRE!!!" the team heard Backup Staff call out in agonizing pain, followed by a long and loud groan.

The next sound was like a large pitcher of water was being poured into the toilet.

Senior 1 had to cover her mouth not to hurl. The rest of the team had turned pale with disgust. Another short round of smaller plops and then two very large plops about ten seconds apart was followed by complete silence. No one on the team could talk, let alone look at each other. No one could go back to their computers and start working either. They all just sat and stared at the desk or the wall or the floor. Five minutes passed in complete silence. Manager started wondering to himself if Backup Staff was ok. Maybe he had passed out with loss of fluids? Manager looked over at the door and through the gap under the door, he could clearly see that Backup Staff was slowly moving his feet. Manager breathed out a sigh of relief.

Another three more minutes passed in silence. Manager couldn't take it anymore. He started getting up to go check on Backup Staff when the silence was broken at last. "Umm, guys?" Backup Staff called out in a weak voice. "Umm. I don't really know how to say this...Umm, there's no toilet paper in here."

Staff 2, who was closest to the bathroom door and had been covering his nose for a couple minutes, quickly jumped up and volunteered to go upstairs to get some. A couple minutes later, he came back with a full roll he'd pulled out of a stall upstairs. "I hope Inventory Manager uses that stall tomorrow morning without realizing the toilet paper is gone," Staff 2 said to the team as he pushed the roll under the door – It fit through with at least a half an inch of clearance.

"Thank you!" Backup Staff said, uncomfortably.

"Do you think we could get a courtesy flush?" SM asked. He wasn't joking. The odor was spreading through the room and it was foul.

> **Senior 3 pinging SM:** *That was kind of mean.*

> **SM pinging Senior 3:** *Maybe, but it was 100% necessary. Just wait until the stench hits you over there.*

The team heard Backup Staff push the handle down to flush the toilet. The water started flowing, but the toilet did not flush properly.

"Oh boy!" shouted Backup Staff, frantically. "Plunger! Need a plunger!"

Luckily, there was a plunger next to the toilet and the team soon heard the suctioning sound of the plunger at work.

"Good thing this isn't the first time I've had to use a plunger," muttered Backup Staff. The problem with the tile floor and the gap at the bottom of the door was that it was almost like a microphone. The acoustics projected all the sound from the bathroom into the cave.

At last, the sound of a slow, full flush came through and the sound of ripping toilet paper resumed. "Disaster averted," said Backup Staff, quietly.

Another slow flush and then the water from the sink turned on. The sink sputtered for about five seconds before the team heard Backup Staff start washing his hands. He soon realized the soap dispenser was empty too and there was nothing to dry his hands on. He emerged from the bathroom with a sunken and sullen look on his face—his arms dripping wet from the elbows down. He made no eye contact with anyone as he grabbed his computer and his bag and quickly and quietly left the room (and the building).

With the door open, the full potency of the foul odor quickly seeped into every corner of the room. Staff 2 started coughing. Senior 1's face was turning greenish like she was going to be sick. Staff 1 grabbed the disinfectant spray – Intern had insisted that she buy a few bottles of it with the groceries given the lack of circulation in the audit cave.

"Wait!" shouted Manager at Staff 1. "If you spray that, this whole place will smell like an airport bathroom with a really bad air freshener for days."

"Do you have any better ideas?" asked Staff 1, as she paused with her index finger ready to push the spray nozzle.

"I guess not," said Manager, and Staff 1 drained the entire can in under a minute.

The team tried the fan in the bathroom, but it was broken. The audit cave had virtually no ventilation.

"What did Passive-Aggressive Senior always say on that job you worked on with him?" SM asked Manager. "I think it is about time to relocate and finish working from home tonight?"

"Yep. I'd say so," Manager replied, then turning to Intern, he added, "Would you mind picking up a fan or two and at least four bottles of good air freshener on your way in tomorrow? I have a feeling we will need them. I authorize charging the expense code for them no matter what SM says."

"I second the authorization is what SM says," said SM, quickly.

Intern happily agreed to pick those items up the next morning and the team did the audit two-minute drill—everything saved, papers and files put away, desks neatly organized, bags packed and everyone out of the room with the lights off, in under two minutes.

The next morning, Intern had two fans running and three bottles of air freshener sprayed. Even still, the stench in the room was hardly bearable.

Backup Staff arrived late, said he hadn't had much sleep the night before and quietly went to work. He looked at the fans and could smell the air fresheners underneath the awful reek, but he did not apologize for the night before. A few minutes later, he was thumbing through the flags on the stack of check packets on his desk, picking out five or six of them and heading out of the room.

A couple minutes passed and Senior 1 asked Staff 2 where Backup Staff went with those flagged packets.

"I don't know," said Staff 2, a little worried. "I thought we were going to go through those questions with him this morning."

"I'd better run upstairs to make sure he's not doing anything horrible," said Senior 1, as she got up and left the room.

When Senior 1 found Backup Staff, he was in Finance Manager's office.

"Certainly, you must care that you've overpaid on these invoices?" Backup Staff asked Finance Manager, unrelentingly. "You should go back to them and get $108 back now."

"As I said before, I appreciate your concern but the vendors typically give us a credit for overpayment on the next invoice," Finance Manager was clearly annoyed. "This is all very small. We don't really care about that small of an amount."

"How do you know you will use those vendors again?" asked Backup Staff, desperately.

"We do $3 million of business with this vendor every year. For the last time, I don't care about $108," Finance Manager said, raising his voice. "Will you please let this rest? You are grasping at straws here!"

"Backup Staff, I think you've heard now and understood the company's position on these, which I might add is also our position," Senior 1 said, in an effort to diffuse the situation. "If so, please go back downstairs."

> **Senior 1 pinging Manager:** *I need you up in Finance Manager's office ASAP. Backup Staff made another mess.*
>
> **Manager pinging Senior 1:** *He made a mess in Finance Manager's office too?*
>
> **Senior 1 pinging Manager:** *HA! Only figuratively this time.* 😑
>
> **Manager pinging Senior 1:** *Great! I'll be up in a minute.*

Manager told the rest of the team to not be weird when Backup Staff came downstairs, but also not to let him go talk to the cli-

The Good Audit

ent alone ever again.

"What happened?" Staff 2 asked.

"He made another mess in Finance Manager's office," Manager said, as Staff 2 put both his hands over his eyes and started shaking his head.

"Noooo!!!!" Staff 2 moaned.

Finance Manager and Senior 1 were making small talk when Manager arrived. Manager thought this meant the problem was taken care of, but he was sadly mistaken.

"Come on in," said Finance Manager, like a grade school principal to a tough fifth grader who'd been throwing snowballs. "Close the door behind you."

"What's up?" Manager asked, hesitantly, while trying to stay upbeat.

"Your staff seems to think that we should care about $108 out of the millions of dollars he tested," said Finance Manager, condescendingly. "He seems to be very hung up over anything he thinks is wrong – like worse than any new staff I've ever seen, worse than this girl I knew who did a rotation from Tax (tax accountants have no concept of materiality, everything has to basically be to the dollar for them). This Backup Staff guy seems to think we need it to the penny."

"We had this discussion with him yesterday. We are trying to get him to understand the concept of materiality and that we can ignore such small amounts," Manager replied, calmly, trying to appease Finance Manager.

"I don't want Widget Maker to be charged for any of the extra time he spent fussing over those invoices," said Finance Manager, in a rather demanding tone. "I tried to explain to him that it probably cost two or three hundred dollars in audit fees for the time it took him to fuss over the $108 that we will get back anyway. He said that is what you had told him, too. I don't get why he'd come to talk to me if you'd already had that conversation with him."

Finance Manager stared hard at Manager in an effort to emphasize his point.

"We will talk to him about it again and get this resolved," replied Manager, calmly. Saying any more would likely just rile Finance Manager up, so Manager let there be a few seconds of silence to gauge whether Finance Manager was truly upset or if this had just been a good reason to give someone (him) a lecture today.

> **Manager pinging Senior 1:** *I told the rest of the team about my new rule: Backup Staff doesn't talk to the client by himself anymore!*

> **Senior 1 pinging Manager:** *I can get on board with that!*

"Thanks," replied Finance Manager. "We don't want this happening again."

Ok, Manager thought to himself, *He just wanted to give us a lecture today.*

As Manager stood up to leave, he caught a whiff of a really bad smell that almost knocked him over. *Oh no*, he thought to himself, *did the stench from downstairs stick? Did I bring it with me?*

"What is that smell?" asked Finance Manager, whose face clearly showed he was utterly disgusted – Manager froze for a couple seconds and then Finance Manager continued. "I noticed it this morning, I think it is coming from this vent over here. Smells like an airport bathroom with a REALLY bad air freshener."

Manager looked down the vent that was on Finance Manager's wall and noticed that he could not see the bottom of it. For the first time, he realized that the audit cave was two floors directly below Finance Manager's office.

"Really strange," said Manager, turning up his nose. "But you are right…your office totally stinks!"

When Manager and Senior 1 got back to the audit cave they both told Backup Staff that he was no longer allowed to talk to the client by himself. Backup Staff appeared to have expected this and accepted it without any argument. Then, Manager took one of the fans and put it over on one side of the bathroom door aimed at the corner.

"Why are you doing that?" SM asked Manager, inquisitively. "I don't get why you'd point the fan right at the corner."

"Look up," replied Manager, pointing at a vent in the ceiling. "That vent goes straight up into Finance Manager's office."

"You are kidding me!" SM said, bursting out with laughter. "Ok. We need to wait five minutes and then someone needs a reason to go visit Finance Manager's office to see if it is working."

"You could go and tell him our new plan for Backup Staff," Manager suggested.

It was settled. Five minutes later SM went up to Finance Manager's office. He was back in two minutes. When he walked back in the room, he immediately took the second fan so they were both facing the corner.

"I guess that means it is working then?" asked Staff 2.

"Oh Yeah!" replied SM, with the nervous excitement of a teenager about to toilet paper a house. "He had three people in his office all looking totally disgusted and trying to figure out what is causing it. I didn't even have to go in. I heard it all from down the hall, so I turned around and walked back here."

Another half hour went by. Manager noticed that the smell seemed to be getting stronger.

"It seems like maybe things didn't get flushed enough," Manager said, as he covered his nose and walked toward the bathroom. "It may all still be clogged close to the surface or something."

He walked into the bathroom and flushed the toilet with his foot. "Let's get out of here and go to lunch," he suggested. As they walked out the door, Manager ran back in and added, "Let's point the fans back to normal, just in case anyone comes down to check things out."

CHAPTER 11 – REALLY STINKY OVERAGES

The team returned from lunch about an hour later. They were greeted at the stairs to the basement by Finance Manager.

"You can't go down there!" he warned. "There is a MASSIVE problem down there!"

"Oh, what's that?" asked SM, innocently. The whole team figured that Finance Manager must have called building maintenance and they had figured out the room downstairs was the source of the odor that was wafting up into his office.

"There is some sort of sewage leak down there," replied Finance Manager, scrunching his nose up. "Apparently, there is water and raw sewage all over the place. The maintenance guys say that the wax ring of the toilet had eroded away over time and basically there was stuff seeping through to the base of the toilet. The toilet was leaking all over where the fill valve hooks into the base of the tank. He tried to shut the water off at the stop valve, but that broke as he tried to turn it and everything just went out of control. He radioed up to get the water main out front turned off, but by then a lot of water and sewage had flown out into your room."

"No way," said SM in disbelief, wondering if this was karma for what they'd done with the fans and the vent to Finance Manager's office.

"The maintenance guy pulled the toilet off as quickly as he could. I guess there was a ton of poop sitting in the trap that just came out everywhere. Who knows how long that has been there since I know you guys haven't been using it, but I guess it just smelled horrible – almost knocked him off his feet he said. The closet bend at the bottom had cracked and there has been stuff leaking out of it for what appears to be years. Anyway, the whole room down there is a huge mess. Water and sewage everywhere. With the toilet off and the leak appearing to have been there so long, maintenance is worried about toxic gases. He was feeling sick and was taken to the hospital to be monitored. We've also been told to send you all to the clinic down the street to make sure you haven't been exposed to anything harmful. Widget Maker will be footing the bill for those tests and everything else related to the leak."

"Lucky we weren't there when that happened," SM pointed out. "The whole audit team would be in the hospital. At least this way we can still work."

"Sort of," replied Finance Manager. "The downside is that all your stuff down there is ruined. Due to the exposure to the raw sewage, everything that was on the floor—your bags, papers, et-cetera—has to be disposed of. All the computers except one will be salvage—."

"Wait," interrupted Manager, frantically. "Whose computer didn't make it?"

"I'm not sure which one it was," Finance Manager replied. "They said when the stop valve blew out, water shot right out into the room and blasted a computer plus a stack of papers that was about a foot and a half high."

"Great!" Backup Staff lamented. "That was my computer. All my work for the past day and a half was on there – all the expense testing, and those papers were the support for it. We will have to rework all of that. I hope those papers were copies and not originals."

The Good Audit

"They were all originals," Finance Manager groaned. "But weren't you all through them with only $108 of errors?"

"Yeah," answered Manager. "I think we were basically done with them." Then, looking at Backup Staff, who was about to say that he still had questions, Manager added, "I think the few questions Backup Staff had left were not going to change the numbers, so we are good."

"Well, that is some good luck then!" Finance Manager exclaimed. "Once they've been audited, I don't care what happens to them really."

Just then someone in a hazmat suit came up the stairs with a couple sealed plastic bags. "Total loss," said a voice from inside the suit. "We are still trying to contain everything. Here are a few computers from down there. I'm afraid everything else will likely not be available until tomorrow at the earliest."

"There should have been seven working laptops down there," staff 2 piped up. "And one wet one that is dead."

"This is what I could get up here now," said the voice in the suit. "The rest will have to wait until tomorrow."

They quickly figured out that the computers belonged to SM, Senior 1 and Staff 2 so Manager, Senior 3, Staff 1 and Intern were out of luck.

SM had called Partner and was explaining the whole situation. Partner pointed out that they were lucky that most of the information in the audit file was stored on the cloud, "An investment that had actually been worth the Firm's money," and that only a few days of work had likely been lost. He suggested the team all come to the office as most of them would need replacement items from IT.

"Also," partner told SM before he hung up, "make sure we figure out exactly how much this leak cost us. They put us down in that room. They had not maintained it properly. I want hours, I want equipment lists, I want IT time to fix all this. We should be billing them out the nose! If they are lucky, the building hazard insurance will foot the bill and it will be a win-win. Either way, we should look at this as a good thing. I bet we can get another $70k to $80k out of them over this and put our margin back where we had it to begin with."

"Sounds like we will be going back to the office for the rest of the day," said SM, as he got off the phone. "We need to get our computer hardware situation figured out and determine what we lost."

"Wait," Senior 3 desperately called to the person in the hazmat suit. "My car keys and wallet are down on the desk farthest away from the bathroom. Is there any chance you could get those? Otherwise, I am really stranded."

"I will see what I can do," said the voice in the suit, as he turned to head back down the stairs. "But I will not be up here for another couple hours even if I can bring them up. Go get tested at the clinic and then come back to check. I will leave them with Receptionist, if I can get them up."

The team walked down the street to the clinic to be tested. Everyone's tests came back fine. On the way back, Staff 2 and Manager were walking several yards behind the group.

"Well," said staff 2, chuckling to himself. "This just proves that the Backup Staff explosion the other night truly was toxic."

"I don't know if it does that," replied Manager, with a chuckle. "And we probably don't want to mention much about that around the client. Sounds like Partner wants to collect on the time that is lost."

"Won't we just end up working even more overtime, being MORE flexible to get the job done?" asked Staff 2, miserably. "I mean, it isn't like they are going to schedule more people to help us or add more days to the schedule for this audit, right?"

The Good Audit

"Which is exactly why Partner wants to put it on them," answered Manager. "Thousands of dollars of more fees, zero dollars of cost, margin goes right back up to where he promised Firm leadership it would be. It is a big win for Partner and for mine and SM's performance reviews. To top it off, Widget Maker won't have to pay for the overages since it will be covered by insurance."

"Ha. That's funny," laughed Staff 2. "Overages!"

Manager laughed, "Really stinky overages!"

"It seems that every time something is a win for a partner and/or for TAF, the rest of the team seems to be getting the raw end of the deal." Staff 2 observed.

By this point, the team was back to the Widget Maker office.

As the team was gathering what little they had that was not in the audit room, CFO pulled SM aside and said, "I just got off the phone with our insurance agent. They are going to pay for all this, so please just make an itemized list of lost time, re-work, lost computer hardware and anything else there might be and we will submit that to them for reimbursement. I'm really sorry this happened. Originally, I thought we should have had you in a room up here, but others insisted that you'd be fine down there."

I wonder why, thought SM, as he thanked CFO and said, "We will get you that list. I think this puts us a few days behind for sure. Hopefully, everyone understands if we start asking for stuff we were previously provided."

"I will make sure that is not a problem," replied CFO, as she started heading toward the CEO's office. "Now I get to tell CEO about his moose heads and sports memorabilia that was down there. He won't be happy."

The team gathered the three computers that were recovered and headed downtown to the TAF office. Senior 3 went to check with Receptionist to see if his keys had been returned.

"Hey," Senior 3 said to Receptionist.

"Hello! How can I help—" Receptionist interrupted herself. "Hey! You are one of the auditors whose stuff was all down in the basement. I'm really sorry. That totally stinks. Hah – I crack myself up. I heard it was poopy water everywhere and like tons of toxic fumes and stuff. I heard one computer got totally soaked and started shorting out and sparking as it melted away. The maintenance guy is in the hospital. All of you guys lost like all your stuff. Are you the one hoping for car keys and wallet to show up here? I can't believe you don't take your keys and wallet everywhere with you. My keys and wallet are always with me."

At this point, the reception phone had been ringing for almost 30 seconds. "Don't you think you should get that?"

"Oh, I didn't even notice the phone was ringing," said Receptionist, looking down at the ringing phone.

Your whole job is to sit here and answer the phone and you didn't even realize it was ringing? thought Senior 3, *probably because she was so busy focusing on talking to me.*

"It is probably just some angry investor," said Receptionist. "They call all the time wanting to know when they are getting distributions, why legal hasn't sent them anything yet, how they can sell their shares, what exactly the company did with their investment money, all sorts of things."

As she was explaining this, she finally picked up the phone. Senior 3 was very happy that she did. It was the people working the mess downstairs. His keys would be at Receptionist's desk in just over an hour.

"Great!" exclaimed Receptionist. "You can hang out here with me and wait. Are you single? Because if you are, I totally want to date you."

The Good Audit

"I am," replied Senior 3, taken back a bit. He was getting irritated with the receptionist as she did not seem to be able to stop talking.

The receptionist position at Widget Maker had historically been a path into product distribution (marketing). The company rotated through receptionists about every three to six months. If someone could hack it answering the phone calls of angry investors for that long, they could probably make it in marketing. The position was typically filled with college grads who were happy to make ten to twelve bucks an hour because they'd gone to school for totally impractical and useless degrees (from an accountant's perspective) like English, history, art, drama, marriage family and childhood development, psychology, social sciences, or some other non-business or professional degree.

After talking to receptionist for about ten minutes, Senior 3 wondered how or why these people went to college at all – over 70% of them ended up in marketing or some form of sales, another 20% of them got teaching degrees, the other 10% realized their mistake and went back to get a law degree, medical school, engineering degree or an MBA (And as a matter of fact, approximately 71% of all accountants wish they'd done that too, but going back for an MBA was too expensive and didn't seem practical because 95% of accountants do not agree with economists that say sunk costs are sunk – you can always recover sunk costs if you are willing to dive deep enough or be miserable for long enough to get them back (unless of course the company goes bankrupt or the costs were paid to the government). This deep dive was more commonly known as "Partner Track" at The Accounting Firm.

"I've been here for just over two months now. They just offered me a position in product distribution!" said Receptionist. "I will be the fastest person in Widget Maker history to move from Receptionist to product distribution!"

123

"Congratulations!" said Senior 3. "Does it come with a pay raise?"

"It does," replied Receptionist. "But the money doesn't really matter. My degree will finally be useful! I was an Art History major."

"How are you going to use Art History in product distribution?" asked Senior 3, while thinking, *you did Art History, so it was never really about the money*.

"I'm not 100% sure yet, but I will get to be more Artsy" replied Receptionist, with no loss of enthusiasm despite Senior 3's skepticism. "I mean I can make ads and cute little mailers and posters. It is going to be so great! Everyone knows you come here to be the receptionist so that you can make it into a better job that is so much more fulfilling. You are told to just endure the crazy stuff and if you can handle that then you can have a REAL full-time job!"

"I guess that makes sense," Senior 3 replied, understandingly. "We are told that after enduring the staff and senior years, life as a manager is supposed to be somewhat better."

By the time Senior 3's keys and wallet made it to the desk, he'd been listening to Receptionist talk about how great art and marketing were for an hour and a half. In the end, Receptionist wouldn't give Senor 3 his keys until he'd agreed to a date with her. Senior 3 insisted that it be after the audit was over when things "calmed down" so that he'd never actually have to go on the date.

Back at the office, the audit team was compiling a list of overages to give to CFO.

"Remember," said Partner, standing in front of the whiteboard in a conference room. "Nothing is too small to make it on this list. I want an estimate of how many energy drinks SM had left in the fridge. I want to know what snacks we had down there, even if it was moldy organic, non-GMO, gluten-free, no sugar

The Good Audit

added, vegan fruit. If you had any personal mementos in your audit bags, put them down. I want to squeeze every cent within reason out of this."

"Shouldn't we be the ones being reimbursed for loss of personal property?" asked Staff 2, very bothered that Partner would try to collect money on his own personal property. "I had my gym bag down there with my iPod, brand new running shoes, $100 of gym clothes and a soccer ball. You are saying the Firm should get money for this? Is the Firm reimbursing me for the loss then?"

"Hmm," replied Partner. "I suppose you should all make personal lists for stuff like that. Please do that on your own time later tonight. Right now, you are on my time, and this time spent making this list should also be listed."

"Alright then," said SM, enthusiastically (Manager glared at him for being such a suck-up). "Let's start brainstorming this list! Intern, will you please take notes? Here you can use my computer since yours was lost when everything hit the fan...literally, ha! That's funny...except it isn't."

No one in the room laughed, mostly because the delivery was horrible and it was too soon to be joking about what happened.

"I don't have a computer anymore," Backup Staff said, sadly, as he pouted at the end of the table.

"Great!" Partner said. "We have all the work we lost on your laptop. We need to put down all the time it will take you to recreate that, plus all the time to sit and wait for a new computer which will likely be tomorrow so all of this afternoon plus a full half day tomorrow needs to be charged for that line, and just to be clear as you take notes Intern, a half day is 12 hours. As an aside, we really only ask people to work half days around here – you can do whatever you want with the other twelve hours."

Again, nobody laughed...except for SM, but his laugh was totally fake. Manager, Senior 1 and Staff 2 sat silently bothered by the 'joke'.

Partner was continuing with his list of things related to Backup Staff's computer being destroyed. "Plus, the cost of getting a new computer, which includes several hours from our IT team as well as Backup Staff sitting there getting it set up. In fact, since we are on computers, they are over there setting up four loaners for you guys right now. All this time needs to be captured! What else?"

"I got my computer back," said Senior 1. "But by the time I got it, the battery had died, so I lost everything I did this morning."

"Perfect!" Partner said, ecstatically. "Put the time you worked this morning and then the time it will take to redo the work."

"My bag had a thumb drive in it," said Staff 2. "Everything Assistant Controller and Finance Manager provided us for support was on that thumb drive. We are going to have to go back and see what we need to re-request support for."

"Fantastic!" Partner almost shouted. "Keep these loss ideas coming! Put down all the time needed to figure out what we need plus all the time it will take us to redo the work! Nothing like getting paid twice for doing the same thing! It is like working while sitting through a training!"

The brainstorming continued. The full day for the entire team was chalked up as a loss, a couple of monitors were gone, the team realized that all the batteries on the four laptops still in the room would be dead by the time they got them so everything done that morning was lost, all seven charge cords needed to be replaced and it would take IT time to order them, the list went on and on. In the end, the list was a seven-page document and the "costs" amounted to one hundred and ten thousand dollars.

"What does this bring our margin back up to?" asked Partner. "I know we have no control reliance, their system is garbage and we have found 16 STINC's—"

The Good Audit

"18 now actually," Staff 2 interrupted. "Manager found one yesterday and I found another one this morning."

"Awesome!" said Partner, enthusiastically, "I say when we get done with the list, since today is written off anyway, we all go get drinks or milkshakes or something to celebrate!"

Backup Staff's eyes lit up and Manager could see him thinking $20 OF TOKENS FOR THE ARCADE!!!

"Anyway," continued Partner. "Where was I? Ah, yes, how much have we taken in write-offs for those issues we found early on?"

"We took seventy thousand dollars for those," said Manager. "But shouldn't we be trying to go back and bill for those too given how big of a disaster this has all been? I mean we have 18 STINCs. We can't rely on controls anymore."

"That's right!" exclaimed Partner with big, cartoon, dollar signs figuratively popping out his eyes. "We can use this as a time to say 'here is the bill for the mess from the toilet' and then 'here is a *smaller* bill for the mess from your accounting team'! Today, this audit just got $185,000 better! Now, let's go get milkshakes! I will even buy you the large-size ones instead of just the regular ones, as a token of my sincere appreciation for what has come out of today!"

Wow, thought Manager, *we just put $185,000 in your pocket and your great, big token of appreciation is the one-dollar upgrade on eight milkshakes that you will run through as an expense anyway? Thanks – eye roll.*

"I think we should get milkshakes every time something goes wrong on this audit," Staff 2 whispered to Manager, as the team walked out of the office.

"If we did that, it would probably be cheaper for the firm to buy us a milkshake shop at the rate we are going," Manager whispered back.

The next morning, Partner, SM, and Manager went to Widget

Maker to meet with CFO to present their lists of bathroom-caused and client-caused audit overages to her. Partner set both lists side by side.

"As you can see," Partner pointed out, motioning to the bathroom list, "the overages due to the bathroom leak are substantial – please, pardon the pun. We believe this list to be a full representation of the costs we incurred or will have to incur as a result of the incident."

"That list looks very thorough," said CFO, as she blew out a soft whistle. "Good thing this is going straight to the hazard insurance claim, so no need to go through it in great detail. Now, what is this other list then?"

"This list…" Partner hesitated. CFO's stern look when she asked about the audit overage list momentarily put him on his heels.

"As we've discussed several times in the past several weeks," Manager chimed in to save Partner, "we've encountered several…roadblocks – sorry, no pun intended…very bad pun – in completing our audit work."

"Yes," acknowledged CFO, drawing her eyebrows down. "But isn't that kind of stuff typical in an audit, especially a first-year audit?"

"Three or four errors are typical in a first-year audit," replied SM. "I think we are up to 18 – some of which are extremely significant."

"Yes, although several of those shouldn't be on the list because I found them in my review and the team just hadn't fixed them yet," CFO argued.

"We are certainly happy to discuss those and take them off if we come to an understanding that you had identified them prior to our audit," Partner volunteered.

Manager was raging inside, *If she found them before the audit and her team did nothing with them, they are still audit findings,* he

The Good Audit

thought, *Otherwise, if she's smart, she'll just say she found all the big ones. Staff 2 is going to be furious if she claims to have found the $45 million STINC he found.*

"Had you found the $45 million depreciation expense error in your review?" SM asked, emotionlessly.

"No," replied CFO.

"Or, the amortization of goodwill? I think that one was several million dollars," SM continued his line of questioning.

"No, we didn't find that one either," replied CFO, softly.

"Why don't you just send SM a list of the ones you did find and we will take care of it?" Partner suggested in an effort to move on. "With those two errors staying on the STINC, we cannot, unfortunately, rely on controls and we have to do quite a bit more work than originally anticipated. This second list, which, I might add, is quite a bit smaller than the other list, details the additional hours we will have to incur to test around that."

"Can you just combine the lists?" CFO asked. "That way—"

"I don't understand what you are saying," Partner interrupted. "Surely, you aren't implying—"

"No, of course not. I just want to see them all as one list. It will make it easier to get it all paid at once," CFO replied.

"Great!" said Partner. "We will combine the lists and email them over to you."

The auditors stood up to leave when CFO stopped them.

"One other thing," she said. "CEO had quite a bit of memorabilia down there."

"Oh?" asked Partner, nervously.

"It appears that someone on your team had put it all in a grocery sack and set it inside one of the desk drawers, the desk by the door closest to the stairs," CFO said.

129

C.P. Aiden

"I'm so sorry," SM began apologizing, "That must have been Intern. I'm sure she didn't realize what she was doing."

"As it turns out," CFO said with a smile on her face, "doing that saved it all. CEO was thrilled that it could be salvaged. He told me to personally thank the audit team for him."

"He is certainly welcome," replied Partner, energetically. Having a CEO happy with auditors is not something that comes around very often, so Partner was soaking this in.

He's certainly welcome to thank us in person, thought Manager as they walked out the door.

When they walked into the parking lot, Partner stopped Manager before they headed in different directions to their cars.

"Hey. I really appreciate you stepping up to the plate in there with regards to our out-of-scope audit fees. You really sealed the deal for CFO in there," said Partner, gratefully.

Manager was shocked with this rare bit of praise from Partner and was speechless for a moment but finally got out an, "it was nothing, just trying to do what is best for the Firm."

"Well, I want you to know that stuff like that doesn't go unnoticed. I know you've all been working crazy hours, especially for this time of year. I want you to go home early next Friday, like 7:30 p.m., and take your wife out to a nice dinner on me... well, on the Firm. Yeah, really tell her how grateful I am for all your hard work and for landing us that extra bit of fee."

Manager could not have been more shocked but managed to say, "Thank you," before he started walking towards his car.

"Oh," said Partner, chasing Manager down. "But don't tell the rest of the audit team. I can't do this for everyone. This is directly incremental to you securing us that other $80,000."

"Sure," said Manager, still a little confused, as something like this had never happened to him before.

The Good Audit

"And one more thing," Partner added. "I almost forgot – try to keep it under $25 total so you can run it through as an overtime meal."

"Alright," said Manager, not sure if he should now feel thanked or insulted.

As Manager got into his car, he tried to make sense of what had just happened and if it was truly for real. He had spoken up and got The Accounting Firm another $80k with basically no questions asked from CFO and the thank you from the partner was to take his wife out to a "nice dinner" that had to total less than $25 so he could run it through as an overtime meal that he would be taxed on. In addition, if he worked until 7:30 on Friday, he'd be entitled to an overtime meal anyway, so all he was really getting was permission to include his wife on the meal. Where in the entire metro area is there a "nice dinner" for two that costs under $25?!...Wow, just wow...but on the bright side, the partner had actually told him "Thanks" and he could count on one hand the number of times any partner at The Accounting Firm had ever thanked him personally – verbally or in writing. In the end, the insult of only giving $25 to buy a nice dinner for two and the massive disparity between the $25 and the $80,000 was a bigger deal than being told "Thanks". Maybe it really was time to start looking for another job – the people working at clients always got paid way more than the auditors anyway.

CHAPTER 12 – MOVING UP

The following week, things were moving along smoothly. Due to what Partner was now calling "the fortuitous leak in the audit cave", the audit team had been given an upstairs conference room. Of course, the room was still as far away from the accounting department as possible. The company did not have a fridge in this room, so the team had to put their drinks and leftovers in the fridge in the break room which always resulted in 60% of the leftovers, 50% of the soda and 80% of the energy drinks being taken by Widget Maker employees. There was only one small window on the far end. The glass panel that showed out to the hallway had a blind that could be pulled down and SM insisted the team leave it down so that people walking by would not be a distraction.

"I once did a hospital audit as a first-year staff and the door had a half window that went from the doorknob up. It did not have a shade to pull down like this one," Manager said, pointing at the glass panel. "The room was literally right next to the entrance to the operating room."

"That sounds terrible," Senior 3 said.

"It gets worse," Manager continued, now with the full attention of the entire team. "There was only a small table in the room – it fit 2 people to each side. The senior and staff 2 sat on the side looking away from the doorway, leaving me to look out. Unfor-

The Good Audit

tunately, the window was the perfect height to give a full view of the stretchers that were being pushed down to the operating room."

"So, you had to watch bunches of people getting wheeled into surgery?" Staff 2 asked, as he gulped loudly.

"Exactly," said Manager, gravely. "One day, there was an older gentleman who was being wheeled down. His face was turned sideways in my direction. For a split second, I looked into his eyes. I saw the look of death in that man! About two hours later, I had run down to the bathroom which required going past the door to the hallway the OR was in (right around the corner from our room). I looked through the tiny glass slit windows that were on that door just long enough to see two people dressed in scrubs rolling a fully covered body away."

"That poor man!" exclaimed a heartbroken Intern. "That is the saddest, audit story I have ever heard."

"I have no idea if the body was that man or if someone else had died, but the experience has never left me," said Manager, solemnly. "I asked the Firm if I could be taken off all healthcare related audits after that. It was just too much for me emotionally."

"Well, I'm glad they seem to have respected your situation and that they did that for you," Senior 3 pointed out.

"They didn't listen at first," replied Manager, tersely, with a flash of angry bitterness in his eyes. "I had to threaten to file a worker's comp claim to seek professional counseling for the irreparable, mental damage it caused and that I would have to miss two hours of work a week for eight to 12 weeks for said counseling. They agreed to reorganize my schedule if I would forego the counseling. I did, and as you can tell, I'm still pretty much scarred for life – but hey, The Accounting Firm got somewhere between 16 and 24 more chargeable hours, so they have no problem with what it did to me. At least they fixed my schedule. I haven't set foot in a hospital since, except for the birth of our youngest son – same hospital too."

"I think I'm going to try really hard to focus on my work for the next little bit," said Staff 1, putting her head down. "And do my best to forget that story."

The room went quiet, except for the sound of clicking keyboards. Aside from the fact that there was more work than humanly possible to get done with so few people and so little time, everyone was too tired and now, much too depressed to want to be social.

The silence was broken by SM breaking out in excited glee – no one on the team had experienced that emotion coming from SM, so everyone looked up very startled. "Oh boy, oh boy, oh boy," SM let out, as he grinned from ear to ear. "My favorite part of the audit just landed in my inbox. Listen to the email from CFO."

SM,

I've attached the file you requested. Please keep in mind that this file is HIGHLY confidential and contains VERY sensitive and private information that cannot leak inside or outside the company. Please limit sharing this file with only the members of your team who ABSOLUTELY need it for testing. Please do not distribute this to other members of your team.

Thanks,
CFO

"If the file is what I think it is, I think we all absolutely need to take a look!" exclaimed Manager.

"Can we see it? Can we see it?" begged Staff 2 like a little, whimpering puppy that wants a treat – his eyes staring at SM and his chin quivering ever so slightly.

The Good Audit

"Ok," said SM, reluctantly. "But make sure that door is really shut and come over here. I'm not sending this out to everyone because CFO asked specifically that I not distribute this within our team, so you'll have to just look on my screen."

Staff 1 and Intern were just coming back from the break room where they had found that most of the soda was gone and SM only had 1 energy drink left (even though there had been 5 there that morning), so they had grabbed the last one for him. As they walked in, they saw the whole team was on the other side of the room all huddled around SM's computer. All were wide-eyed looking intently at the screen with their mouths wide open.

"Quick!" exclaimed SM. "Shut the door!"

"We just got the highly confidential payroll file from CFO!" Staff 2 shouted out. "You are going to want to see this!"

Manager and Senior 3 were pointing at the screen

"Wow!" exclaimed Manager. "They get paid so much for doing so little!"

"Can you believe what she is making?" replied Senior 3, pointing down lower on the screen. "That is unbelievable!"

"I know," replied Staff 2 in amazement. "This is incredible! Look how good that guy has it!"

"Keep scrolling down," said Senior 1. "I have to see more!"

"Ok," said SM, as he continued to scroll down his screen.

"WAIT!" said Senior 1, with a look of astonishment. "Look at that. I can't believe it. She is making way over 6 figures, even with her flexible work arrangement that only requires 30 hours a week. I guess she didn't have to take a pay cut to put the kids to bed!"

"Yeah," replied Manager. "But he is getting a WAY better deal. Look! He basically does nothing and gets paid so much."

"There is always at least one person from each department that is getting the raw deal," SM pointed out, after he had scrolled down more. "See, look at him, for example. He is really getting owned! Works like crazy and makes half of what his boss makes and 25% less than his peer group."

"Wow," said Senior 3, sadly. "I'm feeling hurt just seeing that."

"I guess that explains why CFO said this could be very costly for the company if it got out," Manager said. "That is just so disgusting. I want to throw up."

"Go to the bonus tab, quick!" ordered Senior 3, abruptly.

"Wow!" SM shouted out. "I could buy a brand-new car with a bonus like that."

Intern and Staff 1 were still standing by the door, staring blankly at each other and the team.

"Get over here," said Staff 2, as he looked up at Staff 1 and Intern. "This is part of audit initiation. Staff 1, did you seriously never see one of these during your internship?"

"Nope," replied Staff 1 in bewilderment. "I can't believe you are all getting so worked up over a little payroll file."

At this, Intern could not take it anymore. She rushed across the room to look at the screen. Staff 2 made room so she could see.

"Wow!" she said, enthusiastically. "I've never seen anything like this. Amazing! Staff 1, you HAVE to come and take a look at this! It shows what everyone gets paid. You will never think of any of these people the same again!"

Staff 1 slowly edged towards the computer. The whole team watched Staff 1 with anticipation. They had seen this reaction in others before and were waiting with great anticipation. As Staff 1 continued to move hesitantly toward the team, SM lost all patience. Flipping his screen around, he exclaimed, "Oh, just look at it already!"

Staff 1 stared at the screen totally speechless. Before she could

The Good Audit

get her wits about her, the conference room door behind her opened. SM quickly retracted his laptop, but it was both too late and too awkward with the entire team standing on the opposite side of the conference table around 1 computer and Staff 1 facing them all.

Inventory Manager walked into the room. "Hey, guys! What are you all doing?" he asked, playfully. "I heard some strange things as I walked past and this looks very strange indeed. I'm not sure it looks like auditing."

"We are auditing," replied Manager, slowly. "A little unconventional, but still auditing."

"Wait a minute," said Inventory Manager, pretending to be somewhat bewildered. "I remember the old auditors telling me about something very secretive in the audit that they all got giddy for...I just can't remember what they called it. Did you get a highly confidential file from CFO today?"

"If we did," replied SM, forcefully, "it would be highly confidential."

"Do you think CFO would be pleased if she heard that said highly confidential file was being closely drooled all over by your ENTIRE team?" Inventory Manager asked, as he cocked his head to one side and stared right at SM.

"I suppose that would not be ideal," replied SM, slowly giving up hope that this was going to end well.

"Well, this is awkward then," said Inventory Manager, as he deliberately stared at SM's computer. "I suppose it could be our little secret if I could take a *tiny*, little peek at the file with you. As you know, I have kept our little, lunch arrangement to myself."

"I don't know what choice we really have," replied SM, slowly turning the screen towards Inventory Manager. "You have to keep this VERY confidential, do you understand?"

"This is amazing! Are you seeing some of these people? Unreal!"

said Inventory Manager, pretending he didn't hear anything SM had just said.

"Didn't this guy used to be at The Accounting Firm?" Inventory Manager continued looking at the screen. "He certainly wasn't making that much when he was with you guys! His bonus is like half a senior's annual base salary."

"His job at TAF was much more difficult too," replied Manager in astonishment.

"Hold on," said Inventory Manager, as he paused to scroll up, then down, then back up again. "We need to filter this thing."

Inventory Manager then took over SM's mouse and started clicking away.

"UNBELIEVABLE!" shouted Inventory Manager, wildly, as a flash of anger crossed over his face.

"Keep it down," whispered Manager, while bringing his index finger to his lips to shush Inventory Manager. "We don't need half the floor out there curious about what is going on in here."

"Do you see this?" said Inventory Manager, calming down just slightly. "Here it is in plain black and white."

Inventory Manager had taken the file and filtered for all department managers in the company and the results were astonishing, at least to Inventory Manager.

"This is what I've thought all along but had no way to verify until now," said Inventory Manager, excitedly, while slapping his hand down on the table. "Every other department manager is making $25-35k more a year than me and Finance Manager."

"Must feel good to be a cost center instead of a revenue generator," Manager said sarcastically.

"I need to go tell Finance Manager," Inventory Manager cried.

"Wait!" SM called out, as Inventory Manager headed for the door. "Remember, this is highly confidential!"

The Good Audit

"Yeah," said Inventory Manager, turning around. "I *was* going to keep it that way, but given the valuable information I just uncovered, all bets are off. I will *try* not to divulge that I got this information from you."

With that Inventory Manager rushed out of the room shouting for Finance Manager down the hall.

> **Manager pinging Senior 3:** *They aren't getting that screwed given that they basically know nothing and do nothing.*

> **Senior 3 pinging Manager:** *I can see how they think they got the raw deal in this. Every other department manager seems to also know nothing and do nothing, yet they are each getting paid better than these two.*

"Oh, dear," said SM in dismay. "That certainly did not go well."

About 10 minutes later, Finance Manager walked in, closely followed by Inventory Manager who shut the door behind them.

"Is it true?" asked Finance Manager in disbelief. "CFO sent you all the payroll data and Inventory Manager and I are really paid $25-35k less than all the other department managers?"

"We can neither confirm nor deny such a statement," said Manager, indifferently.

"I can either tell CFO or tell CFO," replied Inventory Manager with a huge grin on his face.

"Fine," said SM, dejectedly. "See for yourself." SM turned his computer around and showed Finance Manager the company payroll file.

"The best part of the audit is getting that detailed payroll file and having the whole team get all googly-eyed over it," said Finance Manager with a grin. "They keep this information very secret around here. Only CEO, CFO, and VP of HR have access to it."

Inventory Manager and Finance Manager were both looking at the file. "Wow!" Inventory Manager pointed out, animatedly. "CEO is crushing it. $1.5 million in salary, $2.8 million bonus for effectively breaking even and $7 million in distributions on his equity."

"Yeah," said Manager, miserably. "We ran a quick and dirty analysis and if you take out the five highest paid people at Widget Maker, the average pay of all remaining full-time employees is $38,000 a year. CEO is making 297 times the average employee."

"Nothing makes me want to be a liberal more than executive compensation," said Finance Manager, decisively.

"Especially, when you see the ACTUAL tax rate most of the super wealthy pay," replied Inventory Manager.

"What do you mean?" asked Staff 1, innocently. "I thought rich people were in really high brackets."

"I did CEO's personal tax return last year. He ended up paying 12% federal taxes after utilizing a zillion loopholes – that is highly confidential, and I expect it not to leave this room," Finance Manager said, as he looked around the room. "In the end, he paid about $1.4 million in federal taxes on $11.3 million of income. Wealthy people generally complain about the dollar amount they are paying, not the rate – unless they can't find loopholes and have to pay the full 35 to 40 percent federal rate…then they complain about both amount and rate."

> **Manager pinging SM:** *Highly confidential…Just like we expected the payroll file information not to leave this room when Inventory Manager looked at it and then brought back a friend.*

Finance Manager and Inventory Manager were, of course, looking at SM's screen and saw the message. Inventory Manager shot Manager a sideways look and said "Hey…"

The Good Audit

"I did that on purpose – a special reminder for you to keep your mouth shut," said Manager, smiling.

"The loopholes aren't a conservative/liberal thing," Inventory Manager chimed in. "They are a 'secret tricks for the super wealthy on both sides' thing."

"I guess that is fair," agreed Finance Manager. "What isn't fair is how screwed we are compared to our peer group."

Inventory Manager and Finance Manager turned and quickly left the room. "Enjoy looking at the rest of the file! We need to go strategize about how we are going to get CFO to give us both raises." Inventory Manager said, loudly, as he shut the door.

"I can't believe you thought we were like looking at something really bad," Staff 2 said to Staff 1, as he busily started typing on his keyboard. "This is just too funny not to tell other people in the office about."

Staff 1 scowled at Staff 2 and was about to object to him pinging half the office at her expense, but her attempt was interrupted by SM.

"If they tell CFO we showed them the file, then we all get fired," said SM, anxiously.

"Oh well," Senior 3 pointed out, cynically. "Not much we can do about it now. Since we are sure to be fired, we might as well finish looking through the file."

In the meantime, Manager had quickly started looking at jobs on a job posting website. Staff 1 walked past his computer and then quickly took her seat.

> **Staff 1 pinging Staff 2:** *This must be serious, Manager is on his computer looking at finance and accounting jobs.*

> **Staff 2 pinging Staff 1:** *That isn't surprising, I'm pretty sure he checks that about twice a day just to see what is out there and if anything is good enough*

to leave for. He really hates what this job and the expectations of the Firm does to his family life. His wife is at home with three kids for 12 to 16 hours a day six days a week.

Manager was really looking at finance and inventory jobs and quickly putting together a list in an email that he sent to Inventory Manager and Finance Manager, copying SM.

Hey Inventory Manager and Finance Manager,

I appreciate the discussion we had earlier about market compensation. As a prestigious accounting firm, we often hear about jobs in the market related to finance, accounting, and inventory. I've attached a list of jobs that fit your experience levels as well as pay ranges that we have been informed of for those jobs (if not already listed on the job description).

At the bottom of the listing, you will see the median and mean pay for the listed jobs currently available in the market. I've also added the size of each company (in assets and revenue) as two columns on the list so you can see how they stack up against Widget Maker.

Please let me know if this listing fits your expectations based on our discussion. This listing is highly confidential so I would hope that you would keep this information as confidential as you would like us to keep yours.

Thanks,
Manager

SM pinging Manager: *Well played!*

Manager pinging SM: *Thanks!* *Hopefully, it keeps us out of trouble.*

The Good Audit

> **SM pinging Manager:** *Hopefully, but you never know what to expect with these guys.*

The next afternoon, Finance Manager and Inventory Manager strutted into the audit room smiling.

"Guess what?!" Finance Manager asked, eagerly. "Guess WHAT??!!"

Nobody even bothered looking up from their screens. They were all too busy trying to wrap things up before everyone left for Christmas to care about Finance Manager or Inventory Manager being excited about anything.

"Guys! COME ON!!" Inventory Manager exclaimed, as he waved his arms. "We have BIG NEWS!"

> **Staff 2 pinging Manager:** *Unfortunately, we are too busy fixing everything they've screwed up to hear their BIG NEWS.*

Manager had not noticed Inventory Manager and Finance Manager at all as he was deep in thought, staring at his screen and had both earbuds in. Staff 2's ping made him look up as Inventory Manager and Finance Manager anxiously waited for someone, anyone, in the room to give them attention.

"Did you need something?" Manager asked, disingenuously, as he removed his earbuds.

"We don't need anything from you," replied Finance Manager, enthusiastically. "We just—"

"Then why are you here?" Manager interrupted, irritably.

"We came to tell you about our raises!" Inventory Manager blurted out, pompously.

"Go on then," said Manager, begrudgingly, while gesturing for Inventory Manager to continue.

"We took that pay analysis you sent over and, after analyzing and revising it ourselves, we had a sit down with CFO," Finance

143

Manager said, exuberantly. "After a very long discussion, we were able to convince her that we are underpaid based on the market data."

> **SM pinging Manager:** *Great! They probably told CFO the analysis was from us.*

"We know you won't mind that we took credit for the analysis," Inventory Manager said, quietly – as if whispering a secret to the whole room while looking over his shoulder at the door as if someone were about to burst through it at any moment. "We know you didn't want CFO knowing that you'd shown us everything and then given that analysis to us."

> **Manager pinging SM:** *These guys keep surprising me...although this is the first GOOD surprise of the entire audit.*

> **SM pinging Manager:** *HA! So true!*

"So, you really came in here to thank Manager for your raises?" asked SM, quizzically.

"Not at all!" replied Finance Manager, dismissively. "We just wanted to share the exciting news! We each got a $25k a year raise!"

"Shut the front door!" Manager sighed, downheartedly.

"And our annual bonuses will go up $5,000, too!" Inventory Manager added, while rocking back and forth, playing his air guitar.

"I thought CFO was going to tell you that you are paid very well for what you do," stated Manager, still baffled at the thought that these two dimwits had just been given massive raises.

> **Manager pinging Senior 3:** *Which wouldn't be a lie by any stretch of the imagination*

"She did,' replied Inventory Manager, seeming surprised that Manager had guessed exactly what CFO had originally said.

"How did you know?"

> **Senior 3 pinging Manager:** *Ha! I'm really enjoying this.*

"Wild guess," replied Manager, sardonically.

"Merry Christmas to us!" gloated Inventory Manager. "$2,000 extra a month! Well...before taxes, so like $1,400 after tax for me. My wife is going to love Christmas this year."

"Are you sure you want to tell your wife about it?" Finance Manager abruptly asked Inventory Manager. "I mean, my wife would find a way to spend it all without me seeing a penny of it."

Inventory Manager's face brightened a bit, his eyebrows slowly moving up as his eyes opened wider. "That's a good point," he acknowledged, as the thought sank in. "I will have to ask Senior Accountant if she can direct deposit the extra money to a different account. My wife will never have to know."

> **Staff 2 pinging Manager:** *What a bunch of pathetic losers!*

> **Manager pinging Staff 2:** *Whenever I'm having a really bad day, I remember who I'm married to, how lucky I am to have her and our kids in my life, and that collecting a paycheck is the ONLY reason I do this.*

"Great idea!" exclaimed Finance Manager, walking towards the door. "Let's go down there right now and ask her! I'm going to be singing Jingle Bells all the way to the bank – the new bank! Happy Friday! I hope you guys have a good Christmas break! Except that you all have Busy Season to look forward to – I can imagine that has to ruin at least some of Christmas!"

> **SM pinging Manager:** *I am so disgusted, I am speechless...so I am pinging you.*

> **Manager pinging SM:** *SMH, these guys are unbelievable.*

C.P. Aiden

Right before Finance Manager walked out the door, he turned to Intern and Staff 1 and said mockingly, "Your holiday break will be even better than everyone else's as I'm assuming you will both have a couple inventory counts to go to, right? Ha Ha Ha!"

CHAPTER 13 – NEVER EAT BEEF, FISH, OR DIRT AGAIN

"I'm nervous about my inventory count," Intern turned and told Staff 2 as soon as Finance Manager was gone. "They told us at training that messing up an inventory count is about the worst possible thing someone can do, because they typically only happen once a year, and you don't have any chance of fixing it if it is all messed up."

"They really aren't that bad," replied Staff 2, calmly. "After you've done a few, they are kind of a nice break from normal auditing. Sometimes they even make for great stories! I went to training last month with a guy in my start class from another office. He did 22 counts his first year – I asked around and I guess he was horrible at most auditing, but he was quickly becoming an inventory count professional. He had a few crazy ones mixed in there like counting guns and ammo, explosives at a fracking company, diamond-tipped drill bits and lots of other cool stuff. He told us that one had so many errors that he counted an entire toy store, wall to wall – took him all night!"

"I counted $4.7 million in the middle of the night once," Senior 3 said, proudly, "at a casino."

"That seems so cool!" Intern said, as her eyes brightened. "It would be kind of weird to be sitting in a room with all that money around you."

"Actually, it was more like being in a maximum-security prison with piles of money just sitting around you," Senior 3 said, dolefully. "You have to go through at least five locked doors to get in there and the last one is just like one at a prison where the one door shuts and locks behind you before the other one opens."

"How do you get through counting that much money in a vault in one night?" asked Staff 1.

"They have machines that count it," replied Senior 3. "For every five stacks you stick in the machine, you count one manually to make sure the machine is working."

"That's sort of lame," scoffed Senior 1. "My first count was at a gold mine. I got to hold $13 MILLION of gold and I only had to lift and count ten things to do it."

"How does that work?" asked Intern, with bewilderment in her voice.

"Well, after nearly strip searching us—"

"They did not!" cried Manager in disbelief.

"Fine." Senior 1 admitted. "They did make us take everything out of our pockets. We had to remove all metal. I guess gold sticks to almost anything metal and could rub off on like a ring or something. Then, they scanned us with those metal detector wands – they did the same thing when it was over too."

"Was it better or worse than an airport pat down?" asked Staff 1, jokingly (but not really joking).

"Meh," replied Senior 1, indifferently. "About the same."

Then, adding some excitement to her voice, she went on, "It was really cool though. This guy comes out wearing something like a space suit and there's all this stuff heating up in a big kiln. It starts melting away and he takes this stick looking thing and starts pulling away silvery looking stuff and sticking it to one side and then black stuff off to another side – turned out he was separating the silver and the iron from the gold. Then he turned the crucible on its side and poured flaming, hot gold into a mold. They let it cool and then dump it out from there. The thing is like seventy troy ounces of gold, so at the prices back then each button was worth about $1.3 million."

"Did they let you touch it?" Intern asked, curiously.

"I had to pick it up to do the count after it had cooled off enough," replied Senior 1, enthusiastically. "It was totally deceiving though, because it looks like a rock about the size of a softball, but you go to lift it and it is insanely heavy. It totally blows your mind."

"Must have been exhilarating to pick up that much gold," Staff 1 pointed out. "I mean you are standing there holding $1.3 million in your hands!"

"Sadly, it was a bit anticlimactic," replied Senior 1. "It isn't like it is yours and you've just watched the whole process so you are so excited to pick it up, but by the time I was to the 3rd one, my arms were getting tired and it just seemed like another big heavy rock."

"I think it sounds thrilling!" Staff 1 exclaimed. "Make your heart skip a beat type of thing."

"Manager has the best story for making your heart skip a beat," said Staff 2. "You've got to tell them your story about the count up at Sturgis."

"It wasn't exactly at Sturgis," Manager replied, and then went quiet.

"Well, you HAVE to tell us now," Senior 3 pleaded.

"Fine," said Manager, with a sigh. "This story never gets back to my wife, understood? She would make me quit TAF today if she heard anything about it."

C.P. Aiden

Everyone nodded as they anxiously waited to hear the story.

"The observation was in the far northeast corner of Wyoming and the inventory was huge piles of dirt, worth millions of dollars" began Manager. "I had to watch some engineers run around these massive mounds with sticks that had GPS systems at the top. They measured location and elevation to figure out how big the mounds were."

"That doesn't sound so exciting," SM interjected. "What makes their dirt so special?"

"After it bakes out in the sun, (they get less than fourteen inches of rain and have over three-hundred days of sunshine up there) they process it to make it edible," replied Manager.

"Gross!" Staff 1 and Intern both let out at once.

"They sell it to food manufacturers," Manager continued. "Turns out it holds all sorts of food together—like the chocolate almost every cheap candy bar is made with. So next time you chomp down a candy bar you can remember you are literally eating dirt!"

"Disgusting," groaned Senior 3, pretending to hurl. "Does your wife eat a lot of cheap candy bars or something? Or why would she be so upset if she knew the story?"

"Oh yeah, I'm getting to that," said Manager. "To get up there, they had me fly to Rapid City, South Dakota and then rent a car and drive from there the night before the observation. As I got on the freeway, I noticed the biggest motorcycle gang I'd ever seen in my life riding in the left lane. They just kept coming – maybe three- or four-hundred bikes, two in each lane. They let me in as I got on, so there I was in the middle of a sea of hogs."

"Oh, dear, did they do something to you?" Staff 1 asked in a concerned voice.

"No," answered Manager. "I waved as they let me in, they were all really nice – waved at me as they passed – I certainly wasn't

150

The Good Audit

going to try to pass them so I was driving kind of slow. About ten minutes later, another bike gang comes by – this one only about a hundred bikes and they looked mean. I let them go by as fast as they could. Pretty soon I was seeing bikers in both directions – huge groups of them. I thought people must really love to ride motorcycles in South Dakota."

"I had to stop for dinner somewhere," continued Manager. "I saw a sign for a place that has hamburgers and milkshakes. I pull into the parking lot and I'm thinking that this place must double as a motorcycle dealership – there seemed to be at least a thousand bikes and maybe five cars in the entire parking lot. The only thing there is the restaurant, a video rental store (yes, they still had those back then), and like two other stores. I go in to get my burger and shake and as I'm in line I look around to see the entire place is packed with bikers. I was in jeans and a button-down shirt that I had tucked in. I stuck out like a sore thumb and nervously untucked my shirt. This guy behind me starts laughing and then he pats me on the shoulder."

"Did you wet yourself?" SM asked, while laughing.

"Almost," replied Manager. "The guy says in a very loud voice, 'you aren't from around here, are you?' All eyes in the restaurant were glued to me and the whole place went quiet. I tried to be as witty and clever as I could with the assumption that people who are smiling or laughing are less likely to maim or kill you, so I said, 'My shoes are giving me away again!' The whole room exploded with laughter. They put me to the front of the line and while I waited for the food, I explained what I was doing up there and they explained that it was the week of the Sturgis bike rally. They all wished me luck and told me to drive safely. As I headed for the door, the first guy – who seemed to be their leader – says to me, 'Don't pass any big group of motorcycles up here unless they move over for you and wave you on. Don't do anything that might upset any large group of bikers.' I left with a very different opinion of bikers than I'd gone in with."

151

C.P. Aiden

"Overgrown Teddy bears, right?" Staff 2 said, playfully.

"Well, I was sort of thinking that," replied Manager, hesitantly. "As I walked out, I was replaying the whole thing in my mind as I walked towards my rental car. I wasn't paying attention, but one pretty big group of bikers had come out of the store next to the restaurant heading to their bikes. Suddenly, another large group of bikers came rushing out of the store screaming and yelling at the group that had just passed me. All at once, both groups were converging on each other and I was right in the middle of them. Chains and brass knuckles were coming out and I even saw a couple switchblades. The yelling and profanity grew in intensity as the groups moved closer."

"What did you do?" Intern asked, anxiously.

"I put both my hands up, one hand facing each group like a referee and I said, 'I want a good, clean fight here. No gouging out eyes and no stabbing below the belt!' and then I stood there nervously. This was the first that either group noticed me and after some big laughs from both sides, I heard a few confused 'how did he get there?' coming from some of the bikers. When I saw that both groups had stopped where they were, I decided to speak up again, 'fellas, as you can see, I'm not up here for Sturgis and I don't want to be in the middle of whatever is happening here. I'd like to make it home to my wife and sons after I survey huge piles of dirt tomorrow. Is there any way you would be so kind as to pause this so I can get to my car right over there?' Then I looked at the two guys that seemed to be the leader of each group. They both looked at me and then said almost in unison, 'Oh, yeah. Sorry. Go ahead.' I walked to my car and hopped in. The leader of one of the groups stood and directed me as I backed up. They all waved goodbye and told me to drive safely and to be careful out there. I waved, said thank you and goodbye, closed my window, and drove away without looking back – no idea what happened in that parking lot after I left. I said the sincerest prayer, I've ever said, thanking God for the miracle it was that I'd made it out safely."

"I can understand why you wouldn't want your wife hearing about this," said Staff 1, sympathetically. "I just hope my count is not that scary."

"I think Manager's story is an exception. Counts are usually not exciting at all," Senior 3 replied. "What are you counting anyway?"

"Some warehouse full of contacts, prescription glasses, and sunglasses," Staff 1 answered. "The instructions say it is super easy."

"See, sounds like a really boring inventory count," Senior 3 said, cheerfully. "Nothing to worry about."

"Yeah, you aren't Staff 1 from India who just got assigned to count a beef processing facility," staff 2 said, with disgust.

"Wait, WHAT??" screamed Staff 1.

"I guess she's been pinging everyone she knows trying to get someone else to do it for her," Staff 2 began, while shaking his head. "Staff 1 from India got the assignment, realized what it was and emailed Scheduling Lady to see if she could get assigned something else. She just forwarded me the response. Here it is."

Staff 2 read the email from Staff 1 from India asking to be reassigned to a different inventory count.

Hi Scheduling Lady,

I was recently assigned to perform an inventory observation at a beef processing plant. I understand the need to perform inventory observations as part of our audits; however, I come from India where cows are sacred in our religion. I cannot imagine how horrible I would feel going through a plant where I am observing dead cow carcasses. From a religious standpoint, as well as just the fact that this is disgusting, I do not think I should perform this count. Is there any way to assign somebody else?

Sincerely,
Staff 1 from India

"This is the response from Scheduling Lady," Staff 2 said, and then read the email aloud to the team.

Hi Staff 1 from India,

I appreciate your email and understand that this might be troubling to you. Unfortunately, all assignments have been made and are final unless you can get someone to voluntarily trade you for their count. After today, I am on vacation for the rest of the year, so unless you have a solution by end of the day, you will just be stuck with what you were assigned. This is how it works – no exceptions. I apologize for any inconvenience, but my hands are pretty tied – once we assign observations, the Firm will not make changes unless the objection to the count is a really good one.

Thanks,
Scheduling Lady

"How is that objection not a really good one?" Senior 3 cried out.

"Seriously!!!" agreed SM. "Her objection is based on religious grounds. She could probably sue for discrimination."

"She could. She should do the count, sue The Accounting Firm for discrimination and then never work another day in her life," Staff 2 said, jokingly. "I mean, think of the media attention this would get."

"I thought the Firm was all about diversity and inclusion," Staff 1 exclaimed in disbelief.

"TAF is very much about diversity and inclusion and the value that is added by having people of different backgrounds, cultures, beliefs, etc..." Manager said, adamantly, and then contemptuously added, "...during recruiting."

All jaws in the room dropped. Even SM was shocked at the bluntness in which Manager had made the statement.

> **Senior 1 pinging Staff 2:** *I cannot believe he just said that, especially to the whole team...especially in front of SM!*
>
> **Staff 2 pinging Senior 1:** *Seriously*
>
> **Senior 1 pinging Staff 2:** *He's not wrong, you know.*

"Once you are an employee, you are just another cog in the machine," Manager went on. "You are an interchangeable part and all the Firm cares about is keeping clients happy so they can bill outrageous fees. If a client cares about having diversity and the Firm can give them a diverse team, then it is a bonus. Have you ever seen a single example of them practicing what they preach? I haven't."

> **Senior 1 pinging Staff 2:** This conversation is getting too real...we need to find a way to change the subject. Intern is looking a bit pale.

"Me neither," Staff 2 said, timidly. Then, in an effort to change the topic, he added, "listen to this email. Staff 1 from India is pleading for someone to swap inventory counts with her."

> Good afternoon,
>
> I hope everyone is doing well and looking forward to a great holiday season. Sadly, my holiday is being ruined by Scheduling Lady – see email chain below. I cannot in good conscience perform a count at a beef processing facility. I understand that this count is totally disgusting and is likely way worse than the counts you've

been assigned, but I would greatly appreciate if one of you would swap counts with me given the situation.

Thanks,
Staff 1 from India

"She attached the instructions as well," Staff 2 said. "This count looks horrible. You have to go into the meat freezers where the fully skinned carcasses are hanging and verify that they are really dead cows. I guess a few years ago, they just looked into the freezer through a window and there were some things hanging that got counted as cows that were not actually cows. Also, the Company once tweaked their scales so the weight was inflated. I guess a sharp staff 1 who grew up on a cattle ranch in Wyoming did the count a few years ago and challenged the company claiming to have cows that weighed six thousand pounds. As a result, the person doing the count has to grab and hang from one of the hooks to verify the scale is accurate so the instructions say to wear gloves you can throw away right after."

"Poor Staff 1 from India," Staff 1 bemoaned, loudly.

"Do you feel bad enough that you would trade your easy count to do this for her?" Staff 2 asked, bluntly.

"I would, except that I'm mostly vegetarian and think I would throw up the second I walk in the door. I just don't think I could handle that either." Staff 1 said, sadly.

"How is someone mostly vegetarian?" Staff 2 asked Staff 1, "I mean, don't you either eat no meat or you eat meat? Isn't some meat still—"

"I wonder if she has any issue with dead fish," Intern interrupted Staff 2, as she could tell that this discussion was going to be awkward and they'd already had too many awkward discussions that afternoon.

"Huh?" Staff 1 and Staff 2 both asked, with confused looks.

"I was assigned a dog food factory for my observation," replied

The Good Audit

Intern. "The dog food is made from fish parts – no beef. I'm totally fine trading one disgusting thing for another. I will ping Staff 1 from India and let her know."

"You are amazing!" Staff 1 said to Intern, then looking directly at Manager added, "See, there is high quality teaming, inclusiveness, respect for diversity, and all that stuff you say doesn't exist at The Accounting Firm."

Manager thought for a moment as the whole rest of the team waited with great anticipation at how he would respond, "Yes, admittedly, it was all of those things. That was awesome and I am super happy to work with Intern. I think she's done a great thing here; however, all of that is based on the goodness of Intern's own heart, not based on any Firm initiative, but the firm would take credit for it in a heartbeat, if the right people in leadership heard about it."

"Seriously, the Firm won't reward Intern at all for stepping up and doing the right thing," added Senior 1. "In fact, if you told a partner or someone in HR, then this story would be used for their benefit in a fluffy, feel-good TAF Daily Newsletter article about how Intern's behavior is a fabulous example of exercising TAF values and enhancing the Firm's culture by executing the Firm's respect, inclusiveness, and diversity initiatives. The article would say nothing about Scheduling Lady's lack of flexibility towards her or respect for diversity or inclusion that caused the issue in the first place."

> **SM pinging Manager:** *Way to make Intern feel really good about doing the right thing!*

"I do admire Intern's willingness to step up on her own when apparently no one else would," Manager said, sincerely, as he turned to Intern. "I think we should all just go home. Everyone is taking the next two weeks off for Christmas and New Year's anyway. Let's start the Holidays off right!"

"Fine," said SM, a bit disparagingly. "Busy Season will be here soon enough."

> **Senior 3 pinging Manager:** *I cannot believe SM went for that.*

> **Manager pinging Senior 3:** *I had to try. I'm so excited to get out of here and spend two solid weeks with my family! My youngest forgot who I am the other day.*

The team eagerly stood up and headed out for the holidays.

CHAPTER 14 – LEGAL MATTERS

For auditors, the freedom of Christmas and New Year's is short lived. The time is really like a sucker hole – a break in the storm just long enough for them (and their families) to start feeling alive again, only to be rudely awakened by the storm of Busy Season – mandatory 58-hour work weeks from January to March (which generally turned into actual workweeks over 70 hours dragging on to the end of May).

When the team arrived back at Widget Maker, the only person who seemed truly excited for Busy Season was Intern, but that was because interns get paid overtime so she was going to have a very different kind of rainstorm during her time working on a client like Widget Maker for Busy Season.

Even SM wasn't super excited for Busy Season – he admitted that this one was going to be worse than usual. Manager set up a recurring meeting on his calendar from 8:00 to 8:30 p.m. to have a video call with his wife and the kids to tuck them in every night and told the team he was unavailable during that half hour. The first morning back from the break was generally quiet. Typically, the company's finance department did not have anything ready for the auditors to look at and client contacts were busy catching up from their vacations and working on closing the books for the year.

Finance Manager popped his head in the door, "How was everyone's break?" he asked, annoyingly. "Did you all get your batteries recharged?"

Before anyone could answer, Inventory Manager pushed Finance Manager into the room and followed him in. "How's the new hot tub?" he asked, in an effort to remind the team of the awesome raises and extra bonus they got just before the holidays.

"It is great!" Finance Manager replied, happily. "We've been in it every night for two weeks!"

> **Manager pinging Staff 2:** *I was hoping the euphoric feeling of being away from these guys was going to last a little longer.*

> **Staff 2 pinging Manager:** *Me too!*

"That's fantastic!" Finance Manager said to Inventory Manager, and then turning to the team he added, "I guess you guys all got The Accounting Firm Christmas bonus, right? Ha-ha-ha."

"You mean the $25 cash card that comes with a generic note that says 'Happy Holidays, Thanks for all you do! Please enjoy something nice on us this Holiday Season and be ready to come back to work the first week of January'?" Manager asked, sarcastically.

"Yep!" replied Finance Manager. "I don't miss that at all."

Inventory Manager laughed and walked back out the door.

> **Staff 2 pinging Manager:** *He literally just came in here to be a jerk? SMH*

> **Manager pinging Staff 2:** *Yep! Classy dude that guy.*

Finance Manager appeared to have lost his train of thought as he followed Inventory Manager to the door, then paused and turned back to the team. "Oh yeah," he said. "I almost forgot why I came in here. I came to tell you that nothing is ready yet.

The Good Audit

Senior Accountant had her baby so she isn't around. CEO wants to do a new deal with some investors and has asked me and CFO to support that on the finance side, so Inventory Manager and Assistant Controller are the only ones who are going to be able to help you for the next week. Great way to start Busy Season, right?"

As Finance Manager walked out, Assistant Controller walked in. He turned to Senior 1 and said, "I just sent you the year-end Cap Table showing all our investors and their percent ownership in the company. Legal was dragging their feet on whether or not they wanted to give it to you. Lucky for you, my wife has access and I know all her passwords. While they were in a meeting I went and logged onto her machine and sent it to myself and then forwarded to you. If you are going to make selections and ask Legal for support, don't tell them you got this from me."

> **Senior 3 pinging Manager:** *That's just awesome. I'm sure he only violated three or four company policies to get us this.*😎

"Won't your wife see the email you sent yourself in her sent folder?" asked Manager.

"Oh dear!" exclaimed Assistant Controller. "I always forget to do that! It will probably get me into trouble someday."

Assistant Controller ran out of the room, hoping the legal department meeting was still going on so he could go back and cover his tracks. Senior 1 opened the file.

> **Senior 1 pinging Senior 3:** *Great! No wonder Legal didn't want us having this one. The file has names, birthdates, social security numbers, and addresses of all their investors!*

At this point, Intern was trying to print off a restaurant list so she could plan breakfast, lunch, and dinner for the whole week as she would be responsible to go pick up each meal so the team could continue working.

"I think they took my access to this printer away," she insisted, as she pointed at the printer in the conference room.

Staff 1, Staff 2 and Senior 1 all checked and it appeared their access had also been revoked.

"I still have access to the printer way down the hall," Senior 1 said, with relief. "You can send me that list and I will print it. Just run down to the end of the hall and pick it up."

"Great!" said Intern, happily. "I just forwarded it to you so I will head down there right now."

As Intern left the room, CFO walked in. She wanted to hear about everyone's holidays and the plan for Busy Season. She was still there talking to the team when Intern walked back in.

> **Intern pinging Senior 1:** *Hey, I don't think that printed. I got down there and all I could see was a list of people's names and addresses.*

Senior 1 looked at her screen and opened up her print jobs. All of a sudden, she muttered "oh, this is terrible", then she quickly jumped up, rushed past CFO who paused and stared at her going by, and took off running down the hall.

Senior 1 reached the printer at the same time as Legal Assistant. Her print job had not started coming out yet and she looked down to see the printed list of investors and addresses.

"Why did you print this? Where did you get this? How long has it been sitting here?" Legal Assistant demanded immediately as she recognized the file.

"This was printed by mistake," Senior 1 said, cautiously. "As soon as I realized it had printed instead of the file I meant to print, I came rushing down here to grab it. It has been sitting here for maybe one minute."

"You do realize that this has personally identifiable informa-

The Good Audit

tion all over it, don't you?" Legal Assistant asked, callously. "And that anyone could have come past here and taken a copy of this in the time it was sitting here. You aren't even supposed to have this file! I need to report this to Legal Counsel right away. He is not going to be happy that our auditors not only have privileged information, but they also printed it and left it sitting out on the printer for anyone to come and look at or take. We take data privacy very seriously at Widget Maker. This infringement of trust will not be taken lightly. One of the reasons our old auditors were dismissed was because they did not keep confidential information confidential!"

Senior 1 reached out to take the printed sheets, but Legal Assistant picked them up and marched them over to the shred bin, "You don't think you are actually going to get to keep this list, do you?" Legal Assistant asked, condescendingly. "When I find out who provided this to you, someone is going to get fired!"

"We are the auditors," Senior 1 argued, defensively. "CEO signed a letter indicating that all Widget Maker employees will comply with our requests and will provide us access to all documents and records necessary to complete our audit. That listing is necessary for our audit."

"That listing is confidential and privileged," Legal Assistant huffed, angrily.

"We have a signed non-disclosure agreement and the letter signed by your CEO," retorted Senior 1. "We get Cap Tables from all our clients in order to test equity balances. I'm sure CFO would agree that we need this for our audit and that it was ok that I have this file."

"What seems to be the problem here?" CFO asked, as she rounded the corner near the printer. "I was heading down the other hall, but then I heard my name."

"Yes," said Legal Assistant, sternly, as she glared at Senior 1. "Your auditors have a file that is privileged and that Legal Coun-

163

sel specifically told me not to provide to them – the Cap Table."

"You are kidding, right?" CFO asked, sternly. "You do realize that CEO has granted them access to all files, records, and documents necessary to do their audit and they've signed a non-disclosure and confidentiality agreement so there is nothing here that is privileged."

"Well…" Legal Assistant said, slowly. She was flustered that CFO had taken Senior 1's side. She stood quietly contemplating her next move.

"Anything else?" CFO asked, impatiently, as Legal Assistant just stood there.

As CFO was about to walk away, Legal Assistant blurted out, "Yes, actually."

"What is it?" CFO clearly did not like Legal Assistant and she was very annoyed. She turned to Senior 1 and whispered quietly, "Legal is always trying to get us in trouble, they complain to CEO about finance non-stop."

"She," Legal Assistant said, pointing at Senior 1, "left this confidential file just sitting on the printer where anyone in the company could have come past and seen it."

"I see," said CFO. "I saw Senior 1 rush out of the audit room to come down here to pick it up so it can't have been down here too long."

"Long enough for me to get here and pick it up before she did," Legal Assistant said, all snarky. "Legal Counsel will find this lack of respect for confidential information extremely troubling!"

"What will I find extremely troubling?" Legal Counsel asked, as he rounded the corner on the other side of the printer.

CFO spoke up immediately, while glaring at Legal Assistant, "The auditors printed the Cap Table to this printer and Legal Assistant here happened to barely intercept it as Senior 1 reached the printer to retrieve it."

The Good Audit

"You told us not to provide the auditors with the Cap Table as it contains personal information of all our investors. When I got here, it was just sitting on the printer for anyone to come by and pick up. Who knows how long Senior 1 let it sit here?" said Legal Assistant in the most brown-nosing tone imaginable.

"I find it somewhat surprising, even for you, that you'd be instructing your team not to provide information to the auditors," CFO said, raising her eyebrows at Legal Counsel. "Surely you know they have an NDA and a letter from CEO stating that the company will provide them with everything they need?"

"I believe what I told my team was not to provide the Cap Table with addresses or other personal information included on it," Legal Counsel replied, coldly.

"Then Legal Assistant's reaction to Senior 1 seems to be a simple misunderstanding of those instructions," CFO said, while glancing over at Legal Assistant.

"About having access to the Cap Table, I would agree," said Legal Counsel, firmly. "But it appears that our new auditors have nearly the same disregard for the handling of confidential information that our previous auditors had."

"Oh, nonsense," retorted CFO, dismissively, as she turned to walk away.

"I'd like to have a formal meeting with whoever is managing this audit," Legal Counsel demanded. "How's 3 p.m.? My office?"

Without saying anything, CFO turned, threw her hand up in the air and walked off back toward the audit room. Senior 1, not wanting to be stuck with Legal Assistant and Legal Counsel quickly followed behind. CFO entered the audit room and held the door for Senior 1 and then closed it. Throughout the entire audit, CFO had remained very postured and composed towards the audit team.

"I absolutely HATE Legal Assistant!" CFO almost screamed, as

C.P. Aiden

she grabbed Senior 1's arm.

CFO looked around the room to see Assistant Controller staring at her. His mouth was agape and he started stuttering something that no one could make sense of. CFO started to apologize to Assistant Controller, but that wouldn't come out either. Finally, Assistant Controller got something out.

"I don't disagree," he conceded. "But I hope you didn't get her in trouble because when that happens, we don't speak for like weeks and she generally changes her passwords."

"I guess you should go check on her then," CFO said, as she motioned for Assistant Controller to leave the room.

Then turning to the rest of the team, all of whom were staring at her in utter confusion and added, "If any of you encounter any issues with our Legal department, I want to know about them immediately. If you find a speck of dust when you are looking through what they provide you to audit, I want it put on a list that you send me. I am going to bury that arrogant, pompous moron and her boss, too! Acting like she's all perfect and following some established protocol. The only protocol they have is whatever garbage they feel like saying to get themselves to look good or to get out of trouble – they are attorneys after all."

CFO threw her hands up in the air, apologized for her eccentric behavior and turned to open the door. She paused to turn to Manager and SM and said, "You two have a meeting with me and Legal Counsel in his office at 3:00 p.m. Come defensive. Senior 1 can catch you up on the purported incident."

"Ok...," Manager and SM were both still very confused.

"And the rest of you," said CFO, panning the room with her eyes, "please try to find a way to fail some or all of the internal controls that Legal is responsible for. I would love to see a Significant Deficiency letter or even a Material Weakness letter submitted to the board at the end of the audit outlining something really nasty about them!"

166

The Good Audit

Staff 2 pinging Manager: *As you wish... HAHAHA*

Manager pinging Staff 2: *I'm still confused about what caused this whole fiasco, but I think that outburst was the best thing to happen so far this audit.*

Staff 2 pinging Manager: *And the fact that Assistant Controller was in here when CFO burst in like that was CLASSIC!*

After CFO left the room, Senior 1 quickly explained to Manager and SM (and the rest of the team) what happened.

"The Cap Table was literally down there for less than a minute!" Senior 1 insisted. "The timing of it all couldn't have been worse. Legal Counsel was not hesitant to divulge that the former auditors were dismissed, in part, because they did not keep confidential information confidential."

"He is seriously comparing this to that?" SM said in disgust.

"What was that?" Senior 3 asked, curiously.

"That was a newspaper article disclosing an upcoming warehouse deal that had not been made public yet," SM said, all matter of fact, as if everyone should already know what he was saying. "The rumor made the price of the warehouse increase 25% overnight, such that the deal did not happen. Widget Maker was sued and Legal Counsel blamed a member of the audit team for the leak. CFO told Partner and me privately that she thinks that someone in legal sent an email with the details to a reporter on accident – thinking she was sending it to an investor in the warehouse. Any guesses on who 'SHE' might be?"

"Legal Assistant," Senior 1 said, coldly.

"It probably was a mistake," Senior 3 tried to point out. His statement was met with a nasty glare from Senior 1 and the rest of the team shaking their heads at him.

"Legal Assistant blamed one of the audit staff who had been seen walking past a news truck in the parking lot," SM continued. "She said he'd tipped off the reporter. CFO says that is total nonsense as the media outlet parked outside that night was not the same outlet the story broke from and that the name of the reporter who wrote the story was only 1 letter off from one of the big investors in the deal."

"It is so crazy to me that a legal department – the ones that are supposed to be the 'smartest, most professional, most trustworthy' are the ones who leaked and then covered it all up so they wouldn't look bad," said Staff 1 dumbfoundedly.

"Get used to it," Manager purposely mumbled, just loud enough for the team to hear.

Two minutes before 3:00 p.m., CFO came into the room with Finance Manager and Inventory Manager.

"Legal Counsel decided to broaden the scope of the meeting. These two are coming as well. Senior 1 needs to come now too. I'm sure Legal Counsel will be on an especially big power trip in there," CFO explained, carefully. "No matter how upset he gets, don't apologize and just let me handle it. Always remember that anything you say or do WILL be held against you in his court of 'law'."

> **Manager pinging SM:** *Great we are just supposed to go in there, get chewed out and then leave. I love this kind of meeting!*
>
> **SM pinging Manager:** *Yep. Exactly.*

Legal Counsel treated his office as if it were his own personal courtroom – except he was acting as judge, jury and the prosecution. He even gave an opening statement.

"The Legal department is entrusted with the most confidential matters at Widget Maker. We have developed and follow a robust set of internal controls over information and contract management. This is why Legal Assistant was at the printer –

The Good Audit

she was safeguarding the confidential information that I sent to the printer. I'm so happy that I work on a team that would never let something so terrible as this happen to the secure and confidential information with which we are entrusted!"

Legal counsel then began his questioning as he turned towards Senior 1, "Did you or did you not leave confidential information on the printer for an unspecified period of time?"

"The file was printed by accident and sat on the printer for less than one minute," CFO interceded before Senior 1 could say anything. "I was in the audit room when the file was printed and when Senior 1 realized that it had been mistakenly printed. The time between printing and Senior 1 arriving at the printer was very short."

Legal Counsel had not expected CFO to jump to Senior 1's side so early in his interrogation. He stood silent for a few moments and then took his seat behind his desk and switched over to being the judge.

"I want to make it clear to each of you that this type of blatant disregard for personal and highly confidential information ought to embarrass you as professionals. You have staff and an intern. Your protocol should be to send someone down to the printer to retrieve any printed document prior to pushing print. That way, you have someone at the printer catching each piece of paper as it comes out – as Legal Assistant did for me today. They should know exactly how many pages they should expect. They should remain standing by the printer for several seconds after the print job is complete to ensure there are no additional items being printed. Is that understood?"

"I hardly think that is necessary," CFO argued. "We are paying the auditors a blended rate of $150 an hour. I think making them take 10 minutes of monitoring each time they have to print something is excessive."

"Nonsense," replied Legal Counsel, directly. "If we have to follow internal controls that they audit us on, then I say they have to follow my protocol for printing sensitive information."

"Alternatively, you could just have your IT department restore our access to the printer that is sitting in the audit room, and we could print to that one from now on," Manager suggested, politely.

"Nobody asked you to speak," Legal Counsel replied, as he glared at Manager.

"I think that is a great idea," said CFO, cheerfully. Then she turned and with a wave of her arm as she started for the door said, "Case closed."

"I will be sending out a company-wide email reminding everyone of our strict interpretation and enforcement of our data security and privacy policies and will let people know that those found in violation of either policy will be subject to disciplinary action up to and including termination," Legal Counsel called out, as everyone walked out of the room.

"Nobody reads those," CFO called back to Legal Counsel.

CFO silently walked back to the audit room with SM, Manager and Senior 1. As soon as they were in the room with the door shut, CFO started going off about Legal Counsel and Legal Assistant again, "You HAVE to find something to ding them with. His comment on internal controls was such a fallacy I almost threw up! I want them to fail some of those controls they supposedly 'perfectly adhere to' so that he has to eat crow in front of you guys and the Board."

"Shouldn't be too hard..." Manager pointed out. "Assistant Controller knows all of Legal Assistant's passwords and has accessed several files from her computer. We could probably fail them for inappropriate data access."

"Yeah, about that one," CFO replied, carefully. "I don't want them to know about that little trap door because sometimes

The Good Audit

I use Assistant Controller to get me drafts of agreements that Legal Counsel keeps a little too close to the vest. We have all kinds of issues when they sign some crazy agreement that has huge accounting ramifications that they, of course, never consider and never ask my team about ahead of time. Then, they blame us for not telling them about the issues before the deal was signed."

"Ok," stammered Manager, a little unsure of what to think of CFO's response. "We will keep digging. If it is like everything else we've seen in the audit so far, then it won't take much effort to find big problems."

> **SM pinging Manager:** *Good one – way to tell her that her whole finance department stinks right to her face.*

> **Manager pinging SM:** *Not exactly what I meant, but I can see how one could interpret it that way.*

"And with that..." CFO said, shaking her head a little as she headed for the door, "I think I'll get back to running my department."

> **Manager pinging SM:** *You know, we've had a great start to Busy Season. Maybe the rest won't be that bad.*

CHAPTER 15 – SWEET REVENGE: THE AUDITORS STRIKE BACK

By the end of January, the team was getting used to the Busy Season routine – show up between 8:00 and 9:00 am, silence with everyone working until lunch at 12:30 (lunch was ordered at 11:30 and it was either delivered to the Widget Maker offices or Intern was sent out to pick it up), followed by more silent working. Most client meetings happened in the afternoon. Team members would get up and walk out with their computers from time to time and reappear a half hour or hour later, dinner was ordered at 5:30 (again, Intern picked up or it was delivered). Dinner generally arrived by 6:30 at which point the team would take a 15-minute break to eat and walk around the empty corridors of the Widget Maker offices. Manager would step out at 8:00 or so to have a video call with his wife and the kids to put them to bed and then sometime between 10:30 and midnight SM would call it good enough for the day. The team would then pack up and leave together. The cycle repeated day after day with the only difference being that Saturdays the team arrived at 10:00 in the morning and only stayed until 8:00 or 9:00 p.m.

This particular day at the end of January, however, the whole team was starving – it was 7:30 p.m. and dinner had finally ar-

The Good Audit

rived. The auditors were the only people left in the building. Staff 1 was setting everything up at one end of the table while Intern was rummaging through the empty, plastic sacks the food came in.

"Seriously! Why do Thai places never give you utensils and napkins?" Intern moaned, as she threw the bags away. "We ordered takeout and they assume that wherever we are eating the food just magically has that stuff."

"The Thais probably assume that we do what they do, which is to share meals, especially dinner, with family at home," Manager replied. "And at home, you have utensils and napkins."

"And a family to eat with," Senior 1 added, sadly. "We did order family style."

"Aren't we like your family?" SM asked, slightly offended by Senior 1's remark. "I mean, we all see each other way more than anyone sees their family, right?"

"Thanks for that awesome reminder," Manager answered for Senior 1. "The few minutes a day I see them make up for all the hours I have to spend with you."

Then, sensing he had just made things a little too awkward, he added, "I think I will just head down to the break room and grab some utensils and napkins for this not-so-family style meal."

> **SM pinging Senior 3:** *After several conversations like the one we just had, I've learned that people with families generally resent it when you point out that they spend way more time at work and with work colleagues than they do at home or with their spouse or kids. I think they start to feel like they are somehow being used too much by the Firm.*
>
> **Senior 3 pinging SM:** *I guess I could see that.*
>
> **SM pinging Senior 3:** *I don't get it. My dogs are always super excited and happy to see me whenever I*

get home.

Senior 3 pinging SM: *I am not married, but I can only imagine that being woken up by a spouse coming home at midnight every night for four or five months of the year would not be very pleasant.*

SM pinging Senior 3: *That's why I have pets and not a wife.*

Manager texted his wife on his way down the hall.

Manager to his wife: *Hey. Are you up for an hourlong video chat tonight? The team just reminded me how much I hate working Busy Season hours and not getting to be there with you and the kids.*

Manager's wife to Manager: *I'll never say no to a 100% increase in daily time spent with my husband!*

Manager smiled as he rounded the corner of the hallway to the break room. Just outside the break room, there was a large printer and next to the printer was a long set of cupboards with a countertop. The countertop was generally clear except for a small bin that had a stapler, some binder clips, a few pens, sticky notes, and other random office supplies. On this particular night, however, the countertop was covered with papers that seemed to be grouped together.

As Manager approached the printer station, he noticed there were small papers with letters above piles of collated packets. Each paper had a letter or letter grouping assigned – "A through C", "D", "E" through "F", etc. and the groupings appeared to be organized alphabetically from left to right across the counter. There appeared to be packets all the way through "G" which was the stack immediately in front of Manager.

The cover page on the top packet showed an investor's name – investor since 2009 and also had a red "Confidential" stamped

174

towards the lower right corner of the page. *Seriously, all this stuff is just sitting here? As if that confidential stamp on the cover page is some magical deterrent to make people not thumb through the rest of the packet. I think my professional judgment as an auditor would suggest I should continue to investigate this,* he thought as he flipped the page.

The second page of the packet showed the investor's full legal name, residential address, work address, work phone number, date of birth and social security number as well as the investor's spouse with her birthdate and SSN (listed as primary beneficiary). It also showed the number of shares owned with the dates purchased. The next several pages included the share purchase agreement. After that, the packet had a sheet that outlined the investor's qualifications as an accredited investor, meaning the investor had to prove a net worth of over a million dollars excluding a primary residence. This was followed by documents that supported the investor's net worth, including bank statements with account numbers all over them.

I can't believe this is all down here just in the open like this. I wonder who put this out here, Manager thought to himself. *I'd better document this.*

Manager took out his phone and got a couple pictures showing the hallway and all the papers. He then came closer to get the stacks of papers with the alphabetical labeling. Then he drilled down into the packet. He used sticky notes to carefully cover the personally, identifiable information on each sheet so it wouldn't show up in the pictures on his phone.

Once he'd taken about twenty pictures, Manager grabbed the utensils and napkins and headed back to the audit room. He pulled SM and Senior 1 aside and quietly whispered, "You need to come and see this."

SM and Senior 1 followed Manager back down the hall where he showed them the stacks of investor packets.

"I can't imagine why someone would have all these just sitting out here," Manager stammered. "I mean, we got ripped to shreds by Legal Counsel a couple weeks ago just for printing a Cap Table with names and addresses. Legal Counsel would go nuts if he saw this here."

"Not to mention that this probably fails at least a handful of their internal controls," SM pointed out, as he shuddered. "Anyone who stayed late, our whole team, the cleaning crew that comes in at nights – all now have free access to this information. Each packet has enough information listed to steal the identities of the investors the packet is for."

"This is odd," Senior 1 said, slowly, as she looked at the packets. "We made selections from the Cap Table and asked for support for 57 investors. This goes to "G" and there are about 15 or so packets here. I believe each packet I see on top of each stack relates to one of our selections."

"Who was pulling the selections for us?" SM asked.

"Legal Assistant," Senior 1 replied.

"Shut the front door!" Manager cried out. "You mean 'don't leave confidential information sitting on the print tray' Legal Assistant?"

"Yep," said Senior 1. "Legal Assistant herself."

"CFO is going to love this!" exclaimed SM. "This is fantastic news!"

"This is a significant deficiency in internal controls, is what it is," Manager said, excitedly. "We just need proof that Legal Assistant is the one doing this so we can pin it on the Legal department!"

"The documentation part and all the extra work this will make us do will really stink," SM asserted. "But seeing Legal Counsel's face when we tell him we will have to send a letter to the Board because of his department's actions, not to mention that this is

The Good Audit

a thousand times worse than what Senior 1 did, will make it all worth it!"

"We need photographic evidence that Legal Assistant or someone in Legal is the one printing these out," Manager said. "Let's go tell the team to be on the lookout tomorrow morning."

The next morning, Staff 2 burst into the audit room, "She's—" Staff 2 stopped immediately, as he realized Assistant Controller was talking to Senior 1. He rushed to unlock his laptop screen.

> **Staff 2 pinging Manager:** *She's down there.*

> **Manager pinging Staff 2:** *Who's she?*

> **Staff 2 pinging Manager:** *You know...all those packets of papers.*

Manager slammed his laptop lid down and ran out of the room. With his phone in hand, he was careful rounding the corner to the break room, acting like he was texting someone as he headed for a drink. He paid no attention to Legal Assistant, but when her back was turned, he quickly raised his phone slightly and snapped a couple pictures before returning to the audit room.

> **Manager pinging SM:** *Time to have an impromptu meeting with CFO.* ■ *Got what we need!*

Finance Manager and Inventory Manager were both in CFO's office when SM and Manager poked their heads in the door.

"Great, you are all here," said SM, directly. "We have something very important to discuss with you."

"If it is audit-related, I don't know if we can handle it today," CFO answered, dejectedly. "Legal Counsel has been all over us this morning because someone found an investor's K-1 from 2 years ago on the company's internal shared drive."

"You are going to love this then," Manager said, smiling. He and SM walked in, closed the door behind them, and sat at the table

177

in CFO's office.

"Do you know the printer down by the break room?" SM asked, excitedly.

"I'm familiar with the printer," answered CFO, a bit bewildered. "What about it?"

"As it happens," Manager spoke up, "At this very moment, and all of last night, there are several investor packets sitting out on the wide-open counter just outside the break room. The packets include all information necessary to steal the identity of those investors. Legal Assistant has been printing them and organizing them to respond to our sample on the Cap Table. That still doesn't excuse that she left 15 packets out last night and she's printed more today. Why she didn't just provide them electronically to us through the secure, audit-evidence portal is anyone's guess."

"No way!" said the astonished Inventory Manager. "Are you 100% sure?"

"I have photographic proof," Manager replied coolly, as he tried to contain his excitement. "See. Look at this." Manager pulled out his phone and showed the others the photos he'd taken.

"Wait here. I will be back," said CFO, calmly. "I might be 10 minutes or so."

CFO left the room and the others sat whispering quietly about how crazy it all was. About seven minutes later, they heard CFO walking down the hall talking to someone.

"Do the auditors know?" a voice asked.

"They are the ones who noticed it last night and documented that it was Legal Assistant printing them this morning," CFO replied. "They are in here now and can show you more."

"I'm happy to look at what they have, but I saw enough already when you showed me those packets sitting out by the break room for any passerby to look at or take," said the voice.

The Good Audit

CFO walked in and she was followed by CEO who greeted SM and Manager with a cold "Hey, guys".

They all sat down and CEO asked for the details about how the packets were discovered, what evidence the auditors had gathered and what the ramifications were. SM quickly explained the events of the night before and the morning and Manager showed the photos taken.

"It is going to be pretty hard, even for Legal Counsel, to explain his way out of this one," CEO admitted, with a sigh.

"We believe this represents a significant deficiency in data security and protection," SM explained. "This incident will likely be formalized in a letter from The Accounting Firm and reported to the board."

"I understand," CEO said, dryly. "However, I am working closely with Legal Counsel on a very big deal that is supposed to close this week. Is there any way we could let this ride for a few days before going and getting Legal Counsel all worked up about it?"

"I'd like to see how long they leave those out for," CFO said, sternly. "I'd also like to see the draft agreement for this big deal you are working on, as I haven't heard a thing about it until now!"

"Oh, I was always under the impression that Legal Counsel gave you the draft well in advance," CEO said, a little defensively. "I will send it over. In the meantime, I agree. Let's see how long they leave those printed packets just sitting there."

The packets were, in fact, the support for the auditor's Cap Table selections and Legal Assistant brought them into the audit room a week later. She set them down on the table and reminded the auditors that the packets contained highly sensitive information, were not to be copied and were to be kept "under lock and key" when they left each night.

"Just like they've been left under lock and key on the counter by the break room every night for the past week?" Manager asked, snidely.

"I have no idea what you are talking about," said Legal Assistant, before she furiously huffed out of the room.

"Well, this is going to be fun," muttered Manager. Then, turning to SM, he said, "I guess we should go down and tell CFO that the packets have left the counter!"

"Let's swing by the break room counter first just to be sure," SM suggested, "And then head into CFO's office."

As expected, the counter was cleared with all the office supplies now neatly organized to one side. SM and Manager hurried down the hall to CFO's office, but as they neared the office, they heard that Legal Counsel was already in the room.

"You didn't need to print them," CFO told Legal Counsel, curtly. "You could have just uploaded them to the private and password-protected, audit-evidence portal on the shared drive rather than leaving the packets out in the open for over a WEEK! There needs to be some consequences here!"

"There will be," Legal Counsel replied, abruptly. "Starting with all audit requests for the legal department need to come through me."

"I was talking more along the lines of discipline within your department," CFO said, tersely.

"This is Office Manager's fault," Legal Counsel argued.

"How is that?" CFO asked in astonishment.

"She is responsible for making sure everything is organized and properly put away each night," Legal Counsel replied. "She should have seen the stacks of packets and locked them up. In addition, you and your team also acted irresponsibly. You knew those packets were there and did nothing for a week."

"After discussing with CEO, we determined to let it play out to

The Good Audit

see just how long Legal Assistant would let this go on," replied CFO. "We wanted to see if your love for policing access to sensitive documents extended to your own department. Apparently, it does not. Again, what are the consequences going to be?"

"Office Manager has been fired," answered Legal Counsel.

"WHAT?!" CFO shouted in amazement.

"Receptionist will be promoted to Office Manager. Legal Assistant is already over in Product Distribution telling them they need to look for a new receptionist. It is all done," Legal Counsel answered, with a nasty smirk on his face. "When the auditors take this to the board, we will simply tell them that the source of the problem was discovered and the person responsible was terminated. End of story."

SM and Manager had been standing in the hall right outside CFO's office. They heard Legal Counsel telling CFO to have a great day. SM and Manager rushed out of sight and back to the audit room. They had heard enough.

When they reached the audit room, they found Staff 2 thumbing through the investor packets and documenting his testing.

"Poor Office Manager," Manager added.

"Oh, don't worry about her," CFO said, as she walked into the room. "Product Distribution heard she was being fired as Office Manager and they are making her Manager of Widget Branding now. Legal Counsel was not happy, but Marketing VP stood her ground."

"Great," Manager said, seriously. "I'm glad Legal Counsel's self-preservation will not ruin anyone else's career this time around."

"Well, Legal Counsel insisted that they do this as a termination and then a re-hire," CFO clarified. "That way he can tell the board the 'person responsible' for the significant deficiency was terminated."

181

"About that," Staff 2 spoke up, "I think we may be looking more at a material weakness, not just a significant deficiency."

> **SM pinging Staff 2:** *Dude, you don't just go announce to any company's CFO that you THINK they have an MW. She is going to freak out.*

"Really?!" CFO was intrigued, "If it has to do with Legal, that would be fantastic!"

"It may be more than just Legal, but they are certainly a big part of this," Staff 2 explained. "Half the support they gave us doesn't match the Cap Table and nothing really matches the amount of cash received from the investors. The equity amount per the Cap Table is over seven million dollars off the actual equity balance recorded. This is a big mess."

"I'd generally be very unhappy about the potential for a material weakness, but given who will have to own it, I'm feeling pretty good," CFO said, cheerfully. "If you have incremental fees for this work, will you be sure your team labels the hours 'Work based on Legal Department differences'? I'd like to track that closely so I can tell CEO how much more the Legal department cost us on the audit."

"Absolutely," SM replied.

> **SM pinging Staff 2:** *You are so lucky*

"I wonder if Partner will be upset we have to document a material weakness or happy that CFO just gave us permission to bill more fees," Staff 2 asked.

"That is a no brainer. He doesn't have to write the 10-page memo on the material weakness, but he does get to take the extra fees all the way to the bank," SM replied, smirking.

CHAPTER 16 – ANOTHER STEAMING MESS

The audit continued. By the end of February, the team was averaging about five and a half hours of sleep a night and working roughly sixteen-hour days with brief stops for breakfast, lunch, and dinner. Senior 3 deleted the dating app off his phone because he was tired of matching with people and then having them get annoyed when he asked if they could wait to meet him until April when he was done auditing.

"Sleep is no good," complained Staff 1. "All my dreams are full of spreadsheets, calculations, random number generators, and a life-size ten-key that chases me around all night."

"Auditing nightmares," replied Staff 2. "Nothing like pretend auditing all night after you've been auditing all day!"

"I just need a little break!" Staff 1 sighed, loudly. "We've been heads down auditing since Manager got Legal in trouble. I wish something exciting would happen to provide a jolt from the rut we are in!"

Just then, Inventory Manager burst into to the audit room and happily announced that Inventory was finally closed for December.

Staff 2 pinging Senior 1: *March 1st and we finally get to start working on Inventory! Yippee!*

"I've provided you all the inventory roll-forwards and a detail for the inventory items you requested," Inventory Manager announced, proudly. "They are on the secured, shared drive because that is the way we do things in finance!"

Inventory Manager had a silly smirk on his face and the whole audit team couldn't help but laugh at him making fun of the Legal Department.

"While you are here," Staff 2 asked Inventory Manager, politely, "Can you show me how I can reconcile this detail to the GL? Just for one example."

"Sure," replied Inventory Manager, hesitantly. "But this better not take long and you need to understand it 100% after the first time. I don't like repeating myself."

Manager pinging Staff 2: *Except when he gets a raise.*

"Hey! That wasn't nice," Inventory Manager blurted out at Manager, as he saw the message come in on Staff 2's screen. "Did I tell you my $5,000 raise that I turned into a $25,000 sports betting account is now at $50,000?"

"Let's just look at the detail for Widget #7," Staff 2 said, trying to move on from having to hear about Inventory Manager's wildly, successful, sports betting account again. "When I look at the total here, I am about two-hundred thousand dollars off the general ledger."

"That's easy to understand," Inventory Manager replied, a little condescendingly. "This is just the sub-ledger detail you have – which is all you asked for. You are missing all the 'fix-it' entries I book on top of this to make the assets actually match the invoices."

"I believe the request said 'Subledger detail reconciled to the

GL' if I am not mistaken," Staff 2 said, getting a little annoyed.

"You really should look at what I send before you ask so many questions," Inventory Manager was agitated. "Look! Look! At the bottom of the listing, there is one cell that is labeled 'fix-it' for $2,500.73. You should reconcile to the GL to the penny now."

"Yes, I see that," Staff 2 said, distraughtly. "But—"

"You understand then?" Inventory Manager smiled as he interrupted Staff 2. "Good, I will leave you to it."

"Wait," Staff 2 cried, desperately, as Inventory Manager turned towards the door.

"What is it now?" Inventory Manager asked, impatiently.

"I need to understand the 'fix it' entries," Staff 2 said, calming down a little bit.

"WHAT?!" roared Inventory Manager. "I just explained that! You are not doing very well at understanding everything 100% the first time! You are as slow as my Warehouse Managers who book every other invoice incorrectly so that I have to fix it."

"I understand your explanation," Staff 2 said, as his frustration began to boil again. "What I mean is that I need the detail of the 'fix it' entries for all of these so I can test the full population."

"Why didn't you just say so?" Inventory Manager asked, in the bluntest tone possible. "Also, to clarify, you need that for JUST the Widget #7, correct?"

"No!" said Staff 2, immediately. "I need them for all the inventory items we picked if they have 'fix it' entries."

"That is terrible," Inventory Manager said, with a scowl. "All the inventory items have 'fix it' entries. Why do you think it takes so long for us to close? I already spent hours pulling the details for you and now I have to go back and do more details for you! This is turning into too many questions and too much time!"

C.P. Aiden

"I'm sorry, but I need the details for all of my selections," Staff 2 said, timidly.

"Fine!" Inventory Manager said, as he let out an aggravated sigh while walking towards the door. "But this is the end of me helping you!"

> **Staff 2 pinging Manager:** *He seriously thinks that is all the questions I "get to have" for inventory?*

> **Manager pinging Staff 2:** *What?*

> **Staff 2 pinging Manager:** *Did you hear what he just said?*

> **Manager pinging Staff 2:** *Who?*

> **Staff 2 pinging Manager:** *Inventory Manager*

> **Manager pinging Staff 2:** *Sorry, I was busy so wasn't paying much attention.*

> **Staff 2 pinging Manager:** *He called me as slow as his Warehouse Managers*

> **Manager pinging Staff 2:** *Oh, I heard that part, that was kind of funny actually.*😆

> **Staff 2 pinging Manager:** *He said I can't ask any more questions.*

> **Manager pinging Staff 2:** *Well, the way he stormed out of here, I would suggest being careful asking more questions if you value your life. Ha-ha.*

> **Staff 2 pinging Manager:** *SMH. You are incredible.*

> **Manager pinging Staff 2:** *Thank you.*

An hour later, Staff 2 received all the 'fix-it' entry details from Inventory Manager.

"He seriously said this was going to take tons of time – HOURS!!! he said," blurted Staff 2, when the email came in. "Now, 59

The Good Audit

minutes later here they are."

"At least he sends you stuff," Senior 1 said, emotionlessly. "Assistant Controller won't send me anything anymore without Finance Manager's approval. He got in a bit of trouble over sending the Cap Table last month."

"Failure to delete sent emails will get him every time," Manager said, laughing.

The following morning, Staff 2 was ready to send out his Inventory selections.

Hi Inventory Manager,

Thank you so much for all your help and clarification yesterday. I have now reconciled all the detail you provided to the trial balance and made selections for my testing based on those details. For each selection, please provide the following:

Purchase Order(s) associated with the selected item

Invoice(s) for the selected item

Payment(s) associated with the selected item

For 'fix-it' entries, please provide the back-up/support for how you determined those entries.

Warm Regards,

Staff 2

A couple hours later, Senior 1 returned to the audit room from a long meeting with FRM.

"Inventory Manager saw your email just a few minutes ago," Senior 1 said to Staff 2, as she walked in.

"How do you know that?" Staff 2 asked in a bewildered tone.

"He burst into FRM's office raging just as we were about to wrap up 10 minutes ago," Senior 1 replied, seriously. "Saying he was

C.P. Aiden

extremely unhappy would be a gross understatement."

About 20 minutes passed and Manager walked into the room, looked at Staff 2 and just shook his head.

"I went looking for Finance Manager and couldn't find him," Manager started explaining. "I headed back this direction and then I heard all this shouting coming from FRM's office."

"This can't be good," Staff 2 said, nervously.

"What exactly did you do?" Manager asked, directly. "Inventory Manager is losing his mind. FRM and Finance Manager are both in there trying to calm him down without any success."

"I asked him to reconcile inventory, that's it," Staff 2 said, with a look of total shock on his face.

"He's all worked up now, and the entire finance team is all crowded into FRM's office," Manager replied, hopelessly.

> **SM pinging Manager:** *I wonder what he will do when Staff 2 looks at the support he gets for the selections and it is all garbage?*

> **Manager pinging SM:** *Staff 2 may lose a few fingers or a knee on this job if he isn't careful.*

> **SM pinging Manager:** *Look out! Here they come.*

FRM walked in, followed by Finance Manager, followed by Senior Accountant, followed by CFO and Inventory Manager. CFO quietly shut the door behind her as Inventory Manager's lower lip quivered in anger.

"I would like to understand exactly how sample selections for inventory were made," CFO said, as she stared back and forth between SM and Manager. "From what I understand, I don't think you have done this very efficiently and the expectations that Inventory Manager dig up so much support for each selection is absurd."

Staff 2 almost lost it. He stammered for a moment, trying to get

188

The Good Audit

something out, but right about when he could control his emotions enough to get real words out of his mouth, Senior 3 kicked him hard under the table so instead of his protest, he leaned back in his chair, groaned in pain and checked his shin for blood.

Staff 2 pinging Senior 3: *That is going to bruise!*

Senior 3 pinging Staff 2: *Better than what Inventory Manager would have done to you if you had said what you were about to say.*

"Perhaps you could help us understand how you organize the inventory reconciliation," Manager suggested to Inventory Manager, calmly. "Often, you know better than some random auditor how items in an account are organized."

Staff 2 pinging Manager: *I am not some random auditor. I am Staff 2 and he is incompetent. Nothing he sent me reconciled to the GL.*

Manager pinging Staff 2: *Keep your mouth shut or I might have to break your other shin. It isn't about how much they, or the support they sent, stinks. It is about getting their buy-in for the process so we don't have to deal with drama like this.*

"Staff 2 made his selections based on widget numbers, but many widgets are made up from several invoices of component widgets, so for each asset he selected, I was going to have to pull an average of seven invoices – so a total of 42 invoices" Inventory Manager told Manager, as he started to breathe normally and calm himself down. "On top of that, I had to pull all of the 'fix it' entries for each of the six items selected as well, so in total I was pulling 48 items of support."

"Is there a better way to organize this?" Manager asked, casually.

"Would it be possible to select based on invoice instead of on widget number?" Inventory Manager asked Manager, graciously.

189

C.P. Aiden

Manager pinging Staff 2: *Boom! Buy in! How many invoices would we pick if we did it by invoices?*

Staff 2 pinging Manager: *34*

"If we picked by invoice, we would need thirty-four invoices and the specific 'fix-it' entries for those assuming we don't find issues with the ones we select," Manager replied, and then cautiously asked. "Would that be ok?"

"Works for me!" Inventory Manager exclaimed. "Thanks!"

Manager pinging Staff 2: *Crisis averted.*

Staff 2 pinging Manager: *So glad it took having 10 people in the room so he could get his sample size from 48 to 34.*

"Staff 2 will send over those new samples," Manager told Inventory Manager.

"I will get my team pulling them right away! I really appreciate how down to earth you are Manager," Inventory Manager said. Then, looking directly at Staff 2, he added, "I'm glad somebody on the team can be practical with stuff like this."

Senior 3 pinging Staff 2: *Breathe, just breathe!*

Staff 2 pinging Senior 3: *Raging on the inside, pretending to smile on the outside. I'm getting better at this.*

Senior 3 pinging Staff 2: *By the time you finish your first year as a senior, you will be a pro!*

An hour and a half later, Staff 2 had support for all 34 invoices selected.

"How is this possible?" Staff 2 wondered in disbelief. "I was getting nothing and then magically, Manager says almost the same things I was telling him and all the support shows up in an

The Good Audit

hour?"

"Manager power," Manager replied, with a chuckle.

In the end, Staff 2 discovered that 18 of the 34 invoices did not match the amounts recorded in the system.

With his head in his hands, he let out a loud, frustrated sigh, and then asked, "Does anyone want to go down to visit Inventory Manager with me?"

No response. Everyone kept their heads down and eyes on their laptops. Staff 2 asked again with no response and then stood up and walked down the hall. He returned a few minutes later and slammed his laptop down on the table.

"Did Inventory Manager shut you down again or something?" Senior 3 asked, somewhat playfully.

"He isn't there!" Staff 2 shouted, hysterically. "It is 6:23 p.m. and he has gone home for the day! He claims to be SOOO busy. He claims to be working like crazy so he can't do anything for us! We are all here until midnight or after every day and he is so busy that he is 'just drowning' and that 'extra' hour and fifteen minutes is just killing him to the point he can only do something for us if Manager throws a pity party for him with half the finance department in the room! This is unreal."

> **Manager pinging Senior 3:** *My wife tells me that big firms working their people until past midnight every night for months and those people just doing it because they are told they have to if they want to have a job is what is unreal.*

"Sounds like tomorrow morning will be lots of fun then," Manager said to Staff 2, sarcastically. "What time does Inventory Manager show up?"

"Usually around 9:30," Staff 2 replied – he was still extremely agitated.

The next morning Staff 2 paid Inventory Manager a visit

C.P. Aiden

promptly at 9:33 am. He told the team he'd give Inventory Manager three minutes to get his computer up and running.

"Good morning!" Staff 2 chirped, happily, as he walked into Inventory Manager's office.

"It was a good morning until I saw your email," Inventory Manager snapped at Staff 2. "You wanted to know why some of the invoices didn't match. We already went through this and I already sent you the whole file of 'fix-it' entries. I seriously have no time to explain everything to you over and over again!"

After trying to explain that he couldn't make any sense of the 'fix-it entry' file and getting his head bit off again, Staff 2 walked slowly back to the audit room.

Later that morning, Finance Manager came down and asked Manager and SM if they could join him in CFO's office.

"Shut the door," CFO said, sternly, as they walked into the room. As Manager closed the door, CFO jumped right in, "I'm very concerned that Staff 2 is asking WAY too much of Inventory Manager. He has been in here three times in the past couple days telling me about how he keeps having to explain the same things over and over again to Staff 2, how there are way too many samples, that Staff 2 is trying to single him out by finding things wrong with what he did—"

"I don't think finding something he did wrong would be singling him out at this point," Manager interrupted. "Our STINC, even after we took those 12 entries off that we discussed you guys 'knowing about' before we found them – the ones you guys had just forgotten to book – is still at 25 things identified that are not correct."

"I am trying to have a serious discussion here," CFO volleyed back – clearly, she was not amused by Manager's interruption. "Inventory Manager is threatening to go look for another job because Staff 2 has just handled everything so horribly and it is stressing him out. If you guys can't fix this, then we don't want

192

Staff 2 coming back next year!"

There was a super awkward pause. Finance Manager just stood with an annoying, cheesy grin as he stared back and forth between Manager and SM. Manager was too upset to say anything else. He wanted to give CFO a piece of his mind about how little help Inventory Manager had provided, how everything was a huge steaming pile of mess and how Inventory Manager seemed to complain about having to do anything, but he held his tongue, knowing that such a response would go way over CFO's head and would result in more escalation of a really stupid issue.

"That's all," CFO said, shorty, as she motioned to the door. "You can go now."

"What was that all about?" Staff 2 asked, anxiously, when Manager and SM walked back into the audit room.

"We just had a very serious 'discussion' with CFO," SM said, slowly. "You can't ask Inventory Manager any more questions".

"What?!" Staff 2 was astounded. "That is going to be a big problem because I just finished going through everything he sent me and there are three big errors within Inventory that I need to go discuss with him."

"If you go down and talk to him," SM said, a bit sternly, "they will ask us to take you off the audit for next year."

"Then for sure I'm going down there," Staff 2 snapped back at SM immediately. "I'm not joking. This whole thing has been such a mess, I'd be happy to be rid of it."

"You are going to help Senior 1 find the errors in her review of your work so that she can go down and talk to Inventory Manager," SM ordered. "And that's the end of it."

"Great!" Staff 2 rolled his eyes. "I'll show them to her right now."

> **<u>Staff 2 pinging Manager:</u>** *What did I do that was so horribly bad that they don't want me back next*

year? I made selections, I asked for backup for inventory items selected, I asked him to explain the differences, that's all!

Manager pinging Staff 2: *I think he feels threatened by you.*

Staff 2 pinging Manager: *Because I ask a bunch of questions about why nothing makes sense? This is an audit. What did he expect? Us to come in here and look at his huge mess and give him a giant gold star?*

Staff 2 quickly explained the three issues to Senior 1 who then walked down the hall to meet with Inventory Manager. Less than 10 minutes later she walked back in the room.

"How did that go?" Staff 2 asked, anxiously.

"Fine." Senior 1 replied, trying to avoid giving out any more information.

"Oh, come on!" exclaimed Staff 2. "You can't just go down there to tell him, the one who wants me kicked off the audit, about three things he screwed up on and then just walk in here and only say 'fine'. There has to be more."

"I told him I noticed a few things in my review and wanted to confirm with him if what I was seeing was correct," Senior 1 said. "I explained the three items and he agreed they were wrong and needed to be adjusted. He was really nice to me."

Staff 2 was raging now. "He just has it out for ME!!" he shouted. "He is nice to everyone else on our team."

"I don't think he likes SM," Manager pointed out lightly.

"He'd probably take me over Staff 2 though," SM replied, with a grin.

"NOT HELPING!!!" Staff 2's face was flushed and his right arm was shaking.

The Good Audit

"Lighten up, Staff 2," Manager said, calmly. "Sounds like we need a pick-me-up this afternoon."

The team went for ice cream and a much needed half hour break from Widget Maker. As the team walked back into the Widget Maker's office, Manager jokingly put his arm around Staff 2 and said, "See Staff 2, we are going to put all of this behind us and never talk about it again."

Just then CFO rounded the corner ahead and walked straight toward the audit team. "Which one of you is Senior 1?" She asked with a smile on her face.

"I am," Senior 1 said, timidly. Senior 1 was a little happy that CFO had forgotten who she was after all the nonsense that happened with the legal department in February.

"I just spoke with Inventory Manager," CFO announced. "He has nothing but wonderful things to say about you. He said you were the easiest person to talk to of any auditor he's ever had to deal with, except Manager. He wants you to do all the inventory testing from now on. He pointed out how very smart you were in finding three mistakes during your review of what he was certain was a huge mess that Staff 2 gave you!"

"Which was a super cleaned-up version of the huge pile of garbage Inventory Manager gave me," Staff 2 whispered to Manager, who just turned and shook his head.

"Let's go get some air," Manager whispered back to Staff 2, and the two of them turned back down the hall and left the building.

195

CHAPTER 17 – THE BEST IS YET TO COME

Manager and Staff 2 were on their third lap walking around the parking lot. Staff 2 was still raging, "Why do we even take on clients like Widget Maker?" Staff 2 asked, furiously. "They are all incompetent, they give us no help or support, they expect us to fix all the problems that they are either too stupid to figure out or that they know about and try to hide from us, they make us follow all their made-up protocol meant to passive-aggressively try to show us who is in charge, they get mad at any question, they try to say the errors we found aren't errors because they knew about stuff but just didn't record it before we started the audit! In the end, Partner and AQR will show up to FINALLY do their review. They create huge fire drills for nothing and then they will ignore the 30 plus errors we've found during the audit and give the company a clean opinion! How stupid are they?!!"

"That was quite the monologue, Staff 2," said a voice from behind them. "I take it you've had better days?"

Staff 2's face went pale. Manager turned and looked back, "Oh, hi Partner," Manager said, in as cheerful of a voice as he could muster. "We were just out here taking laps and working out a few things."

"Well, from the bit I just heard, I think there are probably two or three more laps in order," Partner said, staring right through Staff 2 – Staff 2 wished he could melt away into nothingness

The Good Audit

on the spot. Instead, he muttered something that neither Partner nor Manager could understand and then started lap number four.

"I'd better go after him," Manager told Partner, as Partner headed into the office.

"Just make sure you both charge this time to some administrative code," Partner reminded Manager, sternly. "I wouldn't want time for babying this mental breakdown to be charged to the client!"

"I am SOOO totally fired!" Staff 2 said, gloomily, when Manager caught up to him. "I cannot believe he was right behind us that whole time I was going off."

"Judging by where his car was parked, I think he probably came in about when you were complaining about the client claiming the errors we find are stuff they already know about," Manager pointed out.

"Great," Staff 2 said, sarcastically. "He basically didn't hear about anything that is wrong with the client, but he heard everything that is wrong with him and the rest of the partners....so, so fired. Totally going to get fired, should just go in and pack-up-my-stuff kind of fired."

"I will talk to him," Manager said, calmly. "This isn't the first time a staff or senior has yelled at Partner, and you weren't even yelling directly *at him*, you were just out in a totally open parking lot venting *about him*."

"You have to be kidding me," Staff 2 said in disbelief. "Nothing could have been worse than that."

"There has been," Manager assured Staff 2. "Last year, there was a team that was all working until like 2 am every day to wrap up a job. Partner came in and started doing what partners do which is to pick every nit possible. He wanted the team to add a bunch of the same documentation to several files before he signed off on things. It was going to take Angry Senior about three hours to do and it was already 1 am. Angry Senior just totally lost it. He stood up in front of the entire team and screamed at Partner about how totally useless it was, then told him he wasn't going to do it (using every expletive in the book) and then walked out and drove home."

"That can't be true. Angry Senior still works at The Accounting Firm," Staff 2 replied. "Wouldn't they have fired him on the spot?"

"In all my time at the Firm, I've only seen one person get fired, and that was for harassment," Manager continued. "He walked into a room full of me and five women and said something really crude and inappropriate and then started making advances towards the female senior."

"Sheesh!" muttered Staff 2. "What did you do?"

"I told him to go take a 30-minute walk to cool off and we called HR." answered Manager. "When he got back, I told him to go to the office to get something and when he got there, they took his computer and fired him on the spot."

"Unbelievable," said Staff 2, shaking his head disparagingly. "I still think I'm fired."

"The Firm is making way too much money off of you to fire you," said Manager. "They just want everyone to think they could get fired at any time for any reason, to keep you working at an 'optimal fear efficiency'. Partner knows you basically just about wet yourself and now you are going to go back in and keep your mouth shut and head down which equals more efficiency from you and higher profitability for him."

As they walked back into the office, Staff 2 went to the break room to get a drink. All the ranting outside had made his throat scratchy he told Manager. As Manager walked back into the audit room, he tried to start explaining what had happened to Partner.

The Good Audit

"Let's just move on," Partner cut Manager off. "We have plenty of work to do and I don't want to bother with something as trivial as Staff 2 incessantly ranting all over the parking lot. We don't have long to finish this audit and I just left about 30 comments in the planning documents I finally reviewed."

> **Senior 3 pinging Manager:** *What happened out there?*

> **Manager pinging Senior 3:** *Nothing I can really share, but it was epic.*

> **Senior 3 pinging Manager:** *That is not fair. I feel like we just missed the biggest drama of the entire audit*

> **Manager pinging Senior 3:** *We were only out there for another 15 minutes after Partner came in and he already has 30 comments in planning?! The best is yet to come. And, btw, this is why we were supposed to get Partner and AQR to sign off on planning at the APE so this wouldn't happen. Mega-fail*

"Anything major in your comments on the planning files?" Manager asked Partner, politely.

"Well, I don't like how we laid out our method for testing inventory," Partner replied. "I think we are going to have to redo it all."

Staff 2 had just walked back into the room. His shoulders sunk down, his jaw dropped and real tears started welling up in his eyes. He literally ran out of the room.

"Was it something I said?" Partner asked, mockingly. "I mean I sure wasn't about to cry about any of the stuff he screamed about me to the whole parking lot a few minutes ago."

> **Senior 3 pinging Manager:** *Oh snap! You HAVE to tell me now.*

Manager ignored Senior 3's ping. "The inventory work he did is what got him out in the parking lot to begin with," Manager replied, carefully. "We did change the approach from what was in planning, so we will go update that—"

"Did the approach change to what I'm asking for here?" Partner interrupted. "Because I want it done this exact way and if we didn't do that, then it is back to the drawing board."

"We didn't do it exactly that way," Manager began. "But—"

"No buts," Partner interrupted again. "It has to be this w—"

"Our testing resulted in 3 large STINC's" Manager now interrupted Partner. He did not like where Partner was going and so he had to strike now. "I think, given the STINC's, we could probably all agree that for this year the testing was adequate. Could we leave a note to update next year?"

"Fine" Partner agreed. "But I wish someone would have consulted with me before doing all this work. I am happy we have STINC's. Nothing says you did an audit well like finding mistakes the client made."

> **Senior 3 pinging Manager:** *Oh, we did try to consult with him on the method. He just ignored us.*

> **Manager pinging Senior 3:** *seven times. I have SEVEN calendar invites in my email that he declined.*

> **Senior 3 pinging Manager:** *Do you think we should mention to him that finding errors has not been all that hard and there could possibly be tons more if we had to dig deeper?*

> **Manager pinging Senior 3:** *Nope, but you'd better start making a list of things Partner should look at before he just goes diving into everything and blowing it all up.*

> **Senior 3 pinging Manager:** *Would have been nice to know he was going to show up today so I could*

have that list started.

Manager pinging Senior 3: *He was going to show up sometime before the end of the audit.*

Senior 3 pinging Manager: *Yeah, but we still have a couple weeks. This is the earliest I've ever seen Partner show up for the end of an audit. I'm used to 12 to 36 hours.*

Manager pinging Senior 3: *Which is just one more reason I said the best is yet to come*

"I'm almost through planning," Partner said. "What else am I required to review?"

"I started a list of things you need to review," Senior 3 volunteered.

Manager pinging Senior 3: *Liar*

"Give me just a minute to finish it and I will send it right over."

"Ok," replied Partner. "But you'd better make it quick. Otherwise, I will have to start poking around myself for stuff to review."

Manager pinging Senior 3: *Faster*

Manager pinging Senior 3: *Faster*

Manager pinging Senior 3: *Faster*

Senior 3 pinging Manager: *Stop it! I am trying to focus here. If this list isn't done in like two minutes, we are toast.*

Manager pinging Senior 3: *Better hurry then.* 🙂

If the audit file was like a well-organized community with clean streets, well-manicured lawns, and well-maintained buildings, then Partner's review was like a tornado had come down all of Main Street. In a little less than three hours, Partner had annihilated nearly everything he had touched. The entire audit file only had about 45 comments in it before Partner arrived and most of those were little things – 'add this' or 'take this part out' or 'can you explain this in a little more detail?' type of comments that would be equivalent to fixing a pothole or a crack in a sidewalk.

"Well, I have an event at 6:30 tonight," Partner said, as he started packing his computer up. "I will be back tomorrow afternoon and expect the vast majority of my comments will be addressed by then. Have a great night!" With that, Partner strode across the room and out the door.

After Partner had been gone for two minutes, the team started to assess the damage.

"There are now 468 comments in the audit file!" cried Senior 1 "And 145 of them are to me!"

"I have 168," Senior 3 tried to console Senior 1 without success.

"Guys," SM said, solemnly. "I am afraid that clearing so many comments by tomorrow afternoon will require an ALL-NIGHTER."

He paused to look directly at Senior 1 and then added, "for ALL of us."

The entire team groaned.

"It is 6 o'clock right now. Here is what I suggest," SM continued. "Let's get our dinner order to Intern ASAP. I'm going to head home really quick to let my dogs out for 10 minutes. Manager and Senior 1, I suggest that if you want any time with your families tonight you do the same. Senior 3, you may take a 30-minute nap under the table. Staff 2, you should start clearing comments – especially those related to Inventory, Staff 1, you can take a 30-minute nap in the Mother's room since you live too far away to go see your family – I hear the recliner in there is super awesome. Intern, will you please go pick up dinner? Does that sound ok to everyone?"

The room was silent for a full minute as SM looked around at everyone. As SM got up to leave, Manager finally said something.

"Look," replied Manager. "20 minutes with my family right now and then doing an all-nighter will do way more harm than good. My wife has the kids in a routine and I generally see them in the mornings. Going home now will just throw the kids off and make my wife super mad."

"I'm going home at 8 p.m., like my flexible work arrangement with the Firm spells out, the flexible work arrangement I took a 15 percent pay cut for!" Senior 1 jumped in. "I go home no later than 8 p.m., put my kids to bed and then finish up whatever work stuff I need to after that. Tonight is no different."

"You don't get it," SM replied. "This is an extenuating circumstance and we need you here with the team tonight. That is why I'm giving you right now to go home and put your kids to bed and then come back."

"My kids don't go to bed at 6:00 p.m.," Senior 1 snapped back. "They go to bed at 8:30."

"Can't they go to bed early for one night?" SM asked, with a puzzled look on his face.

"My children aren't like dogs!" Senior 1 exclaimed, with a look of horror. "I can't just go home and let them out for 10 minutes to do their evening business and then expect they will just come in, lay down and be fine the rest of the night. They have routines. They need me there. They need support, love, and care."

"Isn't your husband home to do that?" SM asked, insensitively.

"Children need their mother! My husband is a good man, but he can't do everything." Senior 1 was really getting angry now. "I worked this out with the Firm and I'm sticking to my agreement no matter how many pointless comments Partner left during his three and a half hour 'review' here. I have an agree-

C.P. Aiden

ment and I expect the Firm to uphold that agreement."

"Those agreements are great for when things are normal," SM continued to argue. "But we are in a real bind here and need you to be a team player until things can go back to normal."

"Normal?" Senior 1 was dumbfounded. "Normal? You have got to be kidding me! NOTHING about this job is normal. Normal would be getting home by 6 p.m. every night. Normal would be getting to spend holidays and weekends with your family instead of at work. Normal would be having hobbies outside of work. Normal would be having a life. This...working 90 hours a week, taking a 15 percent pay cut just so I can put my children to bed at night while still working just as many hours as the rest of the team, clearing over 400 Partner comments in less than 24 hours just because he says he is coming back tomorrow and would like them all done. This is not normal, it is insanity!"

"Can't you just be a team player for once?" SM asked, coldly. "We really do need you here with us to get this done. This is an emergency. Not staying will be viewed as an act of insubordination."

"No!" Senior 1 exclaimed, forcefully.

"What do you mean, no?" asked SM, condescendingly.

> **Manager pinging Senior 3:** *You know earlier how I said the best was yet to come? It just got here.*
>
> **Senior 3 pinging Manager:** *I know, I get to take a 30-minute nap and then work all night. Ha-ha*
>
> **Manager pinging Senior 3:** *You know what I'm talking about.*
>
> **Senior 3 pinging Manager:** *Yeah, it is awesome, she's standing up to SM and super sad at the same time to see Senior 1 quit on the spot. I'm assuming that you, like me, don't want to get in the middle of this one.*

Senior 1 immediately stood up trembling with anger, pulled

204

out her employee badge, closed her laptop, handed both to SM and said "I'm done" before walking out of the room, leaving the office, getting in her car, and driving away.

SM stood in silent shock for over three minutes before speaking, "I can't believe she would just walk out on us like that. This is a total emergency!"

"We aren't saving lives," Manager interjected. "And when I texted my wife about the prospect of an all-nighter just because Partner decided to show up today, her response was 'time to go find a job that doesn't try to constantly enforce unrealistic expectations at the expense of any and all personal life'."

"We are saving our jobs!" SM replied. "Partner laid out an expectation. If we don't deliver, our entire careers will be in jeopardy."

"You are kidding me. That is the dumbest reason I've ever heard for doing an all-nighter. I am pretty sure that if Partner didn't fire Staff 2 today for what happened in the parking lot, we won't get fired for not clearing every single comment by tomorrow afternoon," Manager replied.

> **Senior 3 pinging Manager:** *You HAVE to tell me what Staff 2 did.*
>
> **Manager pinging Senior 3:** *Go take your nap.*

"Fine," SM conceded. "Let's work through what we can between now and 2:00 am and then all agree to be back here by 8:30 in the morning to wrap up whatever is left, but if it backfires, it is all on you, Manager."

SM left to go let his dogs out, Manager walked down the hall to an empty office to call his wife, Intern left to pick up the dinner order, Staff 1 headed to the Mother's room, Staff 2 lifted his screen back up and started going through Partner's comments on Inventory and Senior 3 crawled under the table and curled up on the floor for his nap.

C.P. Aiden

Forty-five minutes later, the whole team was back in the audit room, eating dinner and attacking Partner's comments.

"These are worse than SM's comments on the APE agenda," Staff 2 blurted out, not caring that SM was sitting right across the table from him. "He literally wrote out a whole paragraph telling me how to correct my punctuation to 'make it grammatically correct' and what he is telling me is so not grammatically correct."

"This comment is even better," Senior 3 said. "Listen to what he says, 'We say that the difference between the invoice and what was recorded was $2 million. Would this be an error then?' The next sentence says, 'We determined this is an error in the accounting records of the company' How hard is it to read one more sentence? It would have taken less time than typing out that question and now I have to waste my time to type out 'Great question! Please see next sentence.' Seriously, this is unbelievable."

By 1:50 a.m., the team had cleared all but 75 of Partner's comments.

"Seems like we should be in great shape for tomorrow," Staff 2 said, optimistically. "We cleared almost 400 comments tonight!"

"You are ignoring the five percent rule," Manager said, discouragingly.

"What is the five percent rule?" Staff 2 asked, with some hesitation in his voice.

"Ninety-five percent of all partner comments are completely asinine," SM explained. "They are mostly due to the fact that Partner comes in and only takes three and a half hours to look through stuff that took us weeks to do. Partner has almost zero understanding of how the client operates and he also doesn't read everything very thoroughly during his cursory review. The other five percent are the comments that are legitimate. They

206

The Good Audit

identify huge holes in what we did and any one of those comments can take us hours to address. I think we only had six or seven of those tonight and they weren't big jackpot comments either."

"A jackpot comment is one that takes someone on our team at least a full day to clear and one that requires us going back to the client for additional support. We typically go for low hanging fruit first," added Manager. "So, it is likely that more of the five percent rule comments are still left in the open 75."

The team quickly packed up to head home for a few hours of rest. The next morning, the team continued to scramble to get through the comments. Senior 3 and Staff 1 both found jackpot comments and rushed to meet with Finance Manager to get those resolved. No sign of Senior 1. By lunchtime, the whole room was in a state of panic when SM's phone rang.

"Hi Partner," SM said. The rest of the team could not hear the other end of the conversation, but SM quickly replied to whatever Partner was saying. "We have over 430 of your comments addressed and we are working to clear out the rest." Then there was a pause followed by SM saying, "No problem, we will see you tomorrow then."

> **Staff 2 pinging Manager:** *We will see you TOMORROW then??!!!! I'm so confused.*

"Partner had something come up so he will not be able to make it out today," SM said. "He sincerely thanks each of you for working so hard to clear out so many of his comments. He will look at all your responses tomorrow when he comes out. Let's get our lunch orders to Intern and wrap up the rest of these comments!"

"If he isn't coming today, I think we could all use a break," Manager insisted. "Let's go out for a team lunch today, and given how late we stayed last night, I'd propose we all leave by 7:30 or 8:00 p.m. tonight?"

> **SM pinging Manager:** *What are you doing?*

207

C.P. Aiden

> **Manager pinging SM:** *I'm saving us from a mutiny. Don't you see how angry everyone is that they worked like crazy to meet some artificial deadline just for Partner to blow it off and not show up?*

> **SM pinging Manager:** *No. I don't see it. Maybe that is something I will learn to notice when I attend the sensitivity training the Firm is requiring me to go to next month due to a small incident with my last team.*

The team lunch cheered everyone up a bit. As they left the restaurant, Manager noticed a familiar figure walking in front of them. The person was talking loudly on the phone. Manager gestured to the rest of the team to lower their voices and pointed ahead.

"The tickets go on sale at 2 p.m. TODAY! It is at Awesome Concert Venue so it will be AMAZING! I have two computers set up on my home network. I have two cell phones connected to my cell phone network, I have two executive assistants at the office who are planning to refresh the page on two computers each. I have blocked off my entire afternoon to ensure that we get tickets to this. Yeah, I know, I am so exci..." Partner's voice was cut off as he closed his car door.

"What Awesome Concert Venue concert tickets are going on sale at 2 p.m. this afternoon?" Staff 1 asked. "Maybe I want to use my phone and computer to get tickets too, if Partner thinks it is a big enough deal to blow us off and not show up at Widget Maker so he gets his tickets."

Senior 3 already had his phone out and was looking it up. "You are not going to believe this," Senior 3's mouth dropped open as he showed his phone to Staff 2.

"Oh yeah, you are definitely going to want to get on those tickets fast!" Staff 2 said, sarcastically.

"Who is it?" Staff 1 demanded.

208

The Good Audit

"Female Teenage Singing Sensation," Senior 3 burst out laughing.

"OOO-KAAAY, never mind," said Staff 1.

"So, he basically told us to work all night last night to get through all his comments and then he decides not to show up so he can spend the afternoon making sure he gets Female Teenage Singing Sensation tickets?" Staff 2 was once again raging. "Unreal!"

"Well, I think we know how we are going to tell Partner that Senior 1 walked out on us last night," Manager said, with a gleam in his eye.

"I don't like where this is going," Senior 3 said, nervously.

At 1:53 p.m., the entire team was logged into the ticket sales website on both their laptops and their phones.

"This is really dumb to have us all on the same network going through the same wireless hotspot." Senior 3 pointed out. "We will all just crash into each other and no one will get through to buy the tickets."

"I'm glad we have such a bright IT guy on the team," Manager said, playfully. "Staff 1 and Intern, why don't you go downstairs to the bookstore and get on their network? Staff 2, why don't you try the other restaurant downstairs? I will try the building wi-fi and the others can stay on the Widget Maker network."

"Do you think this will really work?" SM asked, hesitantly.

"Even if it doesn't, I think we all win," Manager replied. "We should be able to sell whatever tickets we get for two to three times face value in 10 minutes if Partner does get them."

"It will be awesome," Senior 3 said. "If we get tickets it will be like 'Hey Partner, a little bird told us you wanted Female Teenage Singing Sensation tickets and the whole team took 10 minutes today to make sure you got them. Oh, and by the way, Senior 1 walked out and quit last night. How do you want us to deliver those tickets?' He will be so happy!"

Within 15 minutes, the entire team was back in the audit room.

"Eight tickets!" exclaimed Staff 1, as she and Intern walked in.

"Four tickets," added Senior 3.

"I got two," said Manager. "They are on the front row. I hope Partner got tickets because these will sell to some soccer mom for five to seven times face value."

"I got four and they are on the 10th row," Staff 2 said. "But this has me thinking. Partner doesn't need 18 tickets and it doesn't really matter where the tickets are – it just matters that we get tickets. I think we should try to sell the really good ones and split the money. It will be the best spot bonus any of us have ever seen. Like, Manager, you should totally list yours."

"I just put them up for seven times face value," Manager replied.

"You are crazy!" SM exclaimed. "No one in their right mind is going to pay that even for front row tickets."

"Oh wow!" Manager blurted out. "I just got an email from some-one who wants to buy the tickets today, and you would never believe who the email is from…PARTNER!!"

"You are making this up," SM seriously thought Manager was pulling everyone's leg.

Manager turned his screen to show SM and the rest of the team the email. "He wants to meet at 4:00 and says he will bring cash."

"Now the only problem is deciding who is going to deliver the tickets," SM said. "If you show up, Partner will just tell you that you used the Firm's time to buy the tickets and he will only pay you face value for them. Would Partner recognize your wife?"

"He met her at the family activity last summer, so that is risky," Manager replied.

210

The Good Audit

"My girlfriend is at work or she totally would," Staff 2 said. "But she met him at a celebration dinner last year."

"Who has a family member that Partner hasn't met?" SM asked.

"I've got it!" Manager shouted out. "He wants to meet in a grocery store parking lot; how about the same grocery store where Senior 1's husband works – remember, he's a pharmacist or something? SM, we have to call Senior 1. You have to sincerely apologize and tell her that we have a way to get her a huge bonus if she comes back to finish the audit."

"How much will we make off these two tickets?" SM asked.

"About $3,000," Manager answered.

"And I just put my four 10th row seats up and have a buyer," Staff 2 added, "That will add another $2,500."

"The rest of the tickets will add another $2,000 and all but two have buyers now." Staff 1 added.

"OK, I'll do it," SM agreed. "$7,500 to split seven ways makes for a pretty good day at work and I think a thousand dollars might just convince Senior 1 to come back and Partner will never have to hear about it."

The plan went off without a hitch, except that SM had to agree to let Senior 1 leave by 7:30 p.m. every night going forward without question. She would still work from home after the kids went to bed, and her husband got an extra $200 out of the pot because "it wasn't going to look good for a guy working in the pharmacy collecting that much cash from some guy in a super nice car out in the parking lot".

In celebration of their success, the team left at 7:00 p.m. that night, even though there were still 27 comments from Partner left in the file.

CHAPTER 18 – PARTNER'S JOB IS TO SHOW UP AND BLOW UP

The following morning when Partner arrived, he thanked the team for clearing the majority of his comments and then he apologized for not showing up there the day before as he had originally said he would.

"I had a very important meeting that came up last minute," Partner had explained. "Sometimes these things come up and you just have to make adjustments."

> **Staff 2 pinging Senior 3:** *Yep, his very important meeting with a pharmacist and a bundle of cash in a grocery store parking lot was SUPER important! I'm so glad that Female Teenage Singing Sensation tickets are more important than the entire team working most of the night to clear all his stupid comments and that we now know that we were ignored so Partner can live out his teenage dreams.*💀
>
> **Senior 3 pinging Staff 2:** *Given that we each have another $1,000 in our pockets, thanks in part to said very important last-minute meeting, I'm going*

to pretend I'm not angry.

Within two hours, Partner had reopened about 100 of the comments the team thought they had cleared.

Manager pinging SM: *No nit too small to pick.*

SM pinging Manager: *I just hope he's getting close to being done with everything.*

"I don't think any of the memos were included on your list, Senior 3," Partner said. "Especially the Final Summary Memo for the whole audit."

"That is because I was just finishing my review of those," Manager jumped in to save Senior 3 who was squirming in his chair. "I've just sent you all the relevant memos."

"Great!" Partner replied. "I will look at those next."

Senior 3 pinging Manager: *Here comes 200 comments!*

The room went quiet for about 10 minutes as Partner started to review the memos. All of a sudden, Partner broke the silence with something between a shout and a terrified shriek.

"What is this?!" yelled Partner, as he pointed to his screen. "And why is this the first time I'm seeing this?"

Partner was pointing at a description of the material weakness in the Final Summary Memo.

"I sent you three emails about that a few weeks ago," Manager quickly replied.

"And I sent you two or three as well," SM added.

"When?" Partner questioned. "I can't believe I would have missed an email like that from you. You guys need to tell me about stuff like this WHEN it happens. We probably have to consult on this with our Too Smart to Think Rationally group at national. They take weeks to do anything and we don't have that much time before the audit is supposed to be over! This is a huge miss! We could be in some SERIOUS trouble here."

Manager and SM both checked their 'Sent' folders and found the dates.

"February 13th from me," Manager said, pointing at the email, "The subject line said Material Weakness at Widget Maker, and then again on the 15th and 16th."

"Mine were sent late the evening of February 14th and then the morning of February 15th," SM told Partner.

> **Staff 2 pinging Senior 1:** *So rather than do anything for Valentine's Day, he spent the evening sending Partner an email explaining an MW? Big surprise.*

SM and Manager watched Partner as he frantically searched his inbox for emails from them.

"Here they are," Partner said, as he found the emails. "I guess you did send them to me. On something like this, you should really call me just in case I don't see the emails."

> **Manager pinging SM:** *All six emails were unread. How do you just ignore six emails like that? Half of all emails I have sent him over the past three months were unread.*

> **SM pinging Manager:** *While we were all working like crazy that week doing well over the Firm mandated 58 hours per week for Busy Season, he was up at his cabin in Aspen, skiing*

"I did call you," SM replied. "I left you like three messages."

Partner then pulled out his phone and went to his voicemail, "You have 38 new messages," came the voice from his phone. "When do you think you called me?" Partner asked SM, as he

The Good Audit

scrolled down the list of new messages.

"Once each day the 17th, 18th and 19th," SM replied, confidently.

"And I called you the 15th and 16th," Manager added.

"Oh, here they are," Partner said, as he found the voicemails from SM in his new message list and started listening to the first one. "I guess I was in some really important meetings those days somewhere without reception. You guys should have just kept trying to reach though. This type of thing needs to be communicated no matter how many times you have to reach out!"

> **Manager pinging SM:** *Why is it that whenever any partner ditches work for something, they tell everyone else they were "in really important meetings without reception"? And, how is it our fault that he chose to completely ignore 11 attempts to reach him?*

SM ignored the ping as he was frantically searching through The Accounting Firm policies on giving clients material weaknesses.

"Great news!" SM happily exclaimed. "I just found some guidance that says we only have to consult with the Too Smart to Think Rationally Group if we think the company disagrees with us."

"When has any client ever not disagreed with us slapping them with a material weakness?" Partner asked, bluntly.

"When it is the legal department that screws up and tries to cover up their mistakes by acting as though they are so much smarter than everyone such that no one should even question them…and when the finance and legal departments totally hate each other," Manager replied.

"Isn't that last statement true at just about every company we audit?" Partner questioned.

215

"Yes," replied SM. "But in our case CFO specifically asked us to go after the legal department on this and she got CEO's buy-in, which is odd because CEO's almost always ignore finance and listen to legal on everything. In addition, CFO told us to bill them additional fees and label them 'Legal Department's MW'."

"Can't argue with extra fees," Partner said, as he shrugged his shoulders. "I guess if they are willing to pay us more for it and told us to label it that way, we have clear and convincing evidence that they are on board. Let's just add a page or two on that to the Final Summary Memo to cover our bases."

Senior 3 pinging Manager: *Crisis averted*

Manager pinging Senior 3: ha-ha

By the time Partner left that afternoon, the audit file had been blown up once again – over 100 comments re-opened and an additional 372 new comments.

"Seriously, how do you even write that many comments in three hours?" Staff 2 grumbled.

"A partner once told me that if you don't put at least 20 comments on a document or spreadsheet, you haven't added enough value," SM replied. "And if you don't average at least 10 per page on a memo, then you haven't done your job."

"This should be 'an' and not 'a' adds a ton of value, doesn't it?" Staff 2 remarked contemptuously. "Takes longer to write than to fix and just upsets the person the note was left for. We spend hours and hours responding to stupid little nits like this. I've averaged four and a half hours of sleep the last three nights thanks to Partner 'doing his job'!"

"It will be over soon enough," SM said, calmly.

"How can you be calm when there are three hundred and seventy-two new comments in the file?" Staff 2 was almost screaming now. "And how on earth are we supposed to get this all done in time to issue?"

The Good Audit

"This is an audit," Manager said, sardonically. "You haven't been here long enough to know that we NEVER get everything done before we issue our report. We spend another entire month going through what the Firm calls 'archive' which is just a fancy word for finishing everything after the fact."

"This is the typical 'Partner Panic' before a deadline," SM added. "They try to boil the ocean to make sure we didn't miss anything big. The beauty is that after they go through this senseless panic attack, they sign the report and then forget about all the comments they left and we can generally just delete them during archive. That is why they say that time clears all comments. In a lot of cases, doing nothing ultimately clears the comment."

"Then why were we all here until 2 am the other night clearing comments?" Staff 2 asked, sharply.

"Partner wanted us to clear the majority of them, so we did," SM replied.

"What if we miss something?" Staff 2 asked, skeptically.

"Generally, leaving thousands of comments pretty much means we don't miss anything too big," Senior 3 replied. "And as long as whatever we find after the fact isn't huge, Manager and SM hold up the rug while the rest of us sweep whatever we've found under it."

"With these guys, that could end up being a pretty lumpy rug," Staff 2 pointed out, smugly.

The cycle continued for each of the next several days. Partner would show up at 2:00 or so in the afternoon, would reopen about a quarter of the comments the team had cleared, while telling SM and Manager that they could close out and delete the other three quarters, would add more comments – but the number of comments added would be about 25% less than the amount added the day before. Partner would tell the team he expected everything cleared by when he returned the next day. He left by 6:30 p.m. each day so the team "would have enough

217

time to clean up the mess".

The team worked most of each night to get through everything and be ready for Partner's return the next day. The client was getting testy too.

"Don't you understand that I can't be answering all these questions right now?" Finance Manager asked, the fifth day into the cycle when Senior 3 had walked into his office to find out why the company was pre-paying for snack deliveries. "I have to get the financial statements ready for you or you will have nothing to sign off on at the end of the week! You are going to have to figure out the answer yourself!"

As Senior 3 walked out of Finance Manager's office, he ran into Assistant Controller, who was supposed to have the trial balance rolled to the financial statements.

"Hey, do you have that trial balance roll-forward ready for me yet?" Senior 3 asked, cautiously.

"He doesn't have time for your questions either," Finance Manager called out from his office.

"I've been working on it – should have it to you really soon – I've just been busy with some other, personal stuff," Assistant Controller whispered.

"Great," Senior 3 said back.

"Hey, isn't that the same shirt you've had on the last two days?" Assistant Controller noticed, as he started to laugh. "It totally is. Have you not been going home at nights?"

"I've got to see this!" Finance Manager exclaimed, as he rushed out of his office door. He started to sniff the air around Senior 3. "It smells like the audit room. Have you guys been pulling all-nighters?"

"Well, not technically all-nighters," Senior 3 admitted. "But rather than take a half hour commuting each way, I've been sleeping under the table in there – so I've been getting four hours of

The Good Audit

sleep rather than three. Staff 2's been hitting up the couch in the break room and Staff 1 uses the Mother's lounge – I guess the recliner in there is great."

Finance Manager and Assistant Controller spent the next five minutes roasting Senior 3 telling him things like, "there is an executive bathroom down the hall by the CEO's office. It has a shower, you should sneak in and use it", or, "I'm going to go ask IT for the security footage to see if you sleepwalk".

Finance Manager walked back into his office laughing. "So, you could take five minutes to make fun of my shirt and the fact that we've been sleeping here to get the audit done, and you couldn't take 30 seconds to answer a question?" Senior 3 called after him.

"Pretty much," Finance Manager responded, as the door to his office swung shut in Senior 3's face. Senior 3 slowly walked back to the audit room. Right as he entered the room, Inventory Manager saw him and followed him in.

"So, I hear you've all been sleeping in random places in the office every night," he said, with his huge annoying grin.

"How did you hear that?" Staff 2 asked.

"Finance Manager pinged me." Inventory Manager replied.

"How did he find out?" asked Staff 2.

Inventory Manager looked at Senior 3 and, while still grinning, raised his eyebrows. "I wouldn't say it is exactly my fault," Senior 3 said. "Assistant Controller noticed I've been wearing the same shirt for a few days, so I sort of caved and told them most of us have been sleeping here the past few nights."

"It is so hilarious!" said Inventory Manager. "Everyone is talking about it. Seriously Staff 2 – the couch in the breakroom? That is so totally disgusting! I bet even CEO knows by now. Although, if he doesn't, I guess I can tell him during our meeting in three minutes."

"Before you go," Manager interjected, as Inventory Manager made a move to exit. "Is there any chance we will see the inventory reconciliation today? The one that was supposed to be provided two weeks ago? The one that we cannot issue financial statements without?"

"Meh. Probably not," Inventory Manager replied, nonchalantly. "CEO has reprioritized my time to a deal the company is trying to do."

"Great," Manager said. "We are supposed to issue financials at the end of this week. Any idea on when we might get it?"

"It is basically done, except that the first three times I pulled the trial balance, I found errors." Inventory Manager replied. "Assistant Controller basically doesn't know how to do much of anything. It seems crazy to me that an Inventory Manager would be catching errors in the books this late in the game."

"We are up to forty-seven errors, or Summary of Things Identified that are Not Correct, or STINC's, as we call them," Staff 2 said, proudly.

"Well, I'm not an auditor and I'm up to five in the past day and the only thing that stinks around here is this room," said Inventory Manager, covering his nose. "Assistant Controller told me he booked those five and another two entries this morning."

"You mean to tell me that we are less than a week from issuing financial statements and you guys are still pushing entries through the system?" SM was horrified.

"Basically," Inventory Manager laughed. "The trial balance is still all good except for all the changes they've been pushing through – like almost daily. The good news is that every time they book a new entry, Assistant Controller adds a column to his consolidated trial balance, so he is TOTALLY keeping track of it all."

SM went into panic mode and he ran down the hall to Assistant

The Good Audit

Controller's office. Finance Manager and FRM were both in his office looking at a huge spreadsheet.

"I need you to pull me a fresh trial balance and give me the file you have that you are tracking all your adjustments in!" SM exclaimed, as he burst into the room. "And I need it ASAP."

"That's funny," Assistant Controller said, while shaking his head. "We are just looking at that file and trying to figure out why it doesn't match the current trial balance."

"We audited the original trial balance you gave us two months ago," SM blurted out. "If you are telling me that you've been manually making adjustments to get to the numbers that will show up on your financial statements, then there is a whole ton of stuff we haven't audited. We need to test all that – like TODAY!!!"

"If you guys could figure it out, that would be a huge help to us," Assistant Controller said, sheepishly. "I spent all morning looking at it and can't figure it out. These guys have been in here for 30 minutes and we still don't have a clue."

"Just send it," SM was nearing a breaking point. "We will work some excel magic and let you know."

They all walked back to the audit room together with a plan to project the file up on a big screen so that everyone could work through it at once. Five minutes later, Staff 2, who was ignoring the big screen and the conversation about what numbers should be where, had figured out the problem.

"There are 98 inventory accounts that have changed since we got the original trial balance that do not show up anywhere on Assistant Controller's entry tracking," he explained to Manager, SM, Finance Manager, and Assistant Controller. "Somebody has been posting to inventory accounts without telling anyone… and I bet I can guess who it is. In addition, someone else has been making adjustments to equity."

221

"Where is Senior 1? Go get her," Finance Manager said, quickly. "She will have to go talk to Inventory Manager."

"We are going to have to test every single one of these additional entries separately," SM said, somberly. "If we are going to issue the financial statements, we need support for each of these entries before the end of the day."

"Half of them you've already done," Assistant Controller pointed out.

"How so?" asked SM.

"Forty-seven of them relate to audit adjustments, or STINC's, as you guys call them," Assistant Controller started.

> **Staff 2 pinging Manager:** *Actually, we call them Widget Maker STINC's, but I won't say that to his face.*

> **Manager pinging Staff 2:** *I think deep inside, they all know.*

"Another 59 of the entries relate to the adjustments we found, but just hadn't booked before you guys also found them and proposed them as adjustments," Assistant Controller continued. "They are the one's CFO made you take off your STINC."

> **Manager pinging SM:** *Our favorite part of the audit.*

> **SM pinging Manager:** *Seriously – unbelievable that there are 59 of those compared to our actual 47 STINC's!*

"That leaves 67 entries that you haven't tested yet," Assistant Controller said, happily.

> **Senior 3 pinging Manager:** *Final week of the audit and we have to test 67 additional detailed entries. Great!*

"Of those 67, looks like 42 of them are hitting inventory accounts," Staff 2 pointed out, after carefully sifting through the entries. "Another eight are hitting equity, so that leaves 17 random entries."

"Oh, those other 17 are easy," Assistant Controller said, as Inventory Manager walked in. "Those are the 17 that Inventory Manager told me to book to fix his reconciliation."

"Can you please provide us the support for those 17 entries then?" Staff 2 asked Inventory Manager, politely.

"What do you mean by support?" Inventory Manager was confused. "I just looked at the accounts and figured out they were wrong because actual inventory didn't match what our books said."

"Do you have any sort of calculations or any way to show how you got to these adjustments?" Staff 2 kept pushing the issue.

"I have calculations for some, others I just had Assistant Controller book so that my reconciliation would roll," Inventory Manager answered, nonchalantly. "That whole big reconciliation file I haven't sent you yet will support those."

"You should know that you can't just book things so they roll," Manager scolded Inventory Manager.

Inventory Manager rolled his eyes and said, "That was only like four of the entries and the ending balance makes more sense my way because it matches what you guys counted as part of your inventory observations."

The Widget Maker team went back to their offices to start pulling support for the final 67 entries. They started sending everything piecemeal to the audit team. Nothing was labeled so it was anyone's guess which support related to which entry on the list. Inventory Manager had a meltdown after pulling support for 30 entries and FRM helped track down the rest.

"Wow," Staff 2 was surprised as he saw the email from FRM with the support for the other 12 entries. "This is the first time the whole audit that FRM has done anything useful – he actually labeled the entries!"

"Even if he gave us support," Senior 3 said, pessimistically, "we still have to make sure it is all right, and the odds of that with these guys, especially with FRM, Assistant Controller, and Inventory Manager being involved, are pretty low."

The whole exercise took from first thing in the morning to about 4:30 in the afternoon. The team was starting to feel that the end was near when Partner walked in.

> **Senior 1 pinging Senior 3:** *Oh, dear, what is he doing showing up at 4:30?*
>
> **Senior 3 pinging Senior 1:** *Never a good thing when the partner shows up to work this late in the afternoon. For most of the year, they are already GONE by this time. It generally means we will be here all night.*
>
> **Senior 1 pinging Senior 3:** *I'm leaving at 7:30 no matter what.*

CHAPTER 19 – THE BEST HAS ARRIVED

"I just got off the phone with AQR," Partner announced, as he started setting up his laptop. "He is wondering whether or not we are issuing financial statements tomorrow given that he has not reviewed anything in the audit file and he hasn't seen draft financials yet."

"He hasn't seen draft financials because we haven't seen draft financials," SM replied. "We spent most of the day today testing a surprise 67 adjusting entries to the trial balance."

"Wait, what?!" Partner was speechless for a moment. "You mean to tell me that their deadline is tomorrow and we don't even have a draft?"

"We were supposed to get it this morning, but then this other stuff blew up," SM explained. "We literally got done with testing all these other entries five minutes ago. However, now that we have a good adjusted trial balance, we are expecting financial statements from them in about an hour."

"Buckle up then," Partner sighed. "Looks like we are all in for a very long night!"

> **Senior 3 pinging Staff 2:** *Here we go!*

> **Staff 2 pinging Senior 3:** *Does he think we haven't been having very long nights up to this point? I've averaged four hours of sleep a night for the last two*

> **weeks and that is because I have been sleeping on the super lumpy couch in the break room!**
>
> **Manager pinging SM:** *Do you think we should warn Partner that Senior 1 goes home early per her agreement with the Firm?*
>
> **SM pinging Manager:** *He already seems a bit upset and stressed. I don't know if I dare bring that up right now.*
>
> **Manager pinging SM:** *Ticking time bomb.*

"Can you get a meeting with CFO and Finance Manager right away?" Partner asked Manager.

"Sure," Manager answered, as he got up to head down to their offices.

"Also, can someone please put a packet of workpapers together for AQR to review?" Partner asked.

"We sent him a task via the online audit file a couple days ago," Senior 1 said, as she started clicking through the tasks on her screen. "We had also sent him planning related stuff right after the APE. I guess he didn't get to it during his European vacation after all."

"Not only did he not get to it," Senior 3 cut in, "he hasn't even accepted the invitation to the online audit file. This is why he doesn't think he has anything to review yet."

"Will you please ping him and walk him through how to accept that invitation?" Partner asked Senior 3. "He's not that tech savvy, so he could use your help."

"Sure, I'll ping him right now," Senior 3 replied.

> **Senior 3 pinging Senior 1:** *Wouldn't AQR have to accept invites like this for all his clients? How many times does he really need someone to show him how to accept the invite?*

The Good Audit

Senior 1 pinging Senior 3: *I don't know – he "isn't tech savvy"…but Partner just asked YOU for some tech assistance.*

Senior 3 pinging Senior 1: *Not funny!*

Senior 3 pinged AQR which eventually led to them getting on a phone call.

"Can't you just take over my screen?" AQR asked, grumpily. "That is what all my other teams do."

"Sure, will you please go to your instant messenger page you have up with me and—"

"I closed it already. I thought we were done with that when we got on the phone," AQR interrupted.

"I just pinged you again," Senior 3 continued. "Please hit 'Share Screen' on the bottom right, and then once that pops up, please also hit 'Share Control' on the top right of that screen."

Senior 3 clicked 2 buttons and then told AQR where his task was and what needed to be reviewed. He then hung up.

"You sounded like a regular IT service desk rep there," Manager teased, as he walked back into the audit room followed by Finance Manager and CFO.

Senior 3 pinging Manager: *I AM NOT AN IT GUY!*

"Hi!" Partner greeted CFO and Finance Manager, as he stood up to shake their hands. "I understand we are almost through the audit!"

Staff 2 pinging Manager: *Almost through?! He just told us to buckle up for a long night.*

Manager pinging Staff 2: *You will start to see the differences in what and how a partner tells the client vs. how and what he tells the audit team.*

"Yes," CFO replied, happily. "It has been a huge effort on both

C.P. Aiden

ends and we really appreciate the work both teams put in to get us here."

> **Senior 3 pinging Manager:** *Both teams? Seems like we've been the only team really working here!*

> **Manager pinging Senior 3:** *I dare you to say that out loud.*

> **Senior 3 pinging Manager:** *Not a chance!*

"We certainly understand and appreciate all the hard work and hours your team has put in to support us through this process – especially given this is our first year doing this audit," Partner continued, pleasantly. "First-year audits are always a bit painful, it seems."

"So, are we on track to issue by end of the day tomorrow?" CFO asked, cautiously.

"I believe we need to get through the financial statement tie-out tonight and tomorrow and AQR will probably have some comments for your team to get through tomorrow morning," Partner replied. "But I think, assuming we can get a draft of those financial statements in the next little bit, then we can plan to issue our report tomorrow."

> **Senior 3 pinging Manager:** *HOW IS THIS HAP-PENING?!! AQR has looked at nothing! He is going to have like 200 comments tonight!*

> **Manager pinging Senior 3:** *Plus, we haven't even seen the financial statements. They are probably garbage like everything else they've given us so there will be hundreds of changes for them to make and then we will have to check in those changes.*

> **Senior 3 pinging Manager:** *I can't believe Partner is telling them all this.*

> **Manager pinging Senior 3:** *It is his signature on the report. If he wants to sign it tomorrow and get*

The Good Audit

this thing over with, no complaints here.

Senior 3 pinging Manager: *Except that to issue financial statements by tomorrow night, we are all going to work the next 24 hours straight.*

SM to Intern: *Hey Intern, please restock the fridge with energy drinks. Looks like we will be going through a lot of them tonight and tomorrow.*

"We would have had the financial statements to you this morning, but your team had us chasing random journal entries down all day," Finance Manager pointed out. "I should have them over in about a half hour."

It was nearly 7 p.m. when the team finally got the draft.

"Guys," Partner said, solemnly. "We now have a draft of the financial statements. The financial statements are the end product of all our hard work and it is important that they are accurate so that we can be comfortable signing our report that says the financial statements are correct. I am afraid that getting through all of this will require an ALL-NIGHTER."

He paused to look at everyone around the room and then added, "for ALL of us."

The entire team groaned.

"It is almost 7:00 o'clock right now. Here is what I suggest," Partner continued. "Manager, Senior 1, and Staff 1 I suggest that if you want any time with your families tonight you run home for a half hour. The rest of you should find someplace around the office that is quiet and take a 30-minute nap. Does that sound ok to everyone?"

"I'm going home at 7:30 p.m., like my new flexible work arrangement spells out – the flexible work arrangement I took a 15 percent pay cut for!" Senior 1 said, starkly.

"I thought it was 8:30 p.m.?" Partner asked Senior 1.

> **SM pinging Partner:** *You don't want to go down this path.*

> **Partner pinging SM:** *Why not?*

> **SM pinging Partner:** *Senior 1 will quit again*

> **Partner pinging SM:** *What do you mean AGAIN?*

> **SM pinging Partner:** *After your first round of comments, I suggested an all-nighter and she refused to stay. I told her it would be treated as insubordination given the extenuating circumstances we were in. She gave me her computer and her office badge and left for a day and a half.*

> **Partner pinging SM:** *We really need everyone here tonight to get this done. She will listen to me – I'm a partner, she will totally cave to the pressure.*

"You don't get it," Partner replied. "Clearly, you see that this is an emergency. There is no way this is getting done by tomorrow unless we all pull together tonight."

"That is not how it sounded when you were talking to CFO," Senior 1 retorted.

"Well, of course, I have to keep the client happy," Partner replied. "I told her what she needed to hear."

"Even if it was all a HUGE lie?!" Senior 1 was now furious.

> **Staff 2 pinging Manager:** *Oh SNAP! The best just got here!*

> **Manager pinging SM:** *I guess we should have warned him.*

> **SM pinging Manager:** *I pinged him and tried to warn him. The good news is, now this is all him so we won't get blamed for it AND we get some high-quality entertainment out of it all too!*

The Good Audit

> **Manager pinging SM:** *This is her life! She is trying to balance between her family and this job that demands everything without giving anything in return. I can't believe you'd call that entertainment.*

"Let's talk about the issue at hand. This is an extenuating circumstance and we need you here with the team tonight." Partner said, trying to move away from the fact that Senior 1 had just called him out in front of the entire team. "Why don't you take an hour. Go home, put your kids to bed, eat a quick meal and then come back?"

"My kids don't go to bed at 7:00 p.m.," Senior 1 snapped back. "They go to bed at 8:30."

"Can't they go to bed early for one night?" Partner asked, with a puzzled look on his face.

"THEY ARE CHILDREN!" Senior 1 exclaimed, with a look of horror. "I can't just show up at home and expect them to go to bed an hour and a half early just because that would be convenient for you and this audit! They need me there. They need support, love, and care FROM THEIR MOTHER!!"

"Isn't your husband home to do that?" Partner asked, insensitively.

"Children need their mother! My husband is a good man, but he can't do everything they need done." Senior 1 was shaking with anger. "I worked this out with the Firm and I'm sticking to my agreement no matter what. I expect you and the Firm to uphold that agreement."

"Those agreements are great for when things are normal," Partner continued to argue. "But we are in a real bind here and need you to be a team player until things can go back to normal."

> **SM pinging Manager:** *This conversation seems vaguely familiar. So strange. Partner is making a real fool of himself.*

231

Manager pinging SM: *VAGUELY familiar? You are joking, right? This is almost word for word the discussion you had with her less than two weeks ago.*

SM pinging Manager: *I wasn't this big of a jerk though, was I?*

Manager pinging SM: *I'll repeat...almost word for word!*

"Normal?" Senior 1 was dumbfounded. "Normal? Why is it that people that have been at The Accounting Firm for a long time always think this type of thing is NORMAL?! Working all night to meet some unrealistic expectation because the client didn't get us everything we need on time is not NORMAL! What you are asking is insanity and I can't believe that you and The Accounting Firm have manipulated so many people into thinking that this type of thing is ok!"

"Can't you just be a team player?" Partner asked, coldly. "We really do need you here with us to get this done. This REALLY is an emergency—"

"No!" Senior 1 exclaimed, forcefully

"What do you mean, no?" Partner scoffed, condescendingly.

Senior 1 gathered her things together and once again stood up trembling with anger, pulled out her employee badge, closed her laptop, handed both to Partner and said, "I'm done. I have an agreement with the Firm – it is enforceable. I took a MASSIVE pay-cut just for the so-called 'privilege' of going home by 8:30 p.m. each night and then that agreement was revised to 7:30 p.m. You have shown to me tonight in front of the entire team that you will not uphold your end of the agreement. No amount of cash in a grocery store parking lot will bring me back this time! I will see you in court!"

Senior 1 then walked out of the room, left the office, got in her car and drove away – this time for good.

> **SM pinging Manager:** *I am finally seeing how big of a jerk I have been. I am so sorry! Do you think that if I come to my senses the Firm won't make me go to sensitivity training?*
>
> **Manager pinging SM:** *Probably not.*
>
> **SM pinging Manager:** *This is horrible.*

Partner stood in silent shock for several minutes before speaking. "I can't believe she would just walk out on us like that! If she does file a lawsuit, I expect each and every one of you to support the Firm in telling the truth about this incident – that this was a clear act of insubordination and that my termination of Senior 1 was justified and absolutely warranted! Am I clear?"

"I don't think we can say you terminated her as it was very clear that she decided to quit," SM stood up. "I also think she had some fair points in that she does have an enforceable agreement with The Accounting Firm that you would not uphold."

"Seriously!?" Partner was stunned.

> **Senior 3 pinging Manager:** *I can't believe it. SM finally grew a backbone.*

"We are not saving lives here," Manager said shaking his head.

"This is important to my life!" Partner lashed back angrily.

"Saving lives and saving livelihoods are not the same things," Manager replied, calmly. "I think I'm going to take that hour you offered Senior 1 now."

"I think we all should," SM added.

Each member of the team stood up and one at a time walked out of the audit room, leaving Partner alone to think by himself for the next hour.

SM and Manager were the first to return and they walked back into the audit room at the same time.

Partner had calmed down a bit at this point. "So how did you guys get her to come back?" he asked.

"We got her a pretty decent cash bonus," SM replied.

"How much are we talking?" Partner continued to push the issue.

"I think she ended up with about $1,400," Manager said.

"You guys don't have that much to give in your employee rewards budget, do you?" Partner asked.

"No, sadly we only get a few hundred dollars each to give out as 'thank yous' for ALL the staff and seniors, we have on all our teams for the ENTIRE year," Manager lamented. "The $1,400 came from a source outside that budget."

> **SM pinging Manager:** *We can't let him know that HE was that source!*
>
> **Manager pinging SM:** *I know. How do we get him off this?*

"So, what on earth was she talking about when she referenced cash in a grocery store parking lot?" Partner was confused. "Did you guys set it up as a surprise?"

Intern had walked into the room in the middle of the conversation and her face lit up as she finally had an opportunity to give Partner an answer that would get her noticed, "Are you talking about the Female Teenage Singing Sensation tickets?" she asked, eagerly.

"Wait a minute..." Partner hesitated, "...not a word of this to the rest of the team, but I bought Female Teenage Singing Sensation tickets in a grocery store parking lot from some pharmacist guy...but how would Senior 1 know something like that?"

Before Manager or SM could get Intern's attention to tell her to stop, she had already blurted out, "That was Senior 1's husband."

The Good Audit

"But I paid way more than $1,400 for those tickets," Partner was now very confused. "And the whole team knows I bought them?"

"Pretty much," Staff 2 said, casually, as he walked back into the room.

"This does not get around the office, understood?" Partner demanded.

"I used to buy and sell concert tickets in college," SM said, trying to defuse the situation and move on to the more pressing issue of financial statements. "The team desperately needed a break and everyone was trying to think of a way to get Senior 1 back, so when we heard those tickets were going on sale, it just made sense. We pooled our money, took a 15-minute personal break, got on our personal devices and some of us got tickets. Having Senior 1 back really saved our bacon this past week!"

"That is brilliant!" Partner exclaimed. "So Senior 1 came back because the team pulled together, threw some money at her and cheered her efforts? What do you think it will take to get her back this time?"

"Well," Manager said, solemnly. "I don't think any amount of clapping is going to bring Senior 1 back from where you sent her."

"Someone offer to give her $2,500," Partner said, quickly.

Staff 2 texted and then read the response from Senior 1 aloud to the room, "Try adding three zeroes! My attorney says that if we get good press on this, we should be in for a settlement at least that big."

"I can see that," Senior 3 said, carelessly. "Imagine the headlines, 'Pyramid Scheme, Apprenticeship Model, or Indentured Servitude?' or 'The Accounting Firm Sued as Partner Refuses to Honor Flexible Work Arrangement of Working Mom' or something like that."

"She left here an hour ago, and she's already talking to an attorney?!" Partner exclaimed in dismay.

> **Manager pinging SM:** *There is nothing partners at big firms hate more than getting sued. We need to do something to switch gears here or we will be here all night talking about his strategy to have all of us defend his really stupid actions and then we will still have to issue financial statements by tomorrow.*

"Hey," SM piped up. "Looks like we have draft financial statements at last! Let's get working on them!"

"I just sent them to AQR," Manager said, eagerly. "Intern, I also emailed them to you. Please print two copies – one for Partner to markup and one for us to start the tie-out on. Partner, you may want to go into the room down the hall as our plan was to have the rest of us all tag-team the tie-out in here with the financials projected on the big screen."

Once Intern had printed the copies, she handed one to Partner who got up and walked down the hall.

> **SM pinging Manager:** *Nice touch sending him away!*

The team worked tirelessly, going through each number page by page to make sure everything was right. As each page came up, the team would rush to agree each number on the page to anything the team had audited.

"We just need to tie these numbers somewhere," SM had explained. "It doesn't really matter what they agree to in our file, they just need to agree to something."

"So, if a number on the balance sheet that is supposed to be an asset agrees to a liability in our audit work, we are good?" Staff 1 asked, with a confused look on her face.

"I mean, it needs to be within reason," SM replied. "If we can't find support for a number, we need to flag it. Intern, that is your

The Good Audit

job with that second printout."

By the time they were done at 4:43 am, the 43-page financial statements had about 120 flags.

"I guess we should try to get some rest now for a couple hours," Manager told the team. "I will go down and see if Partner has anything for us, though, just in case."

"He left us a present by the door," Staff 2 pointed at the floor. There was the first copy of the financial statements with 50 or 60 flags sticking out to mark where Partner had left comments. Partner was nowhere to be found.

"Great," Senior 3 groaned. "He probably got through that in about an hour and then took off for home at around 9:00 p.m. I guess when he said we all needed to work an all-nighter to get this done, he was referring to all of us, not all of him."

SM and Manager flipped through Partner's flags. They were able to answer about 15 of the comments, another 21 overlapped with numbers the team couldn't find either and the rest were questions for the Widget Maker finance team.

"Let's spread out and get a couple hours of rest," Manager suggested again.

This time the team spread out through the office to find wherever they could to sleep. Staff 2 discovered that CEO's office had a very plush leather couch.

"This is awesome!" he whispered excitedly to himself, then pulling out his phone he set five alarms that would wake him up before 6:45 a.m. so he could vacate the office before any chance of CEO arriving.

It was 7:15 when Staff 2 woke up and someone was outside CEO's door humming. Suddenly, Staff 2 heard Senior Accountant's voice, "Good morning Executive Assistant," she said. "Do you have a key to the mother's room? It appears that somebody has locked it."

C.P. Aiden

"I do, but first let me see this sweet little BAAABBBYYYY!" Executive Assistant cried.

The baby started wailing uncontrollably. "She wants to be fed," Senior Accountant indicated.

"Well, let's go get that room open for you so you don't have to do it out here!" Executive Assistant exclaimed. "You never know who is lurking around this time of the morning."

CHAPTER 20 – THAT'S IT? THE ANTICLIMACTIC PUSH OF A BUTTON

Staff 1 swatted the phone that was buzzing on the end table next to the recliner in the mother's lounge for a third time. "I don't want to wake up yet!" she screamed at the phone. The phone buzzed again and she picked it up, "What?!" she asked in a nasty tone.

"GET OUT of there," Staff 2 shouted on the other end of the phone. "No time to explain, just move it."

Staff 1 made it out of the room and rounded the corner of the hallway and almost crashed into Executive Assistant, Senior Accountant, and Baby. "Isn't she the sweetest baby in the whole world?!" Staff 1 asked, with dazed excitement.

"She won't be sweet for long if this mother's room door is still locked," Senior Accountant said, as she rolled her eyes.

"I've got it covered," Executive Assistant said, firmly. "We are going to get that door open!"

They got to the door and saw it was cracked open.

"That's strange," Senior Accountant muttered. Then, she turned to Staff 1 and asked, "Did you see anyone in this hallway just

C.P. Aiden

now?"

"Nope," Staff 1 answered. "Didn't see a soul." After that, Senior Accountant always claimed the Mother's lounge was haunted.

In the meantime, Staff 2 had vacated CEO's office as soon as Senior Accountant and Executive Assistant started down the hall towards the Mother's lounge. After calling Staff 1, he walked slowly towards the audit room. He and Staff 1 arrived about the same time and they could not have been more shocked at what they saw when they walked in.

The top half of SM's body was sprawled out across one side of the table. He was snoring loudly and a large puddle of drool had soaked through the top inch of the three-inch stack of papers he was using as a pillow. Manager was sleeping propped up in the corner of the room. Senior 3 was curled up under the table fast asleep with his laptop bag under his head as a pillow. However, the most shocking figure of all was that of someone who was thumbing through a stack of papers in the middle of the table and pulling sticky flags from certain pages.

Staff 2 and Staff 1 stood in silence and stared while Assistant Controller continued for 30 seconds or so. When Assistant Controller had been through the entire stack of pages, he turned around and almost fell over at the sight of the two auditors.

"What is going on?! What are you doing, taking all our flags off the financial statements?" Staff 2 asked, suspiciously.

'Oh, nothing really," Assistant Controller replied, innocently. "I needed a few flags to use on the draft I have printed out" – he held up a stack of papers in his other hand that appeared to be a fresh copy of the financial statements – "and I saw that it looked like this stack had plenty of flags on it so I could probably use a few."

"If you just needed a few, why didn't you just take the first 10 or 15?" Staff 2 asked, skeptically, "Why did you go flipping through the entire thing, picking out specific flags? Clearly, you could

The Good Audit

tell these were flags on the financial statements – the same financial statements we FINALLY got a draft of last night."

At this SM woke up with a start. "Wh-What is going on?" he asked, very much dazed and confused.

Before Staff 2 could do anything, Assistant Controller quickly said, "Just comparing notes on the financial statements," and ran towards the door.

"Pulling our flags off isn't going to make the questions go away!!" Staff 2 shouted at Assistant Controller, as he ran out the door and down the hall.

The shout woke up Manager. Staff 2 quickly explained what Assistant Controller was doing when they walked in. Before they could figure out just what to do, Partner walked back in.

"Hey, guys. I thought this was an all-nighter?" he asked, laughing at himself. "I assume you saw that I left the financial statements outside the door last night? I also went in and closed all the cleared comments, except 13 that I reopened."

"Really?" Manager asked. "That must have taken all night!"

"Oh, it did. I just got done and walked down here," Partner said. "I feel like a real part of the team now putting in time like the good old days!"

> **Senior 3 pinging Manager:** *Fact 1 – he looks like he showered. Fact 2 – he is wearing different clothes than yesterday. Fact 3 – The new shirt is ironed and he is totally going with the half-tucked look to try to make it appear like he's been here all night. Fact 4 – he was nowhere to be found at 4:43 am when we got done.*

"That's crazy," Manager responded. "I'm so sad we couldn't find you at around 4:40 am when Staff 2, Senior 3 and SM all got in a huge argument over who could sprint the fastest. They decided then and there to have a race out in the parking lot."

C.P. Aiden

"I must have been so into what I was doing that I didn't hear a thing," Partner said, feigning disappointment.

"Staff 2 smoked them," Manager went on. "It was really a team building experience, gave us all renewed commitment to our work and to the Firm."

"I should have suggested that Senior 3 and I be given a 1 step head-start for every year out of college we've had longer than Staff 2," SM chimed in.

"It is funny how much you start to appreciate The Accounting Firm and team spirit when you are sprinting through an empty parking lot at an empty office building with your co-workers at 4:40 in the morning after working through the night," Staff 2 added. "And we certainly appreciate that your car was moved, Partner, because it would have been right in the way where it was parked last night."

> **Senior 3 pinging Manager:** *You guys are totally making all this stuff up. I can't believe SM and Staff 2 are going along with this story.*

> **Manager pinging Senior 3:** *I am so excited for Partner to repeat this as some feel-good story at some office event.*

> **Senior 3 pinging Manager:** *He won't do that.*

> **Manager pinging Senior 3:** *He will and what will make it even better is that he will tell the story as if he were a part of it.*

"That is a great story!" Partner exclaimed, awkwardly ignoring Staff 2's comment on his car being moved. "Will one of you please write it down and send it to me?"

"Well, now that we are all up and here, where are we on the financial statements?" Partner asked, as he rubbed his hands together in excitement. "Today is issuance day!"

"Funny you should ask," Manager said. "Assistant Controller was

242

just in here going through everything."

> **Staff 2 pinging Manager:** *Understatement of the audit!*

> **Manager pinging Staff 2:** *It was still a true statement though.*

"Looks like we also just got about 50 comments from AQR, as well," Senior 3 said, as his whole body slunk down into his chair.

"I think in all then we have about 137 comments to get through today," Manager said. "And then we will be DONE!"

SM and Manager saw Finance Manager and FRM walking down the hall, so they called them into the room.

"Hey, guys," Manager said, as they walked in. "We have several comments from our review of the financial statements to go over with you so that we can issue our report today. Can SM and I stop by your office in a few minutes, Finance Manager?"

"We have a meeting this morning that we have to be in," FRM said, belligerently, and then, seeing that Partner was in the room, he added, "otherwise we totally would."

"Yeah, the meeting is mandatory for all employees," Finance Manager added.

"So, no one is going to be able to help us this morning?" Manager asked in dismay.

"They serve free breakfast at these safety meetings, so they get a good draw," FRM said. "And CEO sends out an email saying that if you have to miss the meeting, you have to get manager approval."

"Let me get this straight," SM cut in. "You guys want to be done with the audit and have us issue our report today, but instead of helping us with these last questions, you are going to a *SAFETY* meeting? What is that all about?"

"Well, the safety meetings are generally about pretty common-sense stuff – like 3 points of contact going down stairs. Oh, and at this meeting, they are announcing a new company rule – no texting while walking up and down stairs," Finance Manager said. "That is why we have to attend this one. CEO wants everyone there to hear the new rule."

"But you already know the new rule," Manager pointed out.

"I didn't," FRM said. "Until just now anyway."

"So, now you both know the new rule, there is a way to get out of the meeting (I mean, Finance Manager, you are FRM's manager. You could just approve him not going), and you are still going to go to the meeting rather than work to get these financial statements out the door?"

"You guys will figure it out," Finance Manager said, as he headed for the door. "I don't see why I should penalize FRM and make him work on the audit while everyone else on the team gets to go to the meeting."

"I'm wondering if I could chat with CFO this morning," Partner asked, politely, as the two were about to leave.

"She's speaking at the meeting," Finance Manager replied. "So, she won't be available until noon. Have fun."

"Have they been like this the whole audit?" Partner asked in disgust.

"That was pretty mild," Staff 2 said, thinking about all he'd been through with Inventory Manager. "They were being polite with you in here. They've basically treated us like garbage the whole time."

"Hmm," Partner said, thoughtfully.

> **Staff 2 pinging Manager:** *Here it comes. Partner is finally going to stand up for us and tell these guys how horrible they are at accounting and how treating us like this isn't going to be tolerated anymore.*

> **Manager pinging Staff 2:** *Wait for it... wait for it...*

"We should find some way to quantify the inefficiency that they've caused based on their attitude and incompetence. We'll have to label it something else, of course – responsiveness/re-work or something like that," Partner said, seriously. "And then we will have to charge them additional fees for whatever we come up with."

> **Manager pinging Staff 2:** *And there it is!*

> **Staff 2 pinging Manager:** *Unbelievable. SMH. So disappointed.*

> **Manager pinging Staff 2:** *At the end of the day in a partner's world, EVERYTHING revolves around getting more fees.*

"Let's table that for now. SM, can you work on that after the audit is over?" Partner asked. "Right now, we should focus on getting these financial statements out the door."

The rest of the morning was a blur for the entire team. At one point, Staff 2 had 38 excel workbooks open as the team searched everywhere for answers to Partner's and AQR's questions. By the time the safety meeting was over, the team was down to 50 comments, but as Partner had pointed out, "Eight or 10 of these are total game changers. Make sure we get those answered first."

Manager and SM were already sitting in Finance Manager's office when he walked back in whistling to himself. He jumped when he saw auditors sitting in his office.

SM and Manager went through all the remaining questions with Finance Manager. The answer to all but three of those questions was some form of, "oh, that is the wrong number" and sometimes included "that is the number still in there from last year and the year before. Oops." Finance Manager told SM and Manager he would have answers to the other three questions by the

C.P. Aiden

time they had the 'audit close meeting'.

The entire Widget Maker finance team and TAF Audit team attended the meeting, except Senior Accountant, who had left for a trip to Bermuda with her family – her second such trip since having the baby.

"I wish I could be in Bermuda right now," Partner said. "We went for two weeks around Christmas, stayed in our own private villa on our own private beach, it was great!"

> **Manager pinging SM:** *I bet he paid over $20,000 for that trip and never left the villa for more than an hour at a time and worked the rest of the trip.*

"Let's talk about what is left open to get this audit done!" CFO said, eagerly.

"First, I just want to say how grateful we are to your team for their hard work, dedication, and assistance in getting this job done," Partner began.

> **Staff 2 pinging Manager:** *I think Partner should have said what CFO just said and CFO should have said what Partner said.*

> **Manager pinging Staff 2:** *Fat chance! "We aren't firing you" is Widget Maker's only way of saying "thank-you"*

"What is left open?" CFO said, impatiently.

Partner appeared to be reeling from being cut off in the middle of his close-out speech. SM jumped into to save him, "We had three open items with Finance Manager," he said. "Do you have answers for those yet?"

"I have two of the answers," Finance Manager said. "The third will have to wait until I get a hold of Senior Accountant. She is supposed to land in about an hour."

"Alright!" CFO said, smiling. "Finance Manager can go over those

The Good Audit

two answers with you, make the call in an hour and hopefully wrap up the last thing and then we should be good to issue, right?"

"We are just working through the last steps of our internal process as well," Partner replied. "We should be done this evening."

"Great! I guess we can adjourn then," CFO said, as she stood up.

"One last question for all of you," Partner said, as people started getting up to leave. "We have to ask as part of the audit: Are any of you aware of any actual, suspected or alleged fraud at Widget Maker?"

Everyone stood quietly thinking for a moment.

"You mean, like stealing assets?" Assistant Controller asked.

"That would be one way to commit fraud," Partner replied.

"We did have all the sticky notes in the supply room disappearing for a while, but it turned out that Product Distribution stuck them all over their wall down there – they wrote out 'Widget Maker' in huge block letters all over their wall to put in one of their ads."

"We are talking about high dollar fraud," Partner clarified. "Like several hundred thousand."

"I'm sure it was at least a hundred thousand sticky notes," Assistant Controller was clueless and it showed. "It was HUGE!"

"I meant the dollar value of what was taken," Partner clarified, again, starting to get annoyed. "Any high dollar frauds?"

After seeing Assistant Controller embarrass himself, no one else wanted to say anything. CFO looked around the room and then said, "I guess that's a 'no' from all of us."

"Great," Partner said, and then turned to Staff 2. "That should cover it for the fraud inquiry checklist we still need to complete."

247

C.P. Aiden

Partner pinging Staff 2: *Oh, and you don't have to include anything about the sticky notes. That was just ridiculous.*

Staff 2 pinging Partner: *Got it. Thanks!*

Staff 2 pinging Senior 3: *We asked one question about fraud and got one answer. This checklist is seven pages long. How am I supposed to deal with that?*

Senior 3 pinging Staff 2: *I will send you a completed one from one of my other clients that all said 'no' and you can just change the names.*

Staff 2 pinging Senior 3: *Perfect. Oh, and btw, how often do people come out and say "yeah, I know about some fraud here that you haven't found out about yet?"*

Senior 3 pinging Staff 2: *Like never. When you think about it, this group is the group most likely to be doing something bad with the money or the books, it isn't like anyone is going to jump up and say, "YES!!! I stole $3 million this year from the company." Or "YES!!! My boss told me to book a bunch of fraudulent stuff to make our financial statements look better!" Really, we just have to ask to say we did so if there is fraud and everyone gets sued, we get to say "yep, we asked and they all lied to us. Go sue them".*

Staff 2 to Senor 3: *So, this is like the other cover-your-butt stuff that makes up 95% of our audit file?*

Senior 3 pinging Staff 2: *Pretty much.*

By now, the Widget Maker finance team had all left the room. SM, trying to look impressive to Partner said, "While we are

248

The Good Audit

talking about checklists, has anyone done the checklist of checklists?"

"We have a checklist that lists all the other checklists?" Staff 1 asked. "Why does that not surprise me?"

"Yes," SM replied, smiling. "It lists all required and optional forms and checklists. We need to comb through the audit file and make sure we have everything done – well, at least started without any expected issues, by the time we sign our report."

"If we didn't use one of the optional forms, you have to fill out like a paragraph explanation on why we didn't use something that was available for the audit," Manager added.

"I used to just write 'see definition of optional'," Senior 3 joked. "But then some partner told me I had to give a more thoughtful reason."

There were 5 checklists that were not complete after the team had combed through the file. Finance Manager had just been through the last open question with the team and was about to head home.

"I have one more checklist I need to get through with you," Staff 2 said. "It is about consignment inventory."

"Sounds like a thrilling checklist," Finance Manager said, sarcastically. "I think I'll pass."

"Huh?" Staff 2 said, while furrowing his eyebrows and squeezing his nose.

"Yeah, you guys told CFO you had three open items and then your own internal stuff," Finance Manager said. "I took care of those three things so I don't really see this checklist as my problem. Inventory Manager already left for the day and I'm not aware of us holding any inventory on consignment for others. Wouldn't you guys have seen that when you did your year-end observations? Everything should be No or N/A. There, I just did your checklist for you. I'm going home. Text me when you issue

C.P. Aiden

your report."

By 7:45 p.m., the audit team had tied every number in the financial statements, started all (and completed most of) the checklists listed on the checklist of checklists, called AQR and got his ok to issue the report and were just waiting for Partner to give his final ok.

"This is always so stressful," Partner said, as he scrolled up and down the audit file. "I think we are ok to go ahead and issue. SM and Manager, good job. Looks like we will make a killing this year due to all the additional billings we were able to get. You two can take it from here! Please make sure we archive the file on time." Partner then closed his laptop, put it in his bag, and walked out of the room.

Manager copied the audit report onto the third page of the Widget Maker's financial statements, dropped in The Accounting Firm's electronic signature, and printed to PDF which he locked and password protected. He then emailed the PDF to the Widget Maker finance team and said, "We're issued."

Staff 1 had been watching Manager throughout his process. "You mean THAT'S IT??!!" She was flabbergasted. "All that work and all we do in the end is copy a single page into a PDF, email it to the client, and we are done?"

"Yep," Manager answered. "You spent countless hours away from your family, working to the edge of losing your mind, took abuse from Widget Maker that most would call a hostile work environment, and we all gained 15 pounds due to stress just so we could put one page on the front-end of the financial statements and email it to them. They will forward the email to their guy at the bank who will look at the first five pages of the now 60-page document and then file it away, never to look at it again."

"So anticlimactic," Staff 1 said, almost in tears. "I thought it would give me a huge sense of accomplishment or excitement or something."

"You can be excited to come back here for the next three or four weeks as we clean up the rest of this mess," SM pointed out.

CHAPTER 21 – FREEDOM!

The team spent the following few weeks cleaning up the conference room and closing out everything in the audit file.

"I still can't believe Partner finally signed off on everything," Staff 1 said. "I mean leading up to the end, he was leaving so many comments I thought there was no way we'd ever get done."

"Every audit is a fire drill right to the end," Manager replied. "That is why we schedule everyone for a full three to four weeks after it ends – because fire drills always leave a mess!"

Manager scanned across the room and pointed out all the random scattered stacks of papers, random snack food, random unused napkins and utensils left over from lunches and dinners, random pieces of trash and even a 5' x 5' x 5' tower of soda cans in one corner and four long lines of empty energy drink bottles that went from the other corner to the tower.

"We need to give all original documents back to Widget Maker," SM said, as the team looked over the room. "The rest of the papers need to be shredded. Everything else gets thrown away – Intern, please run down to the grocery store and buy a pack of those huge black garbage bags. We will divvy up any remaining snacks when we are done cleaning everything else up."

"Staff 1 can have all the moldy, organic, non-GMO, no sugar

The Good Audit

added, blah-blah-blah fruit she didn't eat," Manager joked.

"There is none of that left in here!" Staff 1 quipped back.

"We'll see," Manager replied. "It smells so bad, there has to be something dead lying around."

"It smells so bad in here because nobody showered this whole last week and half the team slept in here each night," Staff 2 suggested. "I hope that the first thing people did when they got home at 8:30 last night was to take a shower – I know I did."

"I watched TV for an hour last night," Staff 1 said. "Even getting home at 8:30, I sort of felt like a normal human being again."

"I got to put my kids to bed," Manager added. "My wife laughed and we both cried when I went in to put our son to sleep and he asked, 'who are you?' and I was like 'I'm your dad' and he thought for a minute and then was like 'Oh, yeah. I had a dad once'. I was heartbroken."

"I just fell asleep," Senior 3 said. "I slept for 11 and a half hours, but at least I changed my clothes this morning so no one on the finance team will continue to make fun of my same shirt all week."

"No-one is here to make fun of your shirt," FRM had been walking down the hall and had been listening to their whole conversation just outside the door. "But someone or some THING in here smells like it still needs a shower."

"Where is everybody?" Senior 3 asked, as he tried to deflect the shower comment. "You are the first Widget Maker finance person we've seen all day."

"They are all out on vacation for the next few weeks," FRM replied. "I would be gone too, but I am going on a three-week cruise next month, so I had to save my vacation time. I'm ok with that though, because with everyone else in finance gone, it is like I am almost on vacation anyways. My plan is to go to the gym four hours a day. In fact, I'm on my way there now, and then

I'm leaving by 2 p.m. every day."

FRM went to leave, but caught a whiff of something truly awful. "What is that?" he groaned as he covered his nose and mouth. "It is coming from over there I think," he continued, as he motioned his other hand toward the corner closest to the door.

At first glance, there were just huge stacks of paper in the corner, but as Staff 1 pulled one of the stacks away, she suddenly stood up, cried out, "I'm going to hurl", covered her mouth with both hands, and ran down the hall towards the bathroom. About halfway down the hall, she stopped at a section of cubes, grabbed someone's trash can and lost her breakfast.

Staff 2 and Manager went to the corner to investigate.

"Oh, MAN!" Manager shouted. "Do you see what this is?!"

"Who gets to tell her we told her so?" Staff 2 asked. "This has been here since the day we got moved up to this room from the cave!"

"Audit food group number seven," Manager laughed. "Moldy, organic, no sugar added, non-GMO, Vegan, Gluten-free fruit!"

"You know what is weird about this though?" Staff 2 asked, while he bent down to take a closer look. "The sticker labels on the fruit are the only things that don't have mold on them. Makes you wonder what they are made of?"

"Probably not organic, no sugar added, non-GMO, Vegan, Gluten-free material," Manager replied, with a smile. "We should ask Staff 1 if she believes me now – I've always thought the stickers taint the fruit."

"I don't want to think about it right now," Staff 1 said, as she walked back into the room. "But I can tell you what is tainted for sure – that trash can I picked up down the hall. Is intern back with those big black trash bags yet?"

"I am off to the gym!" FRM said. "Let me know if you need anything...um...anything related to the audit...um...which is over."

The Good Audit

"I'll just go this way," he added, as he turned back down the hall away from the loaded trash can. "There is a dumpster at the north end of the parking lot."

"We were thinking of putting all this down in the old audit cave," Senior 3 called out to FRM, as he rounded the corner away from the room.

FRM's head popped back around the corner and he said, "I think that is still blocked off...but you can go check if you want to."

"Nah," Senior 3 replied, quickly. "I never want to go down there again."

The trash bags arrived and the team went to work. Things went slowly, but the audit room started looking like a conference room again.

A few weeks later, on the last day the auditors were on site at Widget Maker, Finance Manager and Inventory Manager walked in together.

"What are you guys doing here?" Inventory Manager asked. "Don't tell me we are starting next year's audit already."

"Didn't the audit get over several weeks ago?" Finance Manager followed up. "The last few weeks in Europe almost erased the audit from my mind."

"We've spent a fair amount of time cleaning things up," SM said, shortly.

"Just proves my point that audits are garbage," Finance Manager said to Inventory Manager. "If it takes several weeks with a team of six people to clean it up, that is A LOT of garbage."

> **Staff 2 pinging Manager:** *Good thing they didn't see the dumpster outside, it is overflowing.*

"Garbage in, garbage out, right?" retorted Manager, who was not amused and was finally able to express that he never had been.

> **Staff 2 pinging Manager:** *Do you think we should*

255

C.P. Aiden

> *tell them that all of Legal Assistant's investor print-outs made it to the dumpster.*

> **Manager pinging Staff 2:** *Nah, I think when you put them in the big trash bag with the moldy fruit and shook it up, you secured them way better than Legal Assistant ever did.*

"So, what is next for everyone?" Finance Manager asked. "Are you moving onto bigger and better clients?"

"Yes. No question about that, but we all have vacations for the next couple weeks," Manager replied.

"Where to?" Inventory Manager asked.

"Senior 3 is going backpacking," Manager answered. "The rest of the team is going to various vacation destinations, mostly to sit on the beach, do nothing, and regret their decision to ever become auditors – SM to Australia for his first vacation in three years, Staff 2 to Cabo, Staff 1 with her family to San Diego, and Intern to Miami."

"Nice. Freedom at last! Go blow all that money you haven't been able to spend for the past six months on hollow trips to sit and do nothing!" Finance Manager said, somewhat sarcastically to the team. He then turned to Manager and asked, "Where are you going? Surely, you have some huge thing planned with your family?"

"I do, and it is SOO much better and way cooler than all the places these guys are headed to. Rather than sit around and do nothing, we are going to do ALL the things. I haven't really been there for quite a while, so I'm looking forward to it – it is one of the best-kept secrets in the world, but it really shouldn't be." Manager replied, mysteriously.

"Well, wherever it is, I hope you really get to enjoy it," Finance Manager said, as he and Inventory Manager turned to leave. "You've all earned it!"

The Good Audit

Senior 3 pinging Manager: *You HAVE to tell me. WHERE are you going?*

Manager pinging Senior 3: *Home.*

Printed in Great Britain
by Amazon